"I think you broke my nose—

Some warning would have been nice." Theia scowled up at Marco.

It wasn't his finest moment. Marco had swooped in for a kiss. Their noses had collided, and her teeth had bashed against his.

"Sorry about that," he said as he leaned in to look at Theia's nose in the light from the streetlamp. "It might be a little swollen in the morning, but otherwise you're good."

"No, I'm not good. You just told everyone we're dating."

"Look, I'm sorry I kissed you and sprang the dating thing on you without asking. But unless you want to spend the rest of the summer hiding from the local matchmakers, pretending we're in a relationship is the best way to—"

"I would have liked a little warning, but you're right," Theia said. "It's a good plan."

His jaw dropped, the words to defend his plan still on the tip of his tongue. "It's a good plan?"

"Yeah. A really good plan. Why? Don't you think so anymore?"

There was a touch of vulnerability on her face when she asked. He saw it in the way her mouth softened, in the shadow that darkened her eyes, and he was overcome with a sudden urg

And right then

the worst ideas he

PRAISE FOR DEBBIE MASON'S
HARMONY HARBOR SERIES

The Corner of Holly and Ivy

"[A] delightful return to a small town that I adore. Frankly, I've never met a Debbie Mason story that I didn't enjoy, and this one is no exception. I had fun with Connor and Arianna, cried a bit, laughed out loud, and experienced the magic of a small-town Christmas season. If that doesn't equal a great Christmas romance, then I don't know what does."
—KeeperBookshelf.com

"Mason takes her romances to a whole new level with plenty of content to make for a more action-packed romance than just two people falling in love. So again this was another fun trip to Harmony Harbor that I'm sure romance readers will enjoy."
—CarriesBookReviews.com

Sandpiper Shore

"Hurray for SANDPIPER SHORE, a Cinderella story loaded with intrigue."
—FreshFiction.com

"Quirky, funny, sweet, and overflowing with a colorful cast."

—*Library Journal*

Driftwood Cove

"Mason rolls out the excitement in the fifth book in the Harmony Harbor series."
—*RT Book Reviews*

"I love second-chance romances, and Debbie Mason has written another good one in her Harmony Harbor series with some pretty significant obstacles between our hero and heroine and their happy ending."
—TheRomanceDish.com

Sugarplum Way

"4 Stars! Harlequin Junkie Recommends! An amazing addition to this sweet and sassy series."
—HarlequinJunkie.com

"I really enjoyed this story…it had a lot of elements that put together made for a Christmas where dreams really do come true."
—RomancingTheBook.com

Primrose Lane

"4 Stars! This is a book worth savoring as it has all the elements of a fantastic read."
—*RT Book Reviews*

"Wow, do these books bring the feels. Deep emotion, heart-tugging romance, and a touch of suspense make them hard to put down, while the humor sprinkled throughout keeps the emotional intensity balanced with comic relief."

—TheRomanceDish.com

Starlight Bridge

"4 Stars! Mason gives Ava and Griffin a second chance at love. There's a mystery surrounding the sale of the estate…that adds a special appeal to the book."

—*RT Book Reviews*

"I loved this book. Debbie Mason writes romance like none other."

—FreshFiction.com

Mistletoe Cottage

"Top Pick! 4 1/2 Stars! Mason has a knockout with the first book in her Harmony Harbor series."

—*RT Book Reviews*

"*Mistletoe Cottage* is anything but typical. It's a fast-paced story with colorful characters, lots of banter, and even more twists and turns."

—*Fort Worth Star-Telegram*

Barefoot Beach

ALSO BY DEBBIE MASON

The Harmony Harbor series

The Christmas, Colorado series

Barefoot Beach

DEBBIE MASON

FOREVER

NEW YORK BOSTON

Copyright © 2019 by Debbie Mazzuca
Excerpt from *Happy Ever After in Christmas* © 2016 by Debbie Mazzuca

Cover illustration by Tom Hallman. Cover design by Elizabeth Turner Stokes. Cover copyright © 2019 by Hachette Book Group, Inc.

Forever
Hachette Book Group
1290 Avenue of the Americas, New York, NY 10104
read-forever.com
twitter.com/readforeverpub

First Edition: June 2019

Forever is an imprint of Grand Central Publishing. The Forever name and logo are trademarks of Hachette Book Group, Inc.

The publisher is not responsible for websites (or their content) that are not owned by the publisher.

The Hachette Speakers Bureau provides a wide range of authors for speaking events. To find out more, go to www.hachettespeakersbureau.com or call (866) 376-6591.

ISBNs: 978-1-5387-3168-0 (mass market); 978-1-5387-3167-3 (ebook)

Printed in the United States of America

OPM

10 9 8 7 6 5 4 3 2 1

For the Mazzucas, LeClairs, Delpapas, Coplands, Armstrongs, and Morglans. There's nothing more important than family, and I'm blessed to have all of you as mine. I love you, all one hundred and fifty of you.

Barefoot Beach

Chapter One

♥

Marco DiRossi's birthday fell on the Fourth of July, the combined celebration ensuring the day had been one of the high points of the summer, his favorite time of year. Summertime when being single in Harmony Harbor had been synonymous with living the good life in paradise. Lazy days spent at the beach soaking up the sun and scoping out the toned and tanned hometown girls, hot summer nights spent at the local bars and seaside cafés flirting with the tourists who flocked to his coastal hometown.

But his love for the Fourth had done a one-eighty once he became a member of the Harmony Harbor Fire Department. Now the holiday represented an uptick in grass fires, minor injuries, and burns.

The summer was also fraught with danger of another kind—his matchmaking grandmother, Rosa DiRossi. She'd been trying to marry him off for years. Her efforts increased tenfold during the summer months, when his hometown became Wedding Central, thanks to Greystone Manor.

Home to Harmony Harbor's founding family, the Gallaghers, the manor also served as a hotel. A hotel that had become, under his sister Sophie's expert and creative management, the premier wedding destination on Massachusetts's North Shore.

Sadly for Marco, at that moment the manor was only a five-minute walk from where he sat in Sophie's backyard. As if on cue, the sound of wedding-day celebrations drifted his way on a warm ocean breeze. His hand tightened around the wineglass stem as he lifted it to his lips.

This year might take the prize for worst Fourth of July, and it wasn't his grandmother's fault. It was his own.

Liam Gallagher, his brother-in-law, best friend, and fellow firefighter got up from the picnic table and started to clear the remains of Marco's birthday dinner.

When Marco put down the wineglass to pick up an empty platter and a bowl of hot antipasto spread, Liam said, "Relax. You're the guest of honor. I'll be in the doghouse if I let you help."

"You'll be in the doghouse with me if you don't." At the sounds of wedding guests chanting *kiss*, *kiss*, *kiss* and clinking cutlery against crystal, Marco sprang to his feet. He wondered what the chances were of moving his party indoors. "Bugs are getting bad. We should probably have cake and coffee inside."

The screen door on the two-story white stucco house banged closed. Marco looked over to see his grandmother carrying a tray loaded down with a coffee urn, mugs, and a bottle of Amaretto. He knew better than to rush over and take the tray.

In her late seventies, Rosa was still strong in mind, body, and spirit. Sometimes annoyingly so. But as he often reminded himself when she got on his last nerve, the traits that drove him crazy were the reason she'd not only survived but thrived when her husband, Antonio, vanished on a rainy summer night.

He'd left her alone with three toddlers to raise and no money. She'd cleaned houses and taken in laundry and boarders until she'd scraped enough money together to start DiRossi Fine Foods and Deli. She worked harder than any woman he knew.

Tonight she wore her favorite blue dress, faded from its many washings. Her dyed black hair fell to her shoulders in loose curls, flattering a face that bore a striking resemblance to Sophia Loren. Rosa looked great for her age, her olive skin barely lined. Until her attention moved to Marco's and Liam's hands and her sucked-on-a-lime expression deepened the creases at the corners of her eyes and mouth.

"Eh, what do you think you're doing? Put those dishes down." Her Italian accent was thick despite the fact she'd moved from Pisterzo, Italy, to Harmony Harbor, Massachusetts, in the fourth grade.

Liam shot Marco an I-told-you-so grin, which faded when he realized Rosa was now focused on him.

"You too. Sit. Sit." She nodded at Liam and then at the dishes. "It's woman's work."

His grandmother was stuck in the fifties, where women had their roles and men had theirs and never the two shall meet.

Liam looked torn. Unlike Rosa, his wife was not stuck in the fifties. Which his ten-year-old daughter, Mia, proved by opening the screen door and yelling, "Daddy, Mommy says hurry up and clear off the picnic table so there's room for the cake." Marco's niece smiled at him. "I made it for you. Mommy said it's your favorite."

Mia had the same long, curly dark hair as her mother and her father's Gallagher-blue eyes. Looking at his niece's adorable face, Marco got a glimpse of what the future held in store for him and her father. They'd have to beat the boys back with sticks. The kid was going to grow up to be a looker just like the rest of the DiRossi women. She was also his favorite little person on the planet, her baby brother Ronan Jr. coming a close second. They'd probably be tied for first place in his heart when his nephew wasn't attached to his mother's hip.

"You gonna give me a hint what kind of cake it is?" Marco asked as he moved the plates and parmigiana to make room for Rosa's tray.

He figured Mia had made him an Italian rum cake. Up until his twentieth birthday, the dessert, with its three layers of sponge cake soaked in a rum-flavored syrup and filled with layers of vanilla and chocolate pastry cream had been his favorite. But then life as he'd known it had ended, and neither he nor Rosa had had the heart to make the cake again.

"Nope. It's a surprise." His niece grinned and then waved over her father. "Come on, Daddy. Hurry up before Mommy finishes changing Ronan."

When Mia disappeared into the house, Liam glanced at his grandmother-in-law, obviously gauging whose doghouse he'd rather be in. He carefully picked up the plates in an effort not to draw Rosa's attention away from unloading the tray.

Marco made a wrong-choice buzzing sound.

Liam glared at him.

Marco didn't know what the big deal was. Rosa hadn't heard him. Lately they'd noticed her hearing wasn't what it used to be. He lowered his voice anyway. "I'm just trying to help. All you have to do to get out of Soph's doghouse is sing to her." The Gallagher boys put the *harmony* in Harmony Harbor. "But that won't work on Ma." Marco had taken to calling Rosa *Ma* when his own mother deserted him.

His grandmother lifted her head to frown at Liam. "Eh, what—"

As Rosa geared up to give Liam hell, his best friend threw Marco under the bus. "Hey, Rosa, did you hear our boy here got asked to be in another wedding? How many is that this year, bro? It looks like you'll beat last year's record after all."

Ensuring that Marco now had his grandmother's complete and disappointed attention, his supposed best friend went about clearing the table.

"*Madonna mia,*" Rosa said, pouring herself a healthy shot of Amaretto. "Always the groomsman, never the groom." She made it sound like he'd been handed a death sentence.

"Ma, what are you doing?" he said when she tossed back the almond-flavored liqueur and then went to pour herself another shot. He reached across the table, picked up the coffee urn, and filled her mug.

"He could have been the groom today. Three years ago too." Liam dropped his bomb just before heading to the house with an armload of dishes.

Marco stifled a groan, shooting a glance at his grandmother to be sure she hadn't heard, followed by a glare at his brother-in-law's back. Liam had to know how badly it would go for Marco if Rosa found out how close he'd come to marrying Callie. At the last second, terror had struck his confirmed bachelor's heart, and he couldn't go through with the proposal.

Callie was a woman with a plan. She wanted a ring on

her finger, a house by the sea, and two babies, preferably one boy and one girl. There was a time stamp on the baby end of things so, no matter how much she loved him, she couldn't afford to wait around until he got his act together. As Liam had alluded, it wasn't the first time Marco had choked at the big moment. There'd been another woman before Callie. He'd loved her too. At least he thought he had.

Rosa took a seat across from him at the picnic table, glancing in the direction of the manor's spa as she did. The Gallaghers owned five thousand acres of land that were bordered by the Atlantic and the woods, which meant they owned the majority of the cottages that lined the gravel road upon which Liam and Sophie's home sat.

For the past year, Marco's mother, Tina, worked at and managed the spa. Room and board came with the job. He did his best to avoid her, but his sister made that difficult to do. She invited Tina to every family gathering, of which there were quite a few. He couldn't avoid the family get-togethers without hurting his sister's and his niece's feelings, something he would never do. So he went. Lucky for him, Tina was at a conference in LA this week.

Maybe lucky for his mother as well, he thought when Rosa returned her attention to him. With one look at her dark, flashing eyes, he knew what was coming. "Your mother, she ruined you for marriage. You don't trust women because of her. She abandoned you. She's a—"

He'd heard it all before. "Ma, relax. I was twenty. She didn't ruin me. The right woman hasn't come along, that's all."

Only he was pretty sure she had, and two hours earlier she had said *I do* to someone else. He lifted his glass of wine, toasting Callie in his mind. Wishing her all the love and happiness she deserved. His chest grew tight as he thought about the woman he might have loved and lost, and he wondered if there was something wrong with him. He wanted what his sister and Liam had.

His grandmother sighed and came to her feet, leaning across the picnic table to pat his cheek. "Time is running out, *mio bel ragazzo*." My handsome boy. "You are thirty-three." She said it like he had one foot in the grave.

"I'm a baby. No one gets married this young anymore."

She snorted and then named ten men he knew, including his best friend and several of his firefighter brothers, one of whom was Callie's new husband. Marco hadn't known how good an actor he was until he'd been greeted with the news of their upcoming marriage at the station four months before.

His sister's voice and Ronan's baby babble drew his attention to the house. Sophie, with the toddler on her hip, walked backward as she filmed Mia, who carried a cake aglow with so many candles it looked like they might need an extinguisher to put them out, which was probably why her father walked beside her with his hands poised to grab the cake. The four of them sang "Happy Birthday," providing the distraction Marco needed.

Or was it? he wondered when Sophie and Liam smiled at each other and then at their children. Marco felt the weight of someone's gaze and glanced over to see his grandmother watching him. Glassy-eyed, she pressed a hand to her heart. He needed a better distraction.

Beaming with pride, his niece set the cake in front of him.

"Italian rum cake, my favorite. Thanks, *cara*. It looks amazing." He leaned over to kiss Mia's cheek and grin at his sister. "Now you can stop passing off the stuff from Truly Scrumptious as your own, Soph," he said, referring to the local bakery. "Mia can bake for you." Unlike him, his sister hadn't inherited the DiRossi passion for food or the cooking gene.

And just as Marco had hoped, Liam couldn't let the jibe against his wife go unanswered. "What are you talking about? She's an amazing baker." Liam began reeling off several examples of his wife's superlative baking skills.

"I might have had a little help with Ronan's birthday cake and the cupcakes for Mia's last day of school," Sophie admitted sheepishly before shooting Marco a *thanks a lot* look.

"Trust me, it's better she buys from the bakery or asks me or Mia to make her cakes and cookies." Rosa chuckled and then went on to regale them with stories of Sophie's disasters in the kitchen growing up.

While his family laughed and argued, Marco smiled and blew out the candles on his cake. They stopped talking to stare at him. Rosa looked like he'd committed a mortal sin.

He raised his hands. "What did I do now? The candles were melting into the cake."

"You didn't make your birthday wish. You need to make one." Rosa picked up a candle and showed it to Sophie. "We need new ones. Matches too."

He sighed, knowing exactly what she wanted him to wish for. "I did," he lied.

She saw right through him and snapped her fingers at his sister. "*Sbrigati!* Hurry up."

He blinked at the forceful note in her voice. Apparently, there was a short birthday-wish window.

"We don't have any more candles, *Nonna*. But it's fine. Marco already made a wish." His sister raised a questioning eyebrow at him.

He frowned at her. "Seriously?"

She rolled her eyes and then lifted her chin at Rosa.

Okay. He got it. She wanted to know what was up with their grandmother. He raised a shoulder. He didn't have a clue why she seemed more anxious than usual about the birthday-wish thing.

"Wish papers, *Nonna*. Remember? I got them for my birthday," Mia said. His niece ran back inside the house without waiting to see if her great-grandmother remembered.

Liam sat next to Marco at the picnic table and held out his arms for his son. Sophie handed him over and then went to help Rosa cut and plate the cake. Marco's grandmother looked not only relieved but pleased. If he believed that birthday wishes came true, he might be getting nervous right about now.

"Any idea what that was all about?" Liam asked Marco under his breath while trying to keep Ronan entertained with an empty mug.

"It's the same thing every year. She insists I wish for the woman of my dreams. I say I do, but I don't."

Liam glanced at Rosa and then nodded as if he'd figured it out, mouthing the name of a long-time member of the Widows Club who'd died five months before.

"Why would—" Marco bowed his head. His best friend was probably right. The Widows Club's biggest regret was that Mrs. Fitzgerald hadn't seen her granddaughters settled and happily wed.

Marco grabbed Ronan's wandering hand and nibbled the little boy's fingers, making him giggle. There was nothing better than a child's laughter to lighten the mood. He looked up when the screen door banged close behind Mia.

She ran to the picnic table with a sheaf of colored papers in her hands.

"Let's eat the cake first," he suggested, uncomfortable

with the idea of them making wishes on his behalf. Especially if they said them out loud. Especially because he knew what they would wish for.

Maybe instead of putting the cart before the horse and wishing he'd get married and live happily ever after, they should ask the wish fairies to grant him the ability to fall in love. He frowned, wondering where that had come from. There was no problem with his heart. Look at how much he loved Rosa, Sophie, Liam, and the kids. But then he remembered the debilitating case of nerves that had swamped him when he'd almost proposed to Callie. So maybe he did need some help in the romantic love department.

"No. We do this now. It's more important than eating."

Marco stared at his grandmother. Other than her family, there was nothing more important to Rosa DiRossi than food. It was a good thing she couldn't read his mind. If she had even an inkling that he thought he needed some help in the romantic love department, not only would today be his worst Fourth of July on record, but any chance of salvaging the rest of his summer would be blown.

While he'd been silently staring at his grandmother, Mia had handed out the colorful squares of tissue paper and markers. He looked at the paper in front of him, then nudged it away with the tip of his finger.

Rosa pushed it back with hers. "You need all the help you can get."

He sighed heavily, shielded the paper with his hand, and wrote *Have an awesome summer just like in the good old days*. He glanced at his niece and sister, who had finished theirs and were rolling them into tight cylinders.

"Are you two writing books?" he asked Liam and Rosa when he'd finished rolling his paper into a tiny tube.

His grandmother didn't respond, but Liam did. "Ronan's fine motor skills aren't fully developed, so he needs help. In case you're wondering, he wants a cousin. Preferably before he's a teenager."

"Thanks a lot—"

Mia interrupted Marco. "That was my wish too, Daddy." She then turned her earnest gaze on him. "You don't have a lot of time, *Zio*. Some people don't get pregnant right away. I'll be a teenager in two years."

"Try three. Besides, you already have cousins on the Gallagher side." Before his sister or grandmother could get in on the conversation, he said, "Now what are we supposed to do? Rip them up?"

"No!" Sophie and Mia cried, while at the same time Rosa set her rolled paper upright on the table. Before he realized what she was up to, she lit a match and touched it to the tip. The paper floated in the air and then whooshed into flames.

He stared at Rosa, who cupped her hands to catch the burning embers. "Are you crazy? Don't catch…What do you two think you're…?" he began when Sophie and Mia did the same. Like Rosa's, their papers rose into the air and burst into flames. "Careful where the embers…"

"We all caught them!" Mia squealed. "Now the wishes will come true for sure."

"Don't you dare light yours." Marco had just finished telling Liam when Rosa leaned over and set theirs on fire before he could stop her.

Above Mia's and Ronan's laughter and squealing, Marco could have sworn he heard screaming. He held up a hand. "Quiet for a sec."

There it was again. Someone was in trouble. Liam handed him Ronan. Marco passed him to his sister and then jumped to his feet. Their pagers went off. They were on call. A recording from dispatch relayed the location of the emergency—Greystone Manor.

Liam pulled out his cell phone as they took off at a run for the manor. "It's my uncle Daniel. He went out on a paddleboard and appears to be in distress on the water," he said once he'd disconnected.

"Heart?" Marco asked as his own began to race. The last place he wanted to be tonight was anywhere near Greystone Manor.

"Could be anything. They never did figure out what happened last fall," Liam said as they sprinted along the path through the woods. He glanced at Marco when they cleared the trees and raced for the bridge. People in their wedding finery stood outside the white tent opposite the pond. "You gonna be okay?"

"I'm fine." He whipped his T-shirt over his head, letting it drop onto the grass. "Just glad I didn't go commando today," he said as he went to unbutton his jeans.

"You and me both. Though I have a feeling the women might be disappointed." Liam lifted his chin at a group of twentysomething women congregated on the beach.

One of them turned, her pretty face stricken. "Can you swim?" she called out. "Our husbands tried to help and got caught in the undertow."

"Everyone wants to be a damn hero," Marco muttered as he looked around for the groom while toeing off his running shoes. "Where the hell is Johnny?" Callie's new husband and a member of their crew.

He spotted the bride at the water's edge. Her back was to him, her wedding gown billowing in the light breeze off the ocean, her long, golden-blond hair streaming down her back. And just beyond her, Johnny struggled to keep himself and a sandy-haired man afloat.

Faint cries drew Marco's attention from the two men. He squinted against the setting sun and made out Daniel Gallagher lying prone on a yellow paddleboard in the distance.

"You're a stronger swimmer than me. You get my uncle. I'll take these two," Liam said as he kicked off his shoes, leaving on his board shorts. They galloped into the cold water. Liam going right, Marco left.

Callie called his name, but he didn't have time to turn around and respond. It was more than that though; he didn't want to see her face. He pushed her out of his mind, focusing instead on Liam's uncle.

Marco dove under the water, coming up several yards away from where he went under. He began to swim out into the harbor, his strokes even and powerful, his kick strong. Liam was right. Marco was the stronger swimmer of the two. It hadn't always been that way. But now his best friend had a family to occupy his free time.

In the distance he heard the sirens as the emergency vehicles raced for Greystone Manor.

Five minutes later, when the searchlights cut across the water, Marco stopped swimming to raise his arm, glad of the light, as night had fallen, the moon and stars buried beneath the clouds.

Daniel lifted his head from the paddleboard, seemingly disoriented. "Where am I?"

"Mr. Gallagher—Daniel—don't try to get up, okay? Just stay down on the board." He didn't want him falling off and into the water. "Can you tell me what happened, sir? Do you have any pain?" he asked as he treaded water to the front of the board. Like most of his crew, Marco was a certified paramedic.

"My heart, I think. I had an attack last fall, you know."

His Irish accent was thick. The older man had returned to Harmony Harbor last summer, after spending the majority of his adult life in Ireland. No one knew why he'd come home.

Marco refocused on his patient. Daniel's color appeared to be good. His breathing wasn't labored, nor were his words slurred. And other than that brief moment of disorientation, he seemed aware of the situation. All good signs. "I heard about your attack, sir. Are you in pain now? Any light-headedness?"

"No. Although it might be the chill keeping the pain at bay."

Possibly. An archaeologist, Daniel regaled him with stories about his digs while Marco swam the older man and his board to shore. For someone who'd been in distress not more than twenty minutes before, he appeared to be doing remarkably well. No sooner had Marco had the thought than things took a turn for the worse.

As soon as he stood up to push the paddleboard the rest of the way to shore, Daniel began to moan. Callie, who'd been standing with the crowd gathered on the beach, lifted her wedding gown and waded out to meet them. She was a nurse.

Of all the things he could have said to her, "You look beautiful" shouldn't have been one of them, but that's exactly what he said.

She stared at him, her eyes glassy. "I wish…" she began, only to be cut off by a man wading out to them wearing a soaked tuxedo.

"Baby, what are you doing? You're going to ruin your dress." Johnny held Marco's gaze as he lifted his wife into his arms and carried her back to shore.

There was a whining sound just before fireworks exploded

in the night sky above them. Red, white, and blue starbursts twinkled down to earth.

Daniel moaned louder when Liam and his father, the fire chief, reached for the board, pulling him the rest of the way to shore. "I'm dying. Call my daughters. Tell them their da needs to see them to say goodbye."

"Daniel, you'll be fine." The chief tried to reassure his brother as the paramedics moved him onto a stretcher with Liam's and Marco's help.

"I'm dying, I tell you. You need to call my daughters, and you need to call them now."

"All right. We will. Just calm down. Here comes Mom, so stop saying you're dying."

An elegant older woman with white-blond hair clutched Rosa's arm as they hurried down the grassy incline. Kitty Gallagher wore low heels and a light-blue pantsuit. The two women had been best friends since grade school.

After leaving Kitty with the chief, Rosa came to Marco's side. She smiled up at him. "You see, *mio bel ragazzo.* Wishes do come true."

He bent down to look her in the eyes. "What are you talking about? You didn't wish Daniel dead, did you?"

She cuffed him on the arm. "*Stupido.* Kitty's grand-daughters, they're coming home to Harmony Harbor."

"What does that have to do with…?" It hit him then what she meant. "No, Ma. I'm serious. Don't even think about setting me up with the Gallagher girls." Looking into her shining eyes, he knew to protest was useless. He grabbed his shoes and jeans and chased down his boss. "Hey, Chief. Any chance I can take my vacation time next week?"

Chapter Two

♥

The new plane Theia Lawson piloted flew like a dream. A good thing since her passengers were a nightmare.

She winced at the muffled sound of stampeding little feet and shrieking laughter coming through the cockpit door and her noise-reducing aviation headset. She wondered why she hadn't anticipated the drama that would result from transporting Penelope Gallagher, her two mischievous twin boys, and Penelope's half sister, Daphne, who'd exhibited all the signs of a fearful flyer, to Harmony Harbor.

No, Theia thought at the crash and bang that practically rattled the seven-passenger Cessna Citation, she shouldn't be surprised there would be drama with members of the Gallagher family onboard. She'd come to know the sisters' father, Daniel Gallagher, pretty well last fall. The man was adept at causing drama wherever he went. Obviously, he'd passed the talent on to his progeny.

The noise level in the cabin decreased exponentially when a measured baritone leveled instructions to settle down and return to their seats in a firm, commanding tone. Theia's boss and best solidus friend, Caine Elliot, had assumed the role of flight-attendant/co-pilot today. He rarely flew as anything other than her passenger, but he'd decided he needed to go undercover to better gauge the situation with the Gallagher girls.

Theia loved Caine like a brother. She credited him with saving her life and then giving her one far better than she deserved or expected after she'd quit the navy. He was kind and generous, brilliant when it came to business.

But he wasn't the same fair-minded, moral man she knew and loved when it came to the Gallaghers of Harmony Harbor. She might not know a lot about business, but his dealings with the family seemed underhanded and vengeful, traits she'd never seen in Caine, though she'd unfortunately witnessed them in her dealings with his grandmother, Emily Green Elliot. Theia had as little as possible to do with the eighty-year-old tyrant who kept Wicklow Developments and her grandson firmly under her dictatorial thumb.

A conversation between another pilot and air traffic control drew Theia from her thoughts about the Elliots' plot to wrest control of Greystone Manor from the Gallagher family. The pilot flying up ahead reported turbulence. There had been a chance of thunderstorms this morning, but she'd factored them in to her fight plan.

She glanced at the weather radar. There was no change in precipitation levels, but that didn't rule out clear-weather turbulence.

After activating the FASTEN YOUR SEAT BELT signs in the cabin, she pressed the comm button on the audio panel and spoke into the mic on her headset. "For your safety, please ensure your seat belts are fastened, as we may be entering an area of turbulence."

She was about to ask Caine to do the same but doubted he'd hear her above the noise. It sounded like the three-year-olds were throwing a tantrum due to being restrained.

"Get hold of your demon spawn before they kick out a window and send us to a watery grave!" Daphne yelled.

Without warning, the remarks triggered a barrage of memories for Theia. A vise tightened around her chest, making it difficult to breathe. Sometimes that was all it took, just a throwaway remark or a simple sound. She held her breath for seven seconds and then pushed it out for eight. In and out until the tightness in her chest finally released.

Pushing the vestiges of murky memories from her mind, she muted the comm on the audio panel. She wasn't back-sliding. This was just a blip. Her PTSD was under control. She hadn't had an episode in almost a year. Switching on her headset to talk to air traffic control, she requested permission to increase elevation.

Her gaze flicked to Caine as he entered the cockpit. She welcomed the grin that curved her lips at the sight of his disheveled dark hair and his untucked white shirt, the look of frustration etched on his handsome face. The Gallaghers had clearly tested the limits of her typically unflappable boss.

He took his place beside her. "Don't even," he muttered as he put on his headset.

She waited until the plane leveled off at the new altitude and she'd checked the radar to respond. "Bet you wish you'd listened to me and drove the Gallaghers to Harmony Harbor instead of flying them to their father's *deathbed*. You're a much better driver than you are a co-pilot. Plus, you look good in Harry's uniform," she said, referring to Caine's personal driver.

"Yes, but I'd have to pay attention to the road. And as you so sweetly pointed out, you have no need of my services. This way, I can spend more time observing Penelope and Daphne."

"How's that working out for you?"

"Smartass," he said without heat.

"So I take it Penelope and Daphne, like the rest of the Gallagher family, have bought into Daniel's deathbed act?" She couldn't believe they'd fallen for it the first time, let alone a second.

"They have, but I'm not convinced the soon-to-be-ex Mrs. Gallagher has. Tara won't allow Daniel's youngest, Clio, to fly over." Tara and Clio lived in Ireland.

"Three daughters by three different wives. He's quite the lad, our Daniel is," Theia quipped, though she honestly wasn't surprised. Daniel Gallagher was a handsome charmer who had a way with women.

Personally, she liked the man. He was interesting and engaging, and beneath his gregarious bravado, she'd caught a glimpse of a man who wasn't as happy or as confident as he appeared, which she found kind of endearing. It didn't mean she approved of what he was doing behind his family's back. In her book, you were loyal to your family no matter what.

Even if that family included an uncle who could barely look at you now and cousins who'd tormented you growing up and hadn't outgrown the habit. Her aunt loved her at least.

Thoughts of her family carried with it the memory of their last visit two and a half years before, days after the accident. Theia cleared her throat in an effort to get rid of the emotion the memories evoked.

"It's probably a good thing there's only two to deal with.

From the little time I've spent with them, there doesn't appear to be any love lost between Penelope and Daphne. I imagine throwing a third sister into the mix would make it that much worse," she said, her voice huskier than usual.

"You're probably right, but it would carry more weight if all three of them were here to demand their shares of the estate be sold immediately."

She pressed her lips together to keep from voicing her disapproval of the plan. It was none of her business, and she had no intention of sticking her nose where it didn't belong. She'd grown fond of the Gallaghers in the short time she'd stayed at the manor last fall, but she loved her job and couldn't afford to lose it. Her salary was more than generous. Without it, she wouldn't be able to make amends to the family who'd lost their husband and father because of her, or to sleep at night, or live with the guilt of what she'd done. What she'd failed to do.

Besides, she considered Caine family. She owed her loyalty to him, not to the Gallaghers.

"I know how you feel about this, T, but you don't know the entire story. Emily—" He broke off to stare straight ahead. "Trust me, I have good reasons for what I'm doing."

She'd known all along that his grandmother was behind this, but she couldn't call him out on it, could she? Emily was his family. And, like Theia, he believed you stuck by family no matter what. As far as she knew, his grandmother was the only family he had left. He was an adult orphan like her.

Actually, she wasn't positive she was an orphan. She'd never known or met her father. Despite her mother dragging her to Ireland every summer to search for the man she'd proclaimed to be her grand passion, the love of her life.

Theia rolled her eyes. As far as she was concerned, romantic love caused more trouble than it was worth. Especially the head-over-heels kind. Or, as she thought of it, the kind of love that made you lose your mind. It wasn't that she was against the whole marriage thing. She wanted a family. Eventually. She just didn't have time for one now. Even if, at thirty-four, her biological clock was ticking so loudly it was getting hard to ignore.

But ignore it she did. She had a debt to pay. And until she'd paid it, she didn't deserve to be happy. She scrubbed her hand over her face, refocusing on the job.

"I'm sure you do have a good reason, Caine. But all I care about right now is that we're flying back to New York at five like you promised." She glanced at him. "We will be, won't we?"

The sooner she was gone from Harmony Harbor the better. Pretending to be someone he wasn't might not bother Caine, but it bothered her. A lot.

"You have a hot date you didn't tell me about?"

"Caine."

"Okay. Relax. As far as I know, we'll be leaving at five. I was a little busy trying to corral the terrors, so it was tough to get a read on how Daphne and Penelope feel about the Gallaghers and the manor. I got the impression they're not overly fond of their father."

Theia laughed. "The master of understatement. They hate the guy. Can you blame them? It sounds like once Daniel was done with the mother, he was done with the daughter."

"Yeah, he's not going to win Father of the Year. Which is why I suggested he tell Daphne and Penelope that he wants them to keep the estate in the family. Given how they feel about him, that should ensure they do the exact

opposite. It works in our favor that they both could use
an influx of cash. Penelope and her husband recently separated, and Daphne was on the losing end of her divorce
settlement."

Since Penelope was a marriage counselor and Daphne a
divorce attorney, Theia could understand how their marital
problems might affect their professional reputations and
negatively impact their incomes. She imagined their careers
of choice also added another layer of conflict to the sisters'
already difficult relationship. Still, she thought her boss
might be forgetting one important detail.

"I hate to be a Debbie Downer, but you do realize that
seven of Colleen Gallagher's great-grandchildren are firmly
in the Save Greystone Manor camp, right? And trust me, if
you think the pushback from the Harmony Harbor Business
Association to your Main Street development is tough, they
have nothing on the Gallagher great-grandkids."

"You hate to be a Debbie Downer?" Caine snorted a
laugh. "T, you're one of the most pessimistic people I
know. But I appreciate you pointing out the possible snag.
It's one of the things I love most about you. Even when you
don't agree with me, you're always looking out for my best
interests. You're the one person I can count on to tell me
the truth."

It hadn't done her a lot of good in this instance. He had
a blind spot when it came to the Gallaghers and the estate.
He'd already found a loophole that would allow him to buy
Penelope's and Daphne's shares. It was how he planned to
get the other Gallaghers to sell that worried her.

Not my monkey, not my circus, she thought. Still, she
couldn't keep herself from saying, "Yeah, you can always
count on me to tell you the truth. I just wish you'd listen
to me now and again, especially when it comes to this. If

you're determined to go ahead with it, you have to handle every last detail. Big or small. You can't allow your grandmother to get involved in any way. Look what happened two years ago."

Theia had been new to Wicklow Developments and hadn't been Caine's trusted confidante at the time, but she'd heard what had happened when Emily had been running the show in Harmony Harbor. It was why Caine had asked Theia to go undercover at the manor last year.

"You don't have to remind me. It's not something I'm likely to forget." Even if it wasn't his fault, it was obvious Caine still felt guilty about not keeping a closer eye on what was going on in Harmony Harbor when a woman whom Emily had hired was murdered. Just not guilty enough to walk away from Greystone Manor. "It's also the reason why—"

Whatever he was about to say was interrupted by chatter over the radio. They were in for a bumpy ride. Caine sighed and went to undo his seat belt. "You got this?"

"You're kidding me, right?" It would take a lot more than a little turbulence and an incoming storm for her to require her co-pilot's assistance.

"Can't blame a guy for trying," he said as he went to unfold his six-foot-four frame from the seat just as an alarm sounded. "What the—"

Theia scanned the panel for the problem, refusing to let the shrill beeping sound mess with her head. "Looks like our fearful flyer decided to calm her nerves with a cigarette. Better get her out of the bathroom before we hit turbulence."

She wasn't sure Caine heard her over the toddlers yelling *fire* and Penelope banging on what Theia assumed was the bathroom door. She didn't bother giving her safety spiel over the comm. She'd let her flight attendant handle their passengers while she avoided the turbulence as best she could. She looked at the weather radar while talking to air traffic control, calculating their chances of making it to Harmony Harbor before the approaching storm.

Ten minutes later, they were through the worst of the turbulence. Better still, it sounded like Caine had calmed the nerves of all four Gallaghers.

She activated the comm, relaying to her passengers that they would be landing shortly and to please keep their seat belts fastened. She imagined Caine had already ensured that they did. Theia silently echoed Daphne's cheer that they'd soon be landing. Not only would Theia be rid of her passengers shortly, but she was confident they'd beat the incoming storm. More important, according to the weather radar, the system would clear out before her departure time of five. She mouthed, *Woo-hoo*.

Caine entered the cockpit looking worse than he had before.

"Not your usual love bite," she said with a nod at the teeth marks on his tanned forearm.

"You're enjoying this, aren't you?"

"No, I—" She broke off, frowning when someone began yelling in the cabin, and it wasn't the terrors. Not the little ones at least. "Is she saying 'fire'?"

Caine turned and ran. In his hurry, he forgot to close the cockpit door. Theia caught a glimpse of Penelope on her hands and knees in the aisle.

"What were you thinking, giving them your purse? You should have taken out the lighter!" she yelled at her sister while patting the carpet under the seat.

Theia's mouth went dry. The threat was real. She'd assumed Penelope was being dramatic.

"I didn't give it to him! H-he must have…*Mon Dieu*, we're going to die!"

"No one is going to die. Out of the way, Penelope, and get the boys buckled," Caine said, taking her place on the floor. Seconds later, he shot to his feet, his eyes meeting Theia's as he rushed toward the cockpit.

"How bad?" she asked, hoping her hat hid the perspiration beading along her hairline.

He had to raise his voice to be heard over the twins, who were hysterically crying. "Can't be sure, but better to err on the side of caution and have the fire department meet us on the tarmac."

A tremor ran through her, and she gave him a jerky nod. She activated her comm, relaying the situation to air traffic control. Caine reached for the Halon extinguisher to the right of the co-pilot's seat.

She glanced back at Daphne, who began her *We're going to die* chant again. Her face was frozen in terror, her hands clutching the armrests in a straight-armed death grip.

"Stop it. Stop saying that! You're scaring the boys," Penelope screamed at her sister. Which seemed to work, at least on Daphne. But the twins instantly picked up where their aunt had left off, and then Theia heard the pounding of little feet and one of those brothers screaming, "Help! Save us!"

Some of Theia's tension eased when Caine, who'd been having trouble getting the extinguisher to release, stood with it in his hand. But no sooner had he turned to head for the cabin than the little boy screaming for help burst into the cockpit, hurling himself at Caine's legs and throwing him off-balance. All six feet four inches and two hundred and twenty pounds of Caine landed on Theia, slamming her forward. Her face smashed into the instrument panel,

while her hands jammed against the controls. The plane
banked sharply to the right.

"Theia!" Caine shouted as the momentum threw him
off her.

She pushed herself upright, her vision blurring as she
absorbed the sights and sounds around her. Caine was
now on the floor, his feet anchored against the backs of
the seats to keep the g-force from throwing him and the
crying little boy he protected with his body around the
cockpit. The twin's brother, mother, and aunt were hysterical in the cabin.

Theia wiped away the moisture dripping into her eyes,
surprised when her hand came away bloody. There wasn't
time to worry about her injury. The Cessna's nose was
down. They were going into a death spiral. She'd been in
one before. They didn't both make it out alive. The faces
of Caine, the Gallagher sisters, and the little boys filled her
mind. Everything inside her froze at the thought that they'd
die on her watch.

"It's not the engine. You're good. You've got this."
Caine's calm, confident voice penetrated the panic that
held her in its icy grip, snapping her out of it.

She forced a grunt of agreement past her lips as she
pulled the throttle back to idle and then brought the nose
up. She squinted past the blood dripping into her eyes, trying to focus on the navigation equipment. A muffled cheer
filled her ears, and then the voice of the air traffic con-
troller. She flew the requested pattern with no problem,
ensuring both she and the plane were fit to land.

Focused on proving that both she and the Cessna were
good, Theia hadn't noticed the quiet that had descended
within the cabin. Caine must have gotten the little boy back
to his seat the moment the plane leveled off. She glanced

at the cockpit floor. There was no sign of blood, other than her own, but she needed to know everyone was okay, and whether the fire in the cabin was out. Instead of reminding her already traumatized passengers that they weren't out of the woods yet, she activated and deactivated the seat belt sign a couple of times to get Caine's attention. Hoping he'd be in a position to notice.

He practically burst through the cockpit door. "Are you okay?"

"Yeah, I'm good. How about you and the little guy?" She frowned at the expression on his face. "What is it? Is the kid not okay? The fire's spread?" Her heart leaped to her throat.

"You're hurt. You're covered in blood. Dammit, T, this is on me. I should have shut the cockpit door. Made sure the kids were buckled in," he said as he rooted around one-handed in the back pocket of the co-pilot's seat. He must have found what he was looking for because he straight-ened, then leaned toward her.

"Caine, I'm good. I'm fine," she said when he began gently cleaning the blood from her face.

Theia never let anyone know when she was hurting or scared. Even Caine, who was pretty much her closest friend in the world. She hadn't told him about the almost inca-pacitating panic she'd dealt with when she first got back in the cockpit. After the accident, she thought she'd never fly again. If it weren't for Caine, she probably wouldn't have. But she'd never let on, never let her guard down, never let him see the crippling fear that would overtake her at the most unlikely of times.

Her uncle, the colonel, had taught Theia to never let anyone see her sweat or see her cry. To show any sign of vulnerability or weakness was to allow the enemy to see it too. Her male cousins had done a good job of beating the lessons into her, as had the navy. She'd learned to hide her emotions very, very well.

"The little guy, the fire, that's what I'm concerned about." She pushed his hand away. "Stop. I need to prepare for landing, and I need to know what we're dealing with."

He made a frustrated sound before he reached for his headset and took his place beside her. "Other than being terrified to leave his seat, the boy's fine. I don't think we have to worry about the rest of them either. I wish I could say the same about the fire. There's no flame, but there is smoke. I can't get the extinguisher to work. It must have gotten damaged when I dropped it. I soaked the area with water, but—"

"You think it's under the floor." She scanned the instrument panel, looking for signs they had an electrical fire onboard. She didn't see anything so far. Although she did see signs of the incoming storm. The winds had started to pick up but not to a worrisome level. Visibility was still good. It wouldn't be long before it wasn't. She contacted the control tower while doing a quick prelanding check of the equipment. "Cessna Citation one three five, ready for landing."

She didn't have to state the runway. It was a municipal airport with only one runway, which could be tricky with crosswinds. She was okayed to land. Her heart pounded at the line of fire trucks and ambulances awaiting their arrival. She prayed they didn't need them.

Her prayers were answered. As soon as they'd taxied to a stop, she unbuckled her seat belt and stood. She locked her shaky legs, fisted her trembling fingers, and gritted her teeth when a wave of dizziness washed over her.

"Get the Gallaghers off as quickly as possible and hold

back the fire department. I want a chance to deal with this on my own." The last thing she wanted was for them to tear her new baby apart for no reason.

"You need to get your head looked at. Let the professionals…All right." Caine held up his hands and then grabbed his black uniform jacket off the back of the seat. Recovering his black hat from the floor, he fitted it on his head and pulled the brim low. "On this plane, you might be the boss, but I'm your boss on the ground. You're getting checked out whether you like it or not."

Theia rolled her eyes as she followed him out the cockpit door and then winced. Maybe she wouldn't fight too hard when he demanded she let the paramedics look her over. She didn't have to worry about him getting the Gallagher party off the plane immediately. They did that all on their own with murmured goodbyes.

No apologies or thanks for the ride, she noticed. Though she supposed she couldn't blame them. She wasted less than a second thinking about the Gallaghers and moved to the seat where the little pyromaniac had been sitting. No sooner had Theia pulled back the carpet than she heard the clump of heavy boots in the aisle. She lifted her head to peek between the seats. A firefighter in full gear filled the space. She gave a panicked yelp at the sight of the hose in his hands and shot to her feet.

"It's all right. I—" A blast of water knocked her on her butt.

Chapter Three

♥

"Close the discharge valve!" Marco yelled into his radio, pulling back against the force of the water blasting from the hose to aim the nozzle at the ceiling. Heads were going to roll for this, and not just his.

"Hang on. I'll be with you in a second," he called out to the woman struggling to her feet. "Don't try to stand."

He gave his head a frustrated shake when her chin jutted at a stubborn angle and she ignored his directive. Teeth gritted, she grabbed the armrest of the chair in front of her, hauling herself upright. Two seconds later, she was back where she started—on her butt in a puddle of water. Exactly what he'd anticipated would happen and why he'd warned her to stay put.

It wasn't just the amount of water causing her to slip. They'd gone with a mixture of foam and water because they'd been told there was an electrical fire. An electrical fire that would soon cause the plane to explode if they didn't get it under control immediately. He'd also been told the plane had been evacuated, so he'd gone in water and foam blasting.

Movement caught his eye, pulling him from his inner tirade at the guy in the tower who'd relayed the misinformation. Once again the woman was pulling herself to her feet.

God save me from stubborn women.

"Ma'am, do me a favor and don't move," he said at the same time his pipe man yelled in his ear that the valve was stuck. Marco swore in Italian at the situation and the woman, who'd ignored him *again* and had gone down for a second time. With her chin-length dark hair plastered to her pale, red-streaked face, she looked like she belonged in a horror movie.

He tamped down his frustration and began moving toward the exit door. "Just stay where you are until I get back, ma'am. I promise, I won't be long."

Blood streamed from the open wound on her forehead, her eyes narrowing as she once again hauled herself to her feet. "No. No way. Just go. I don't want to see you and your hose near my plane again."

Marco's gaze shot to her mouth. He didn't care that those bright blue eyes were shooting daggers at him or that it sounded like she thought he was an idiot and pretty much hated his guts; he needed to hear that voice again. Smoky and sultry, his body responded as if they were tangled in the sheets on a warm summer night instead of in a standoff over six inches of dirty water in a sweltering metal coffin.

"If you so much as put one boot back on this plane, I swear to God I will…" Her eyes went wide as her feet once again shot out from under her. Only this time she ended up flat on her back, the water rolling over her before she got her mouth closed. She jolted upright, choking and sputtering.

Concern for the woman managed to distract him from his crazy fascination with her voice. He called for backup. Most of the crew were nearby treating the passengers and captain. Liam bounded up the metal stairs, and Marco met him at the exit door.

His best friend stuck his helmeted head in the cabin. "What's going—whoa, there was someone still onboard?"

"Not another one," the woman on the floor groaned. She sounded like she was going to lie back in the water but then thought better of it.

Instead of yelling *Sit your ass down before you break something,* like he wanted to, Marco fought with the hose to hand it off to Liam. "Take this," he said, and then turned to stride to the woman's side.

He reached her just as she staggered to her feet. Since she'd done exactly the opposite of what he suggested every single time, he decided to take matters into his own hands. After all, there was a possibility she was in shock. He would have been, given the terrifying ordeal she'd just endured.

They'd been responding to the call at the airfield when one of the crew pointed to the sky and they watched the plane spiral toward the earth at a sickening speed. He'd nearly lost his lunch, and he was pretty sure his knees had gone weak.

"Hang on. I've got you." He bent down, positioning his shoulder against the dripping white shirt plastered to her stomach, and put her in a fireman's hold.

"Don't even think about it, buddy." She pushed forcibly on his head.

He staggered a little, surprised at her ability to move him, at the strength in her slender arms. She was about five six to his six two and a good hundred pounds lighter. Her willowy frame was deceiving. Her attitude, not so much.

He took off his helmet and set it on one of the seats, pushing his fingers through his damp hair while silently counting to ten as he reminded himself what she'd been through. He gave her a reassuring and (go, him) patient smile. "Look, I have a grandmother and a sister who are just like you. They're strong, independent women, and the last thing they'd want is to be carried out of here." He didn't add *Just as pig-headed* too. "But as you've found out, like, three times, your shoes aren't onboard with your plan."

He tapped his forehead. "You've also suffered a head injury that needs to be checked out." At the reminder—not that he needed one, really, but it solidified his plan to get her out of there ASAP, no matter how much she fought him; she probably wasn't thinking straight—he braced his feet and bent to pick her up.

"What do you think you're…? Put me down. Put me down this—oomph." Her breath shot out of her when he carefully tossed her over his shoulder.

She pounded his back. Her delicate-looking hands packed a wallop. He tightened his arms around shapely legs that seemed to have more muscles than the average female, at least the females he dated.

His sister teased him for being attracted to the delicate flowers who needed to be rescued—something this woman was not. He also wasn't attracted to her, which kind of validated his sister's assessment. Except he wasn't totally immune to the woman currently flaying his back with her fists, as his body's reaction to her voice, even now, proved.

"Would you just relax?" he said when she continued to struggle. "We're almost…" His legs buckled. She'd gotten a foot free and kicked him in the crotch. Despite the emasculating pain, he regained control of her legs and her feet and managed to make it to the end of the aisle without falling to his knees. "Keep your head down," he said, an angry snap in his voice as he ducked out the door.

He winced. She might have nearly unmanned him, but less than twenty minutes ago her life had probably flashed before her eyes.

The winds had picked up, noisily whipping the flag over the terminal, rattling the metal staircase he carefully traversed to the tarmac. The plane's captain looked over from where he sat in the back of the ambulance, having his hand wrapped. He blanched and shot to his feet, shaking off the paramedic.

"What happened to her? Is she going to be okay?" he asked as he jogged toward them.

"The only thing wrong with me is *him*. He completely overreacted to the situation, ruined the interior of the cabin, and then decided to play He-Man." She tried to wriggle out of his hold. "Put me down. Now."

The pilot looked relieved. "Don't give him a hard time, T. He was just doing his job."

"He's right, ma'am. Now, if you promise not to kick me again, I'll put you down."

"So, what? If I don't agree, you're going to walk around with me over your shoulder for the rest of the freakin' day?"

"When you put it like that…" He kept his amusement in check as he lowered her feet to the ground. He grimaced when she stood before him. Her hair and face were bloody. Both he and the pilot reached for her when she swayed. She swatted their hands away. "I'm fine."

"Of course you are. You just look like you're auditioning for a horror flick."

"That's exactly what I thought," Marco said, smiling companionably at the pilot. "By the way, man, that was some flying. Honestly, I don't know how you held it together. From down here…" Marco trailed off. He didn't think the woman needed to hear what it looked like from the ground. "Anyway, great job."

"I'd like to take cred—"

Arms crossed and head cocked, the woman interrupted the pilot. "He wasn't the one flying the plane. I was."

Marco laughed. "Yeah, right."

"I'd take two steps back if I were you. Maybe four. Her legs are longer than they look." The other man covered a grin with his bandaged hand.

She stopped glaring at Marco to stare at the pilot. "What happened? Why didn't you tell me you were hurt?"

"Same reason you're pretending you don't have blood dripping in your eyes. We're both stubborn idiots. Now, go get yourself checked out. I'm going to inspect the damage to the cabin. I've got a call in to the maintenance crew." He looked up at the darkening sky. "They probably won't make it until sometime tomorrow."

The observation earned the man a withering glare, which the woman then turned on Marco before stomping off in the direction of the ambulance.

"You're not yanking my chain, are you? It really was her flying?" Marco winced when she stopped. She looked like she was about to turn around and stomp back to him but instead gave her head an irritated shake and continued to the ambulance.

Her co-pilot leaned in to him. "She has excellent hearing."

Marco glanced to where she now sat in the back of the ambulance. "Despite what it sounds like, I'm not a sexist jerk. I just—"

"Yes, you are," she yelled at him while waving off the paramedic.

"I think she just told them not to waste time numbing her cut before they stitch it. She's like some kind of superhero. Oblivious to pain and able to save planes from crashing to the ground," Marco said.

"I wouldn't say that in her hearing, but in some ways, she is. She's a former navy fighter pilot."

"Really? Wow. That's, ah…cool." He went with the opposite of what he'd been going to say. Hot. The woman was hot.

"Trust me, pal. You don't want to go there," the co-pilot said.

"What? You think I'm interested…in her? No. I just met her, and she, ah…" He was about to say kicked him in the groin and maybe quip that he wasn't a masochist, but his gaze had strayed to where she sat talking to the paramedic who was preparing to stitch her cut, acting like she wasn't nervous. Her fingers clenched into fists said otherwise. And that small show of vulnerability intrigued him. He wondered what else she was hiding.

"Hey, what do I know? You may be exactly the man for the job." Grinning, her co-pilot clapped him on the back and walked away.

Marco followed him to the plane. "Okay. I don't know what you think I said, but it wasn't that. Seriously, it wasn't."

"'Methinks the man doth protest too much.'"

"It's *lady*. 'Methinks the *lady* doth protest too much,'" Marco corrected him.

The co-pilot laughed. "If she heard this conversation, she certainly would."

* * *

Theia had no idea what Caine had just said to the man who had ruined her plan to escape from Harmony Harbor at five tonight, but they looked too buddy-buddy for her boss to have threatened to sue the Harmony Harbor Fire Department. Lucky for her—and the overzealous firefighter—there was hardly anyone around to witness her humiliation.

She could only imagine what her uncle and cousins would say if they had seen him throw her over his shoulder. Who does that in this day and age? It wasn't like she was incapacitated or seriously injured.

Self-consciously, she rubbed her butt while squinting at the two men, trying to read their lips. Caine looked far too amused for her liking. And her would-be knight in turnout gear looked…panicked.

Why would he look panicked? Of course. She should have known. Caine was threatening to sue, just doing so in a nonconfrontational manner. Which made sense, she supposed. It wasn't as if the firefighter had purposely set out to flood the plane and put it out of commission for who knew how long. Maybe he was new on the job or not very good at it.

"Stop squinting. You're wrinkling your forehead, and this is difficult enough as it is." The paramedic leaned in to peer at the cut, made a face, and pulled back. "Are you positive you're allergic to local anesthetic? I feel really bad that I'm hurting you. It would be better if you went to the hospital. There's a plastic surgeon on—"

"Don't worry about me. I grew up with three older male cousins and have the scars to prove it. I'd rather a few minutes of pain than an outbreak of hives any day."

"Okay. If you're sure." She leaned in again, gingerly repositioning strands of Theia's hair. "Your hair is all clumped together with blood, so it's hard to tell if you have bangs. If you don't, a wispy side bang would look great on you and hide the scar." The twentysomething woman gave her a commiserating smile. "It never fails, does it? You always meet the hottest guys when you're looking your worst."

Theia frowned. "What do you mean?"

"Um, you're all bloody, and your hair is kind of matted and stuck to your face. Plus, you have no makeup on, and your white shirt and black pants aren't all that flattering, you know."

"I'm a pilot. This is my uniform. It's not supposed to be flattering. It's also wet. And I don't wear makeup." She'd tried once, but her cousins had teased her mercilessly.

"That's cool, you being a pilot and all." She sighed. "I wish I could have been you for five minutes. Not when you were actually flying, of course. Just when Marco carried you from the plane." She fanned her face with the hand that held the needle. "He is so hot. And he's—"

"An idiot."

The paramedic jerked back. "What? No, he's not. He's, like, a hero. He's amazing. Everyone loves him."

"Why?"

"Because he's a great guy. He'd do anything for anybody. And, well, like I said, he's totally hot. Anyone with two eyes in their head can see that."

Okay, so admittedly the guy wasn't hard to look at. He had the whole tall, dark, and handsome thing going on with his thick, wavy hair and masculine, chiseled jaw. But so what? The world was full of good-looking guys. She'd worked with a bunch of them. Not that she'd share that with the head of his fan club.

"Looks aren't everything. Being good at what you do is what really counts, and he isn't," Theia said.

"Wow. I can't believe you just said that about a man

who risked his life to save you. Who ran into danger instead of away from it. For you."

"It's his job. And the only danger I was in was because of him. I nearly drowned. If he had evaluated the situation before coming in water blasting, he would have seen I had it under control." She was eighty percent certain she would have if she'd had two minutes to evaluate the situation herself.

"Just FYI, HHFD was told there was an out-of-control electrical fire onboard and they had seconds to act before the plane exploded. They were also told the plane had been evacuated. Marco's an experienced firefighter and a total pro. He had an equipment malfunction."

"Oh, I didn't—"

"Maybe you shouldn't make disparaging comments about someone before you know the facts." She leaned toward Theia with the needle poised. She didn't look so friendly anymore.

Theia leaned back and put up her hand. "You know what? I'll take care of it myself."

Chapter Four

♥

Theia wondered what the odds were of her would-be rescuer not seeing her as she crossed the tarmac to the plane. She sighed when Marco glanced her way and changed direction, meeting her halfway.

"Don't let me stop you from doing what you have to. I…I'm…" What exactly was it she'd been going to do? Somehow she'd lost her train of thought. It might have something to do with his warm caramel-colored eyes.

The paramedic was right; he was an exceptionally handsome man. The type of man a woman would fall head-over-heels in love with, especially if he was as great a guy as the paramedic made him out to be. Theia blamed the woman for her sudden inability to think straight. No man could live up to that hype. She lowered her gaze from his. "I'm going to check on the damage report."

"And I wanted to check on you. How's your head?" His brow furrowed, and he raised his hand.

She jerked back. "What are you doing?"

He slowly lowered his hand. "Are you always this jumpy?"

"No…well, yes, sometimes." She lifted her bangs, positive that's what he'd intended to do. "See, all good."

"No, it's not all good. Your wound should have been stitched, not glued."

"I know. The paramedic told me glue doesn't work well on foreheads, but I'll take my chances." She tried to shove her hands in her pockets before realizing the water had practically sealed the seams shut. So instead she rubbed her hands self-consciously on her hips while looking around. "She also told me about your equipment malfunction and that you'd been misinformed about the severity of the fire. Sorry for misjudging you and acting like a…well, you know."

His mouth lifted at the corner. Funny, she hadn't noticed his lips until just then. Nice. Actually, she'd go so far as to say he had a beautifully shaped mouth. His bottom lip was full and looked…*Ugh*. What was up with her sudden obsession with his looks? It was the paramedic's fault. Theia should have slapped a bandage on her forehead and called it a day.

"So, what, you thought I wasn't only a sexist jerk but an idiot too?"

"That's about right." She fought a grin. Mostly because he was doing the same and it was kind of contagious. "Just so you know, I still think you're sexist."

"I'm not, but I can see why you might think I am. And if I try to defend myself, I'll no doubt validate your opinion."

A firefighter came around the nose of the plane, waving him over. "Hey, DiRossi, we could use some help with the kids."

"Is he talking about the Gallagher kids? The ones who

were on the plane?" She thought they'd already left for the manor.

"Yeah." He brought his attention back to her. "The other team was treating the aunt and one of the boys. Liam promised them a ride in the engine. He's their second cousin."

"I know. I stayed at the manor last fall. Liam's wife, Sophie, hired me to fly in guests for the manor. But I, ah, got a lucrative contract I couldn't pass up." Even though she barely knew the man, she hated lying. It had been awful leaving the Gallaghers in a lurch last year. She blamed Caine for putting her in this position.

"Sophie's my sister. I remember her talking about you." He rubbed the back of his neck. "My grandmother talked about you too."

She didn't miss the grimace. "Looks like I didn't make a good impression," she said, then frowned as she put two and two together. "Wait a minute. If Sophie's your sister, that means Rosa DiRossi is your grandmother, and I know for a fact I made a good impression on her." She winced, thinking she should have kept that tidbit to herself. She'd made such a good impression on Mrs. DiRossi that the older woman had decided Theia was the perfect match for her grandson.

Marco sighed. "Don't worry. You're off the hook. She has her sights set on Liam's cousins as the future Mrs. DiRossi."

"I'm pretty sure it's still illegal to have two wives. Anyway, Penelope and Daphne don't seem the type to share."

He laughed, turning at the high-pitched whir of a siren. "I think that's my cue. I better go help with the boys. I'll see you around."

"I doubt it. I'm leaving first thing in the morning."

"You might want to tell that to your co-pilot. He seems to think you'll be around for a few days."

"Does he, now?"

Marco held up his hands, his helmet in his right. "Don't shoot the messenger." He began to walk away and then turned to walk backward with the wind whipping through his movie-star-gorgeous hair. "If you start feeling dizzy, nauseous, or get a headache, go to the hospital and get checked out, okay?"

"Hospital sounds like overkill. I'll just take an aspirin—"

He shook his head. "No aspirin or ibuprofen. You could have a concussion or a bleed."

"Good thing you're not a doctor. Your bedside manner needs some work. Thanks for leaving me with that cheery thought though."

"I may not be a doctor, but I am a certified paramedic, so do me a favor and take it easy tonight."

A firefighter *and* a certified paramedic, she thought as she watched him walk around the nose of the plane. Weirdly, her heart started to race. So maybe she did find him a little hot.

"This is a first. I've never seen you drool over a man before, T. You'll be glad to know he seems to feel the same way about you."

"Get out of here. He does not. And I wasn't drooling." Pretending she was scrutinizing the body of the plane for signs of damage, she rubbed a hand across her chin while surreptitiously moving her index finger to the corner of her mouth.

Caine broke into a wide grin. "You are interested."

"I am not. And don't think you can distract me. I know what you did."

"What are you talking about? I didn't do anything."

She repeated word for word what the paramedic told her and then crossed her arms, waiting for him to try to deny it.

"All right, I may have exaggerated the risk to the plane."

"You told them it was seconds away from exploding! Was there even a fire?"

"Yes, but it appeared to be contained. And before you ask, no, I didn't expect the water damage to be quite so bad."

"I don't believe you, Caine. I could have been hurt. There's a lot of pressure in one of those hoses, you know."

"I didn't expect you to stand in the line of fire." He grabbed her hand as she turned to walk away and tugged her back. "I'm sorry. The last thing I wanted was for you to get hurt. It's no excuse, but just before I went back to the cockpit to prepare for landing, Penelope and Daphne were talking about how freaked out they were. They decided to stay a few days at the manor to recover. In my defense, I didn't exactly have a chance to think it through. Things were a little hairy at the time, if you recall."

"Trust me, I remember. But you need to come up with a better excuse because that one's not working."

"Right or wrong, I did what I thought was best for Wicklow Developments. A lot of money and time has been invested in this, T. I don't trust Daniel not to blow it. You can help him stay focused. You're good with him. He likes you."

"He's afraid of me."

"There is that." He smiled. "I promise, it'll be a couple of days at most. I need you to keep an eye on him on and stick close to Penelope and Daphne. We don't have anything pressing scheduled. You can enjoy a few days by the sea. Get some R and R."

"Right, because hanging out with Daniel, his daughters,

and grandchildren will be so restful." She blew out a breath and shook her head. "Isn't there another way? You know how I feel about this, Caine."

"I know, and I'm sorry to have to ask you to go against your principles again. It's just that you're the only one I trust to do this."

She'd heard that before, and it was getting old. Even if she knew it was the truth. Caine must have sensed she was teetering on the edge of refusing because he said, "I'll give you a thousand dollars for every extra day you have to stay."

"Done." Holden's oldest wanted to go to college in the fall. Had he survived the accident, her naval flight officer would have made sure his son had everything he needed. Now it was Theia's job to see that he did.

"I should have known. People would think I don't pay you well. What do you do with all your money?"

"Save it for a rainy day."

He cocked his head to study her. "No, I don't think so. One of these days I'll figure out what—" He broke off when a bolt of lightning crackled above them. "Skies are going to open up any minute now. You want me to call you a cab, or do you want to hitch a ride with Marco?"

"You're not funny."

"I know, but you love me." He looked over her head. "Looks like your ride is here."

She glanced over her shoulder to see a tall, silver-haired man in a well-tailored black suit rounding the plane, an umbrella in hand. He lifted it in greeting. The man's name was Jasper. He was a mainstay at the manor and ran the show behind the scenes. He was also Kitty Gallagher's love interest.

Caine drew the brim of his hat lower. "I'd better take off

before he gets a good look at me." He kissed the top of her head. "I owe you above and beyond the bonus, T. Take it easy tonight, and call me if you have any of those symptoms Marco mentioned."

"Where are you going?"

"I'll rent a car and check on some business I have in Boston. Keep your ears open about the Main Street development. The town hall meetings are scheduled for the fall, and I want to know which way the citizens of Harmony Harbor are leaning."

Caine and his grandmother were developing a modern office tower on Main Street. It was like the Elliots were determined to oust the Gallaghers as first family of Harmony Harbor. But major opposition from the town's business community had shelved the deal until the citizens of Harmony Harbor had been consulted.

"Gotta go," Caine murmured as Jasper approached. He acknowledged the older man with a brief nod and then headed for the terminal at a jog.

Jasper's intent gaze followed Caine before he turned to Theia with a smile. "It's good to see you again, Ms. Lawson. Although I wish it were under better circumstances." His tone was as clipped and proper as she remembered, with a whisper of a British accent underneath.

"I wish it were too. Daniel's daughters and grandchildren were shaken up."

"Quite. But without you in the cockpit, it could have been much worse. Was that your co-pilot you were speaking with?"

"Yes. Yes, it was." She welcomed the splat of raindrops on the tarmac. "We should probably get going. It looks like it's about to pour."

"Quite." He opened the umbrella with an expert flick of

his wrist, then held it over their heads. "Kitty is having a room prepared for you as we speak. She's delighted you'll be staying with us again. Would you like a room prepared for…? What's your co-pilot's name?" he asked as they walked across the tarmac.

No matter how casually he asked his question, she got the feeling Jasper knew more than he let on. He made her nervous. He was always alert, taking in what was going on around him without appearing to do so, turning up where you least expected. Those traits, combined with his bearing, made her suspect he was former military or law enforcement or, if she was given to fancy, an international spy. If anyone could blow her cover, it would be him.

"James…" She caught herself just before *Bond* popped out of her mouth. "…Moneypenny." And that's so much better, she thought, rolling her eyes at herself. Two and a half years out of the navy and she'd lost her game.

"I'm almost certain I've heard that name before."

"He gets that a lot. We better hurry…Ow." She brought a hand to the back of her head.

"Oh dear, stay still. I'll untangle your hair." He gave a sharp tug, pulling out several strands as he freed them from the metal tip of the umbrella. When she objected with a cranky "ouch," he grimaced. "All good now. We'd best be off." Placing his free hand in his pocket, he set off at a fast clip.

Theia glanced at the tarmac to get a look at just how much hair she had lost. There was nothing there. She frowned. He didn't pocket them, did he?

* * *

It isn't easy being a ghost, Colleen Gallagher thought as several guests walked through her while she waited impatiently in the entryway of Greystone Manor for her great-granddaughters' arrival.

She'd been dead for two years, eight months, and one week. She'd died on All Saints Day in the manor's elevator at the age of one hundred and four. She'd been ready to join her family on the other side, but the good Lord had other plans for her.

She had a few of her own.

At the top of her list was to see her great-grandchildren happily married and settled in Harmony Harbor—preferably at the manor. The estate had to be protected at all costs. Founded by William Gallagher, it had been in the family for centuries. She wasn't about to have it lost on her watch. And things were coming to a head. She could feel it in her bones.

Caine Elliot, the CEO of Wicklow Developments, the man who wanted to get his greedy hands on the manor, had set his most dastardly plan yet in motion. He was using Colleen's grandson Daniel against them.

She knew what Daniel was about as soon as she spied him out the window of the tower room on the Fourth of July. He'd been in the middle of the harbor on one of those paddle thingies, pretending to have an attack. He needed money for an archaeological dig, so he'd do whatever Caine asked of him. Even if it meant selling out his own family.

She'd been haunting the turncoat ever since she'd discovered what he was up to. Only that hadn't worked out as she'd hoped. The other day he'd moved from the manor to one of the cottages.

No one else had the slightest inkling what Daniel was up to behind their backs. But at least her daughter-in-law

Kitty had shared her suspicions about Theia Lawson with Jasper, Colleen's old friend and confidant.

While Theia had been staying at the manor last fall, they'd noticed a resemblance to the man they believed to be her father. She had the Gallaghers' blue eyes, you see. And just like Daniel, the voice of an angel. But more telling had been the story of her mother singing for their supper throughout the pubs of Ireland with the father Theia had never known. And then there was her uncommon name. Obviously Daniel had shared his fondness for the goddesses of Greek mythology with Theia's mother, as all his daughters had been named after one.

Colleen wished she could share her thoughts on how to deal with both Daniel and Theia. Jasper and Kitty had the best intentions, but things didn't always go as the couple planned.

And Colleen couldn't order the adults in the family to do her bidding like she used to. For one, they didn't see or hear her. There were exceptions to the rule though: Young children could see her, and Simon, her boon companion, could both see and hear her.

The black cat had arrived within days of her dying. Lately, she'd come to believe there was more to Simon than met the eye. He wasn't your average cat. Of that she was certain.

Wondering where he'd gotten to, she turned and spotted him padding after her daughter-in-law, who hurried from the study. Kitty wore white capri pants paired with an ice-blue top with the shoulders cut out. Despite being in her late seventies, the woman was still as style conscious as she'd always been. Kitty patted her elegantly coiffed hair, looking nervous as she went to open the door.

She'd planned to go to the airport to pick up the girls,

but at the last minute, Jasper had suggested she stay behind. Colleen suspected it had to do with the phone call Jasper had received from Kitty's son Colin, the fire chief, just moments before they were to leave for the airstrip.

"It looks like they'll be here any minute now, Simon," Colleen said. Then, remembering how some of her great-great-grandchildren had reacted upon seeing her for the first time, she looked for a place to hide. The door to the closet just down from the entryway stood half-open, providing her with the perfect hiding place.

Well, it would have been perfect had Kitty held her horses and let the girls and the twins come inside. Instead, her daughter-in-law let out an excited squeal at the sound of a siren and hurried outside, closing the door behind her. Apparently, Simon was as excited as Kitty because he hightailed it after her, slipping out the door before it closed.

No matter how much she wanted to, Colleen couldn't follow after them. If she tried to leave the manor, she'd only bounce off what felt like an electrical force field. It wasn't a pleasant experience. She'd tried at least fifty times with the same shocking result before she'd given up.

She considered hurrying to one of the offices that had a view of the front walkway and parking lot but decided to bide her time. It turned out to be the right call. No sooner had she had the thought than the front door opened.

Marco DiRossi appeared in full firefighter gear with what could only be Penelope's boys in his arms. The children had strawberry-blond hair, a smattering of freckles on their handsome little faces, and mischief in their Gallagher-blue eyes. It was clear they were a handful. No wonder their mother was having a hard time of it.

But at that moment the twins were having themselves

a good giggle over something Marco had said. Colleen wasn't surprised that the lad had a way with children; it was the same with the ladies, as Penelope proved when she followed them inside, smiling up at Marco like he was a hot-fudge sundae with a cherry on top.

Colleen studied her great-granddaughter. It had been so long since she'd last seen her. The gangly, awkward teenager she remembered had become a beautiful woman with a lovely peaches-and-cream complexion, bright blue eyes, and honey-blond hair. She wore a flowy floral top and an ankle-length skirt, which seemed to indicate she was still the sweetly feminine and quietly introspective girl Colleen remembered. She hadn't been surprised to learn she'd become a marriage counselor.

Marco crouched to set the boys on the ground. "You guys were a big help today," he said to the twins.

When he stood to say goodbye, the little boys wrapped their arms around his legs. "No, don't go," one of them said at almost the same time his brother said, "We want to go with you."

"Are you kidding me? The station is boring compared to this place. Besides, you guys haven't spent any time with your great-grandma Kitty."

Kitty gave Marco a grateful smile. As happy as her daughter-in-law was that Penelope and the boys were finally here, Kitty looked ill at ease, perhaps afraid to say the wrong thing and send them packing. Colleen understood her concern.

Prior to Daniel's deathbed summons, the girls had shown no interest in visiting. Even learning they were beneficiaries in Colleen's will hadn't been enough to entice them to come two years before. But they'd both been happily married and doing well at the time and obviously saw no benefit in holding minor shares in an entailed estate. At least until now. Colleen had a feeling it was more than their father's deathbed summons that brought the girls to Harmony Harbor.

"I'm sorry," Penelope said to Marco as she attempted to unlatch the boys from his legs. "William, Weston, let go."

Kitty must have picked up on the frustrated weariness in Penelope's voice and intervened. "Boys, Cook has made a special treat for you." She held out her hands. "Would you like to come with me to see what it is?"

The boys looked at each other and then up at Marco. "Can you come?"

He ruffled their hair. "I have to get back to work. How about I drop by for a visit another day, okay?"

Just as the twins opened their mouths to deliver what looked to be a protest, the door opened and in walked Penelope's sister Daphne. With her beautiful café-au-lait skin, Gallagher-blue eyes, and rich dark-brown hair, Daphne had shown signs of the stunner she'd become early on. A pair of diamond-studded sunglasses held her glossy hair back from a face that wore a distinctly unimpressed expression. Taking that into account as well as the elegant white crop top she wore with form-fitting black pants and high heels, it appeared her great-granddaughter hadn't changed much. Supremely confident and razor sharp, she'd always had a bit of an edge.

Perhaps picking up on the same, Kitty restrained some of her obvious delight at seeing her granddaughter for the first time in years. "Daphne darling, it's so good to see you." She seemed to weigh whether the coolly elegant woman in front of her would welcome a hug.

Daphne solved that by kissing Kitty on both cheeks. "It's good to see you too, Grandmama." She looked around, gave Marco a smile as he said goodbye and headed out the door, then asked, "Papa isn't here to greet us?"

"He hasn't been well, darling. But I'm sure we'll see him this evening. He's as happy as all of us that you've come for a visit."

"Unwell, my eye," Colleen scoffed. "You're not doing Daniel any favors making excuses for him like you do, Kitty."

Jasper and Theia walked in, loaded down with suitcases. Colleen chuckled. The girl was a right mess in her wet uniform, her face pale, and her dark hair standing up at the crown. Even though she'd obviously had a difficult morning, she managed a warm smile for Kitty. As Colleen had noted the last time she was at the manor, Theia Lawson seemed like a nice woman despite the fact that she was working with their enemy.

Kitty greeted her as warmly as she had her granddaughters, which seemed to make the girl uncomfortable. Perhaps picking up on her discomfort, Jasper suggested she retire to her room and freshen up.

"We should do the same," Penelope said, and then glanced at Kitty. "Would you mind sending the boys' treats to the room?"

"Not at all," Kitty said, despite her obvious disappointment.

Daphne took her luggage from Jasper. "I'll do the same if you don't mind."

"I've got it," Theia said when Penelope offered to take their luggage. She lifted her chin. "Lead the way."

"Just give them time," Jasper murmured to Kitty as they watched the women and children head across the lobby. "Come; I have some news you'll want to hear." He took her hand and walked with her down the hall off the entryway.

Curious about Jasper's news, Colleen followed after them.

Kitty turned to Jasper as soon as he closed the door of the study behind them. "Is Theia staying?"

"I believe so, and I have even better news." He held up a plastic baggie. "Not only did I manage to get several strands of her hair, but there's blood on one of the samples. We should be able to get an accurate DNA reading."

Kitty stared at the man openmouthed. "Jasper! What did you do?"

Colleen wanted to know the same.

"As if I'd harm the child. She was hurt earlier. They had a rough flight. One of the twins nearly brought the plane down. It sounds like they take after their grandfather."

Colleen prayed the twins were nothing like their grandfather. They had enough to contend with this week.

"How soon will we know if Theia is Daniel's daughter?" Kitty asked.

"We should have the results back within two weeks."

She chewed on her thumbnail. "Do you think we can get her to stay that long?"

He didn't look hopeful but no doubt realized that wasn't the answer Kitty needed or wanted to hear at the moment. Ever since Ida Fitzgerald had suddenly died a few months back, Kitty had become obsessed with ensuring her family was happy and settled.

"I'll do everything in my power to ensure she does, my love."

Since it was the first time she'd heard Jasper utter an endearment, Colleen surmised he had been as affected as Kitty by the loss. If only they could hear her, Colleen would set both of their minds at ease.

Theia Lawson wasn't going anywhere. She was Caine

Elliot's right-hand woman and confidante. He'd no doubt sent her here to ensure Penelope and Daphne signed over their shares to either him or Daniel. They were all in for a very big surprise if they thought they could settle the matter in a few days.

Colleen chuckled. Sometimes she amazed herself.

Chapter Five

♥

Theia awoke to someone knocking on the guest room door. She turned blurry eyes to the alarm beside the double bed and jolted upright, disgusted with herself. It was nine o'clock. She hadn't slept past five since she'd moved in with her uncle and aunt at the age of twelve.

After being raised by a mother who adopted a hedonistic lifestyle and had no problem sleeping past noon, her uncle's early-morning wake-up whistle had taken some getting used to. Now she embraced it. Not the whistle—never the whistle. But she did love getting up at the crack of dawn and knowing she had the whole day ahead of her.

"Coming," she called to whoever was knocking on the guest room door.

She flipped back the covers and got out of bed. She'd slept in her bra and panties, drying them with a blow-dryer before crawling into bed around nine last night. Her mother would have laughed at Theia's inability to sleep naked.

Theia hurried to the bathroom and grabbed the hotel

robe off the hook on the back of the door. As she stuffed her arms into the sleeves, she cast a frustrated glance at her phone, sitting in a bowl of rice on the white marble counter.

Her phone was the reason she'd slept in. Since leaving the navy, she'd gotten used to being woken up by her alarm. Something else she had to thank Marco DiRossi for. Not only was he responsible for her dead phone, but he was the reason she'd ignored the alarm going off in her head, rolling over to dream about him some more. She was beginning to think the blow to her frontal lobe had done more damage than she'd thought. Since when did she allow a handsome man to mess with her head and interfere with her assignment?

She ignored the obvious answer, which caused a warning sign to flash in her mind, and dug her cell phone from the rice, turning it on as she crossed the room. Nothing happened. The screen remained black. Something else to add to today's to-do list. Which basically comprised two things—run interference with the Gallaghers and get Penelope and Daphne to sell their shares.

She'd dropped the ball yesterday. Though it wasn't entirely her fault. Penelope and Daphne had retreated to their rooms for the rest of the day and evening, claiming exhaustion. Daniel, on orders from his health care provider, was supposedly too weak to receive visitors. It took Theia less than fifteen minutes to discover the orders came from the woman who ran the manor's spa and not Daniel's nephew, the doctor.

Theia didn't push the issue. Daniel was undoubtedly nervous about his daughters' reception. He had good reason to be. Still, she managed to find some sympathy for him. Even if he was a deadbeat dad, she'd gotten the impression last year that he loved Penelope and Daphne. He just didn't seem to know what to do with them. But her sympathy extended only so far. If she had anything to say about it, he was meeting them today. They needed to get this wrapped up sooner rather than later. The less time she spent here lying the better.

Shoving the dead phone in the bathrobe's pocket, she opened the door. Daphne stood on the other side. The woman was stunning. Her flawless mocha skin emphasized her beautiful blue eyes. Her long hair pulled up in a high ponytail, she wore a black stretch crop top and calf-length running pants that showcased her incredible body. Theia wondered what it must be like to wake up every morning looking like a supermodel.

Daphne had it all: brains, beauty, and a family who loved her. Even if her dad wasn't that great at showing it, her grandmother and cousins were. The reminder that the extended Gallagher family would wrap the two women and the twins in their loving embrace added to the pressure Theia already felt. The longer they stayed in Harmony Harbor, the more likely Daphne and Penelope would be to side with the Save Greystone Manor Team.

Theia shifted in her bare feet, a little embarrassed by the protracted silence. She caught Daphne's eye. It appeared the other woman had been staring at Theia for as long as she'd been staring at her. Obviously not for the same reason. Theia probably looked like something the cat dragged in and spat up.

She gave Daphne a sheepish grin. "Slept in and didn't have a chance to brush my hair yet." She fluffed it with her fingers. Sometimes that's all she did before heading out. Her hair might not be movie-star gorgeous like Daphne's, but it was healthy, shiny, and thick.

"Me too."

Theia cocked her head. "Seriously? You didn't brush your hair and it looks like that?"

"No. I slept in too. I'm just heading out for a run now. I'd hoped to get it in before it heats up, but it's already, like, eighty in the shade and the humidity is killer." She shrugged and then picked up a bag by her feet. She handed it to Theia. "Jasper mentioned that you didn't have any clothes with you and asked if I had anything you could borrow. All I have is some extra workout wear. It should fit. We have the same build."

"I wish," Theia murmured, surprising herself. Her body might not be as curvy as Daphne's, but she was in great shape. She should be. When she wasn't working for Caine, she was working out. To cover her murmured discontent, she quickly added, "This is great, thanks. Do you mind if I join you on your run? It'll take only a couple minutes for me to get ready."

She hoped Daphne didn't mind. This would be the perfect opportunity to get a read on the woman. The perfect opportunity to turn her against Harmony Harbor and Greystone Manor. Which was as far as Theia would go. She'd never try to turn Daphne against her family.

"Sure. I'll wait for you in the lobby."

"Great. See you in a few."

True to her word, Theia met Daphne at the entrance to the manor less than five minutes later. With its towers, Gothic-style wooden doors, and stained-glass windows, Greystone resembled a fairy-tale castle. There was even a suit of armor standing sentry in the lobby, with its massive stone fireplace, slate floors, and a grand staircase with a red runner and brass railings.

Theia would never admit it to Caine, but she thought it a shame Wicklow Developments planned to replace the manor with modern, high-end condos. She felt the same about the glass and steel office building they wanted to build on Main Street. With its old-world, seafaring charm, Harmony Harbor was postcard perfect.

She'd better get thoughts like that out of her head, she mused as she offered Jasper a smile. The older man looked up from polishing the entry table when she approached.

"Daphne tells me you two are off for a run." He looked particularly pleased with the turn of events, which seemed a little odd. It wasn't like Jasper knew Theia was lacking in the female friend department. She'd always gotten along better with men than she had with women. The years she'd spent in the navy were no doubt partially to blame. There weren't a lot of women in her previous line of work.

"We are," Theia said, looking down at the hot-pink tank and stretchy ankle-length leggings she wore with her sneakers. It wasn't an outfit she'd choose for herself, but still… "I appreciate you thinking to get me some clothes. I'll stop by Main Street later."

"I didn't wish to overstep, but I noticed you didn't have bags with you. Ms. Daphne came to mind. Probably because you look rather alike."

Theia stared at him. He couldn't be serious. Daphne was beautiful, whereas she was…average?

"For your shopping expedition this afternoon, I'd recommend you stop by Merci Beaucoup," he continued without missing a beat. "Though you may wish to go right after your run instead of waiting until later. Main Street is busy year-round, especially on the weekends, but it gets quite crowded during the summer months."

The older man had just given her the ideal opening for her "down on Harmony Harbor and the manor" campaign. "Tourist towns are such a drag in the summer months, aren't they? Then they turn into a ghost town once everyone leaves."

Jasper looked somewhat offended. "Harmony Harbor draws tourists all year long, Ms. Lawson. Especially here at the manor."

"I'm sure they do." She smiled and then nodded at Daphne, who stood in the entry like a stork, stretching her hamstrings. Theia hoped the other woman had been taking in the conversation. She didn't want to offend the older man for no reason. "I didn't realize how sticky and humid it is here in July. Daphne, we'd better go before it's too hot to breathe."

Jasper's heavy silver eyebrows drew together. "Perhaps you should run on the boardwalk. That way you'll get a nice breeze off the ocean. Take the path to the left of Kismet Cove. You may recognize it, Daphne. You used to love walking on the boardwalk with your grandfather whenever you came to visit."

"Did you come to the manor often when you were young?" Theia asked after they'd said their goodbyes to Jasper and headed outside. It wasn't nearly as hot or as humid as she'd made it out to be. It was actually quite lovely, with a warm, floral-scented breeze rustling through the trees along a path bordered by wildflowers.

"Not often, no. My parents divorced when I was five. We were living in France at the time. After my mother and Daniel split up, the trip became too expensive to make. I came once as a teenager. Great-grandmama Colleen paid for all of us to come. She thought it was disgraceful we sisters had never met."

Theia had a feeling that she wouldn't stand a chance of turning Daphne and Penelope against the manor and the town if the Gallagher matriarch were still alive.

"Did you stay in touch with your sisters?" From her brief interaction and observations of Daphne and Penelope together, Theia didn't think they had. She didn't understand why not. She would have loved to have a sister growing up.

"No. Clio was quite young at the time. Penelope and I exchanged letters for a while. Then our correspondence slowly dropped off. Our mothers didn't encourage our relationship. They each blamed the other for Daniel leaving them. My mother seemed to think Daniel was still in love with Penelope's mother." She rolled her eyes. "Love makes people act crazy."

Theia agreed completely. Her mother was a perfect example. "I guess you see a lot of crazy being a divorce lawyer."

"Yes, and lately in my own life." Her expression soured, and she picked up the pace, her feet slapping against the wooden slats as she reached the boardwalk.

Theia took the hint and enjoyed the view instead of digging deeper into Daphne's psyche. She didn't want to alienate her this early in the game.

Trees arched over the walkway. The shiny green leaves rippling in the breeze provided a cool oasis, shafts of golden sunlight cutting through the shadows. The *snick* of their sneakers on the wooden planks competed with the *swoosh* of waves rolling against the rocky shore. The boardwalk hugged the coastline, moments later providing a startling view of the harbor.

Daphne slowed her pace, no doubt to take in the sailboats dotting the sparkling, crystal-blue water. A horn blasted as a fishing boat headed into the harbor.

"I miss views like this. Growing up, I lived in a fishing port. Harmony Harbor reminds me of my village."

Theia grimaced at the note of nostalgia in Daphne's voice. Clearly, convincing the woman that life in a small town by the sea was far from idyllic was off the table. "Still, there's something special about big-city living, isn't there? You must love New York." Theia picked up the pace in order to leave the stunning views behind them.

"At first I did," Daphne admitted, catching up to her. "But it's begun to lose its appeal. Thanks to my rat-bastard ex, I can no longer afford our condo in Manhattan."

This could go either way. On the positive side, Daphne was obviously in need of cash. While on the other hand, in her present circumstances, she might be more open to moving to a small town by the sea. "You never know; you might come in to a windfall and be able to stay in your condo. The commute would be killer if you had to move out of the city. Your law offices are located in Midtown, aren't they?"

Daphne glanced at her, a frown creasing her brow.

Right. If Theia were a mere pilot and owner of a small air charter service, she would have no reason to know where Daphne worked. "Wow, look at that view," she said in an effort to distract the woman, pointing at the deserted beach below. It was a pretty view with the sea grass fluttering in the light breeze. Though hardly a *Wow* view, at least it seemed to have distracted Daphne. She jogged lightly on the spot, taking it in with a slight smile playing on her lips.

She waggled her eyebrows at Theia. "Now, that's what I call a view. Let's go down and say hi."

"You want to say hi to the seagulls?"

She shook her head with a laugh and then took Theia by the shoulders, turning her slightly to the left. "No. I want to say hi to *him*. The hunky firefighter Penelope seems to have pegged for husband number two."

"What?" Okay, that came out a little forceful. She

cleared her throat. "I mean, come on. She wasn't around the guy for more than five minutes and she pegs him for husband material? If you ask me, he looks like player material," she said, eyeing the man in question as he walked to shore. He pushed his wet hair back from his face with both hands, his biceps flexing, water glistening on his tanned, washboard stomach. He could be shooting a commercial for men's cologne or for the watch on his forearm, which caught the morning light, or the black board shorts that hung low on his hips.

Marco DiRossi was quickly becoming her least favorite thing about Harmony Harbor. He was the fly in her ointment, the rock in her shoe, the pain in her butt. He'd wreaked havoc with her phone, her beautiful new plane, and her peace of mind, and now it looked like he might mess with her plan to get Daphne and Penelope out of town ASAP.

"I hope so because I'd certainly like to play with him." The words came out of Daphne's mouth on a seductive purr.

"Wait." Theia hurried after the attorney, who was taking the wooden stairs to the beach two at a time. "You just said Penelope wanted him for herself. Isn't there some kind of sister code that prohibits you from going after the same guy?"

"Maybe if we grew up together, or even liked each other, she could invoke the sister code. But we didn't, and we don't."

"Yes, you do. You told me so yourself." She wondered if Daphne picked up on the panic in her voice. Theia heard it loud and clear. She worked to smooth it out when she added, "You used to write letters—"

"A long time ago. Now we're basically strangers who share the same deadbeat papa. Besides, she doesn't want

Marco for herself. She wants him for her kids. They adored the guy. And she's still in love with her husband."

Theia clung to that one piece of good news. Penelope was in love with her husband, who lived on the West Coast. The perfect inducement for the thirty-three-year-old mother of two to get this wrapped up as quickly as possible. Caine probably had the goods on the guy. Once he shared with Theia what he knew, she'd develop a game plan.

She looked up at the sound of a deep male voice returning Daphne's greeting. A greeting that, probably due to the overtly sexy French accent she'd wrapped it in, held the hint of an invitation. It was the first time Theia had noticed Daphne's accent. According to the file, the attorney had followed her ex to New York seven years before.

Daphne left all subtlety behind when she reached the man, rubbing his hair dry with a towel. "You're an incredible swimmer. Do they teach you to swim like that in firefighter school, or were you a lifeguard?" Smiling up at him, Daphne smoothed her beautifully manicured hand down his arm, lingering at his impressive bicep.

Theia rolled her eyes. It never ceased to amaze her how some women, no matter how smart and beautiful, turned into idiots around a good-looking guy.

"Thanks. We do water rescue training every couple of days during the summer, and I was a lifeguard for about all of three weeks at sixteen. According to the man who fired me, I spent too much time flirting with the girls." He smiled as Theia reached them. "Hey, how's the head?"

"Fine. How's the hose?"

The corner of his mouth twitched. "Haven't had any complaints."

"I bet you haven't," Daphne murmured in her sex-kitten voice.

"I was talking about his equipment," Theia said, forcing her eyes to remain on Marco's face. Daphne sure as heck didn't keep hers there.

"So was I," the attorney said, twirling the end of her ponytail around her finger.

It took all Theia had not to push Daphne into the water. She was making smart women everywhere look bad. Her obvious attraction to Marco was also making Theia nervous. The last thing she needed was a reason for Daphne to want to remain in Harmony Harbor. Somehow, she had to lower Marco's attraction quotient in Daphne's eyes.

"Saw you out there. Your kick could use a little work, but you're not bad," she said.

"*Not bad*. Who were you watching? He was amazing." Daphne gave her a pursed-lips look, then smiled at Marco, batting her long lashes. Where was the woman's pride? Had her husband stolen that too?

Marco smiled at Daphne and then winked at Theia. "Thanks for the tip. I'll keep it in mind. Enjoy the rest of your run, ladies."

"Are you heading to work?" Daphne asked.

"No. Jolly Rogers for breakfast." He bent to grab a white T-shirt from the sand.

As he did, Daphne turned wide eyes at Theia and waved her off.

Oh no. No way was she letting the other woman invite herself to breakfast with him.

"Enjoy your breakfast. Come on, Daphne. We have to hit Merci Beaucoup, and I need your help. I don't speak French, and I'm clueless when it comes to clothes."

"Apparently you're clueless about a lot of things," Daphne muttered.

* * *

Payback's a bitch, and Daphne paid her back big-time.

Standing outside her room at the manor, Theia transferred the four shopping bags to her left hand and with her right dug her room key from the pocket of her new and ridiculously overpriced white jeans. Once she got over her snit, Daphne took great delight in dressing Theia and spending her money.

In the space of two hours, Theia had spent more on clothes than she had in the past ten years. She was torn between wanting to leave Harmony Harbor as soon as possible and staying an extra couple of days to recoup her losses.

As she opened the door, she noticed a small box on the floor addressed to her. She looked around the room. Nothing else seemed out of place. She closed the door and then placed the bags on the floor to pick up the box. She recognized the bold, masculine handwriting. It was from Caine.

She went to the bed and sat on the end. Opening the box, she smiled when she saw the new cell phone. He must have realized hers was dead when she missed their usual morning check-in call. He'd saved her a trip to the nearby town of Bridgeport.

The phone rang. It was fully charged and programmed. Caine Elliot was not a man who did things in half measures.

She barely got out her hello.

"I've spent the last four hours worrying about you. There is a landline available at the manor, you know."

"I do, but I didn't have a chance. I had the opportunity to spend some one-on-one time with Daphne, and I thought you'd prefer that to me checking in."

After yesterday, when Caine went all juvenile and accused

her of drooling over Marco, she didn't want to bring up the man. And maybe she didn't want to be reminded of Daphne's reaction to him either. Though, in fairness, ninety percent of the female population would no doubt react the same at the sight of the wet and sexy firefighter.

But even if Daphne's reaction were normal, the fact that Rosa DiRossi planned to match one of the Gallagher sisters with her grandson was worrisome on a whole other level. Theia had seen the matchmaking Widows Club in action last year. So, no matter how much she wanted to, she couldn't keep the news from Caine.

Just as she opened her mouth to tell him, he said, "I have some worrisome news. When our IT guy went to put trackers on Penelope's and Daphne's cell phones, he discovered someone had already done so."

"Who would do something like…? Emily." She pressed a hand to her face, groaning into her palm.

"It didn't take you long to figure that out. Now you need to figure out who she's hired to do her dirty work at the manor before things get out of hand."

Chapter Six

♥

Colleen sat in the window seat in the study with Simon curled up beside her. The time had come for Daniel's daughters to be apprised of the entire contents of her will. George Wilcox, the Gallagher family attorney, sat behind the centuries-old mahogany desk sorting papers.

Red-faced and sweaty, he stopped to take off his glasses and give them a polish, nervous no doubt at what would transpire. When she'd first requested the addition of the codicil, he'd warned her against playing God with her great-granddaughters' lives. He told her meddling would get her in trouble, just like it had years before, just like it would if the contents of the memoir she'd been writing at the time, *The Secret Keeper of Harmony Harbor*, ever saw the light of day. She'd written down the secrets of her family and friends, secrets of her own in the book.

She hadn't known it at the time, but George had a point about her memoir. It wasn't until she died and the leather-bound book went missing that the consequences of it being found had hit home. Still, she believed it was important that some of the secrets were recorded for posterity. She hadn't meant for it to be available for all and sundry to read. The problem had been that she'd begun to think she'd live forever.

She chuckled at the thought. She wasn't completely wrong, now, was she? But that wasn't the point. She'd died before she had decided who to entrust her book of secrets to.

Her memoir had eventually been found and was now in the hands of Kitty and Jasper. Her once right-hand man and confidant had been high on her list of candidates to whom she'd leave the book. Kitty had been at the lower end of the list.

In a way, Colleen had been proven right on both counts. She judged her daughter-in-law and Jasper's ability to right the wrongs of the past at fair to middling. Mainly because they managed to make a right hash of things before they eventually turned out as Colleen had wanted them to in the first place.

Like she did with her book, she'd ignored George's warning about the codicil. She had her reasons for what she'd done.

George slipped his glasses back on and did another brief scan of the pages before passing the copies across the polished wood. Penelope and Daphne leaned forward to retrieve them.

Colleen glanced to where Jasper stood in front of the closed door as if barring the girls' hasty retreat. His disinterested expression didn't fool her. He was as anxious as she was to see how Penelope and Daphne would react when they learned the only way they'd be entitled to vote on their inheritance was to remain at the manor for a month and take on jobs of management's choosing.

She'd added the stipulation for several reasons. Most important was that, unlike her great-grandsons, her great-granddaughters had barely spent any time at the manor. The only way they could become proper stewards of the family's greatest treasure was to fall in love with Greystone the same way Colleen had. And for that they needed to spend time here and take part in everyday life.

Truth be told, the blame lay with their mothers more than the girls and Colleen. She'd begged them to be allowed to spend their summers in Harmony Harbor. She'd offered assurances and money, yet nothing worked. All she'd wanted was for the girls to know their father's side of the family. To know that their great-grandmother and grandparents loved them and would be there for them if they were ever needed.

Ronan, Colleen's son and Kitty's husband, had been gone ten years now, but Jasper would stand in his stead. And while Colleen might be an incorporeal being, she'd improved at this ghost gig. She'd help where she could. In some ways, she thought she'd just given Daphne and Penelope the best gift of all. She'd given them a second chance to know their family and to become sisters.

She'd given their father a second chance as well. She just hoped he'd take it. Daniel had never liked a challenge where the odds were stacked against him. He'd rather walk away than be made to look like a fool.

Colleen smiled, thinking she'd have some help on that end. Theia had proven herself adept at handling Daniel last fall. She wondered how the girl would feel if the DNA results proved Daniel was her father. For that matter, how would Daniel feel? Colleen hoped he didn't mess up as badly with Theia as he had with Penelope, Daphne, and Clio.

Daniel's youngest would be here if not for her mother once again intervening. Still, she would have expected Clio to ignore Tara's wishes and hop on a plane, making her way to Harmony Harbor on her own. She was as hard-headed as her mother and father combined.

"It looks like the moment of truth is upon us, Simon," Colleen said when both girls looked up from their papers to stare at George.

Exhausted from running away from Penelope's twins, Simon barely managed to lift his head, but he did manage a rather remarkable facsimile of a stink eye. She supposed she shouldn't be surprised that he wasn't overjoyed the twins would be here for a month if their mother agreed to the terms Colleen had set out in the codicil.

"Is this some sort of joke? No one in their right mind would expect someone to walk away from their life for an entire month."

Colleen sighed. "Leave it to a lawyer to look for a loophole."

"I can assure you your great-grandmother was of sound mind when the will was drawn, Daphne. I pointed out some of the obvious problems that might result from the stipulations, but she was adamant, and I believe she had her reasons. The job you will be given is a paid position, and of course you receive free room and board."

"What about day care? Will there be someone available to look after the boys while I work?"

"Your grandmother and I will be delighted to look after the children for you, Ms. Penelope," Jasper said.

"Are you sure? They can be a handful."

Jasper smiled. "So were your cousins. We'll be fine, and may I say I think your time here will be good for all of you."

Daphne stared at her sister. "Are you seriously thinking of staying?"

Penelope shrugged. "I don't have any reason to go home."

"I know you and your husband are separated, but what about your practice?"

"It's a little difficult to sell yourself as a relationship expert when your marriage imploded as publicly as mine did. I took a leave. Honestly, I don't even know if I want to practice anymore."

Colleen recalled Kitty mentioning something about Penelope's marriage crashing and burning on live TV.

"Unlike you, I don't have the luxury of taking a leave."

"You're really going to stay at the same legal firm as your ex?" Penelope said.

"Of course not, which is why I have to get back to New York and pound the pavement."

"You don't, not really. You told me you're living out of a suitcase at a Best Western. So stay here and figure it all out. We can figure it out together," Penelope added softly, as though afraid to be rejected.

"I don't know."

Jasper's gaze moved from Simon to where Colleen sat, a congratulatory smile hovering on his lips. He might not be able to see or hear her, but Jasper sensed her presence. He knew she'd be here to see how it played out.

"Come on. It might be fun." Penelope bit her lip and then lifted her eyes to Daphne. "We don't know how much time we have left with Dad. I have things I'd like to work out with him. I'm sure you do too."

"We've been here since yesterday afternoon, and he's yet to grace us with his presence. If you ask me, that doesn't sound like a man who wants to make amends to his daughters."

Jasper rubbed the bridge of his nose between his thumb and forefinger before saying, "Your father wasn't up to receiving visitors yesterday, but he's feeling better today. We'll arrange for a visit this afternoon. Does that work for you both? Perhaps lunch on the patio?"

"Is he up to lunch on the patio?" Penelope asked, glancing from Jasper to her sister.

"Leave it with me," he assured her with a faint smile, his eyes once again drifting to where Colleen sat on the window seat.

She sighed. "You have no idea what a snake he is, my boy. No idea at all."

George beamed across the desk at the girls. "This is wonderful news. Just wonderful. I'm sure your great-grandmother is smiling down on you both from heaven."

Jasper raised an eyebrow in the direction of the window seat, as though asking if she was going to make her presence known. She'd done it with Daniel, which was why he was no longer residing at the manor. So she thought it best not to alert the room to her presence. George was likely to have a heart attack if she did.

"You have all the time in the world to make up your mind, of course, but are you leaning toward keeping the manor in the family or selling?" her attorney asked the girls.

"Selling," they both said at the same time and then smiled at each other.

"Oh, I see," George said, appearing flustered. "You are aware that the shares can't be sold to anyone outside the family, aren't you?"

"Yes. Our father doesn't want us to sell, but if we choose to, he'll buy the shares from us."

"But we can also sell them outside the family if we decide to. A trust can be broken when it can be proven it causes undue hardship to a beneficiary." Daphne withdrew what appeared to be a legal document from her purse and handed it to George.

Jasper looked at her like he couldn't believe that either Daniel or the girls would conspire against them.

"The henhouse is overrun with foxes, my boy. And it's past time we expose them."

* * *

"Don't worry, it'll be a couple days at most, T." Theia mimicked Caine's voice as she crossed the bridge over the pond with her phone pressed to her ear. "Well, FYI, it's not days; it's"—she glared at the swan gliding beneath the bridge, which had the audacity to make a loud snorting sound and interrupt her tirade—"a month. I am not staying a month, Caine. You can't afford to keep me on this job for a month. Besides, they told the lawyer they're selling, so we're good."

"No, we're not good. They have a month to get to know their family and a month to fall in love with the manor. An entire month to change their minds. I need you there to keep reminding them that the best thing for them to do is sell."

"But maybe I don't think it's the best thing. Maybe the best thing for both of them is to get to know their family. They're not like you and me, Caine. The Gallaghers are great. They'll be there for them. And from where I'm standing, Daphne and Penelope could use someone on their side for a change." She stopped walking and leaned on the rail, worried that she'd said too much, worried that she'd inadvertently hurt him. "I'm sorry. I just hate lying to everybody."

"I know, and I'm sorry to ask you to. But you're wrong, you know. About the money? I'll give you a thirty-thousand-dollar bonus to stay the month and see the job through. I'll wire ten thousand into your account now."

"It's worth that much to you?" She thought about what the money would be worth to Holden's wife and son. Combined with Theia's savings, she could cover his four years in college.

"Yes. I haven't got a clue who's working for my grandmother. I tried to get her to tell me, but she won't. She says she no longer trusts me to get the job done."

"You know what? I really don't like your grandmother. She's vindictive and mean, and I hate that she can hurt you."

"She's sick, T. She tries to hide it, but I know that she is. I don't think she has long to live, and that worries me."

"Because she'll be desperate to see this through before she dies." A shiver ran down her spine.

"It's the only thing she cares about. It's what's driven her for the last sixty years."

And it's what's driven you your entire adult life, Theia thought. *Emily made sure that it did.* Which was why Theia said, "I'll do it. I'll stay. But this is the last time I ever do something like this, Caine. I mean it. I don't care how much you pay me."

"It's the last time. I promise. The money will be in your account by the end of the day."

"Fine. I'll talk to you later."

"T, you're wrong about something else. You and I, we're family. We always have each other's back. We don't need anyone else."

"I know that, you big dope. I said yes already." She held the phone over the pond, afraid he'd hear her sniff away her tears. She rubbed her nose and then went to bring the phone back to her ear when the swan leaped from the water, gigantic wings flapping, its beak opened wide. She released a startled yelp and pulled her hand back just in time. Its beak brushed the tips of her fingers. "A swan just tried to eat my phone!"

"T, it's me. You're allowed to get emotional. It doesn't mean you're weak, you know."

"What are you talking about? I'm serious. There's a killer swan in the manor's pond."

"Really? Maybe that's an angle you should explore with the twins and Penelope."

"Thanks. But I'll run this op my way."

"Whatever you say, Lieutenant."

She loved Caine, and as she'd just proven, she'd do anything for the guy. But she knew herself. If she didn't figure out a way to assuage her guilty conscience, she'd end up with an ulcer before the month was out.

She crossed the manicured lawn to the path through the woods. She was on her way to Daniel's house. Jasper had asked her to retrieve him for a father-daughters' lunch this afternoon. She'd been only too happy to oblige. She needed some one-on-one time with the man.

And as she thought about the come-to-Jesus talk they were about to have, she realized what she had to do to be able to live with herself. She'd make Daniel into the perfect father. She'd turn him in to exactly the kind of father she'd always dreamed of.

Chapter Seven

♥

W hat the hell happened to you?" Liam shouted as he dragged Marco into the Coast Guard rescue boat.

Marco grunted in response, leaning heavily against the side of the boat as he tried to catch his breath. He needed a minute to recover, but mostly he needed to figure out what to say.

He couldn't share his suspicions with his best friend. His best friend whose father was the chief of HHFD. If Liam thought for a second that someone had deliberately put Marco's life in danger, he'd go to his father whether Marco wanted him to or not. And Marco wouldn't be responsible for ruining a man's career unless he was a hundred and fifty percent certain what happened onboard the freighter was intentional.

They'd been participating in an interagency exercise, simulating a response for a hazardous-material emergency on an offshore vessel. HHFD, their hazmat team, the US Coast Guard, the harbormaster, and three neighboring fire departments were all involved. This wasn't the first time Marco had been used as an alternate on the hazmat team. But it was the first time he'd nearly gotten himself killed doing so.

Two screwups within a three-day window wasn't going to look good on his record. Maneuvering in the heavy suits onboard the freighter had its challenges, but until today those challenges hadn't involved him being tripped by a hose and falling overboard. Between the noise, the thick smoke, and the number of players involved on the freighter and in the water, no one had immediately registered that he'd fallen overboard.

Liam crouched beside him to help remove the equipment that had nearly dragged Marco to the bottom of the ocean. "That was too close. If it were anyone else but you, we would have been too late. You would have—" He ripped the protective gloves off Marco's hands and fired them across the boat.

It was an unusual display of anger from his even-tempered best friend. Anger motivated by fear. It was a reaction Marco understood. His anger would have been far worse had their roles been reversed.

Liam's older brother Griffin, a chief warrant officer with the Coast Guard, turned from where he stood at the helm, his eyes narrowed on his baby brother. His concerned gaze moved to Marco, and he did a quick head-to-toe scan and then raised his eyebrows in an *Are you good?* expression.

Marco nodded and decided it was time to convince Liam of the same. "What are you talking about? It would have taken a lot more than a dip in the ocean in a hazmat suit to take me out. Just ask my niece. She doesn't call me Merman for nothing."

"Shut up," Liam said, taking a look around. "What the hell." He pulled him in for a hard hug. "I don't give a crap what they think."

"Aw, you two are so cute together," Sully, the commanding officer and Griffin's best friend, teased.

The rest of the crew took up where Sully left off. The teasing continued nonstop all the way back to the harbor. After the first five minutes, it got annoying, but it helped lighten the mood and ease the tension stringing Marco's muscles tight. All that changed once they reached the dock and the crew disembarked. Marco gathered up his equipment with Liam's help. They were just about to join the others on the dock when Sully and Griffin cornered them.

The two men, wearing their orange vests and navy shirts and pants, crossed their arms, their expressions serious.

"All right, from the beginning. What happened out there?" Griffin said. He was an older, fairer, taller, and more muscular version of Liam and had a don't-mess-with-me air. He'd been a Navy SEAL for close to twenty years before joining HHCG, and it showed. But growing up, Marco had been almost a permanent fixture in the Gallagher household, and he wasn't easily intimidated by Griffin.

"I know you guys wish I were a Coastie, but I'm not. I report to your dad, Griff. Not you and Sully. Thanks for the ride though." He went to walk between the two men.

Sully grabbed his T-shirt and reeled him back in so Griffin could look him in the eye. "You're a pro. You don't make mistakes, and you sure as hell don't fall off a freighter unless—"

In his gut, he knew Griffin had seen more than he was letting on. "I'll deal with it."

"See that you do, or I will." He blew out a breath and then

pulled him in for a one-arm hug. "You're not invincible, you know. That was too close. You're damn lucky you swim like a fish."

"Just call me Merman," Marco joked, unwilling to let Griffin see how much his obvious concern touched him.

He'd never let Griffin know how much it meant to him that he'd stepped in to fill his big brother's shoes. Griffin had been looking out for him since Lucas joined the army, the same year Sophie and their mom left town. The day his big brother walked out the door of the family apartment was the last time Marco had seen him. Lucas always had an excuse at the ready as to why he couldn't come home.

As soon as they'd climbed out of the cutter and onto the wharf, Liam said, "Who is my brother going to take care of if you don't?" When Marco opened his mouth to say he didn't have a clue, Liam put his hand in Marco's face. "Don't bother trying to deny it. If you don't tell me everything in the next two minutes, I'm calling Rosa and telling her what happened."

Marco pushed Liam's hand from his face. "Do you want to give her a heart attack?"

The more likely outcome would be that she'd drive them insane dogging Marco's every step off and on the job, which meant she'd be dogging most of Liam's too.

Marco sighed when Liam held up his cell phone. "All right, you win. But first you have to promise you won't tell the chief."

"I can't make that promise until I hear what happened."

Marco knew he'd pushed his luck. Once they passed two older men fishing off the wharf, he went through the morning's simulation step by step. As much for himself as for Liam. Marco didn't want to believe that Johnny had intentionally set out to send him overboard. Just

like he didn't want to believe he was responsible for
the malfunctioning disconnect valve the other day on
the plane.

"You have to tell the chief. He needs to open an investigation." Liam looked toward the engines idling in the
parking lot, and his expression hardened. Johnny was
walking toward them in his turnout gear.

One look at Johnny's face told Marco all he needed to
know. He handed Liam his hazmat gear. "I'll handle this."

Johnny held up his hands as Marco strode toward him.
"I swear to God, I didn't know you went over. I didn't
mean for—"

Marco laid him out with a right uppercut to the jaw. He
heard the whispers, the sound of people moving in for a
better look, and reached out his hand to the man sprawled
on the wharf at his feet.

Johnny cradled his jaw in his palm. "You going to hit
me again?"

"Depends what you tell me. I might have you arrested
instead."

The other man's expression went from suspicious to
panicked. "Please, don't. Not for me, but for Callie's and
the baby's sake."

"Callie's pregnant?" He poked around beneath his
surprise to see if there was something more: regret?
Jealousy? There was nothing other than happiness for
Callie. Though it was tempered with concern about the
man she'd married. He'd never been particularly fond of
Johnny. He'd been a jerk to Liam when he'd first transferred from BFD.

"She is. And it's mine," the man in front of him said
with a belligerent thrust of his chin.

"You do a disservice to Callie saying crap like that.

Of course the baby's yours, you idiot. But if you ever pull another stunt like you did today, and like you did two days before with the disconnect valve, you risk losing them."

"Okay. But I'm telling you the truth. I didn't mean for you to fall overboard. I didn't know you had. I just meant for you to fall on your face. I wanted people to know you're just like the rest of us. You're not a hero."

"I never said I was, and as far as I know, no one else has."

"Yeah? You don't think I saw the way my wife looked at you on our wedding day, when you rescued Daniel Gallagher? You don't think I heard what she started to say? She wished it was you she married, not me. She married me because of the baby."

He sympathized with the guy. He really did. But... "This doesn't have anything to do with me, Johnny. This is between you and Callie. And for the record, Callie wouldn't marry you because she was pregnant. She makes good money, has great friends and a supportive family. The only reason she married you is because she loves you." He hoped it was true.

"So you're not still in love with her? You don't want her back?"

"No. We both moved on months ago." It didn't sound like a lot of time even to him. For both their sakes, he wished he could say years.

"But you aren't dating anyone. You haven't—"

"Says who? Not that it's any of your business, but I have a date this weekend."

The guy perked up right away. "Really? Where are you going?"

"Movie Night in the Park," he said in an effort to sound

convincing. One look at Johnny's face told him he'd made a mistake.

"That's great. Maybe we'll see you there. Callie and I are going too."

"Everything good here?" Liam asked, coming up behind him.

"Yeah, we're good. Right, Marco?" Johnny's gaze moved anxiously from Liam back to Marco.

Marco let the silence stretch a little longer. He wanted Johnny to sweat. Just because he sympathized with the guy didn't mean he was getting off with a punch in the chin and a warning. He planned to keep a close eye on Johnny. For the sake of HHFD and Callie and her baby.

As though he couldn't take it any longer, Johnny filled the silence. "I get it, okay? I'll do whatever I have to, to prove you can trust me."

"Yeah, you will." He took the hazmat gear from Liam and handed it to Johnny. "You can take this to the team. Explain how I ended up going for a swim."

"But I thought we were good."

"You said it was an accident. I believe you. So will they. You just might want to forget the part about you wanting me to fall on my face."

For a second, it looked like Johnny might throw the equipment at Marco, but then he got himself under control and nodded. "You're right. Thanks. I appreciate you giving me a second chance," he said, then walked away.

"You know, you could have rescued me before I put my foot in my mouth. I told him I had a date for Movie Night in the Park."

"I was rescuing you. I was on the phone with my father, trying to explain why you just knocked Johnny on his ass without implicating him in your near drowning."

"How did he…?" He searched the parking lot and spotted the chief leaning against the ladder engine. He waved Marco over.

"I didn't think this day could get much worse, but it looks like I was wrong."

"I have some news that might cheer you up."

"What is it?" he asked warily, not trusting the amusement in Liam's eyes.

"Rosa called."

Marco groaned, and Liam slung an arm around his shoulders. "It's good news, buddy. She set you up on a date with my cousin Daphne. The divorce attorney?" he said at Marco's frown.

"I know which one she is. I met her at the beach yesterday." Thing was, it was the hot pilot he couldn't get out of his mind that morning, not the hot divorce attorney. Daphne Gallagher was gorgeous, but he preferred Theia's edgy attitude to the attorney's flirty one. Still, if he wanted to keep the peace at HHFD and in Johnny and Callie's marriage, going out with Liam's cousin was as good an idea as any. There was also the added benefit that he'd keep the peace in his own home.

* * *

Project Daddy Do-Over wasn't going well. When Theia arrived to pick up Daniel yesterday for lunch with his daughters, his yoga-instructor-slash-masseuse had handed her a doctor's note. Daniel was supposedly spending the day in bed due to high blood pressure. Given her sexy bedhead, flushed cheeks, and sparkly eyes, Theia suspected the perky woman with the perky boobs might be responsible for the rise in Daniel's blood pressure.

Theia had turned the doctor's note over and wrote one of her own. If he wasn't on the patio at five for dinner with his daughters and grandsons today, she was going to call a certain member of the Greek parliament and let him know where a certain archaeologist could be found. The message was cryptic enough that his fake doctor wouldn't understand the threat, but Daniel would.

Last year, Daniel had unearthed a trove of gold coins on his dig in a farmer's field, which he'd decided to keep for himself instead of informing the government—or the farmer who'd granted him written permission to dig on his farm for fifty percent of whatever he found. Though the workers on the dig were sworn to secrecy, word soon reached the farmer's ears, and he was holding Daniel's equipment hostage until he paid up. Word had reached Caine around the same time as the farmer. From the beginning, Caine had pegged Daniel as the weak link in the Gallagher family and had put one of the archaeologist's trusted assistants on his payroll. He'd used the information to get Daniel to work for him.

Theia sat on the stone wall that surrounded the patio, waiting for Daniel to show. She was half-hidden among the spidery branches of a willow tree that looked like it had been around longer than the manor. She didn't want to impose on the Gallaghers' family time. She just wanted to ensure Daniel joined them for dinner. Penelope had arrived with the boys moments before. She looked rested. The time at the manor had begun smoothing the pinched look from her face. Kitty and Jasper had taken the boys in hand, giving their burned-out mother some time to herself before she took on her official role at the manor.

So far no one had questioned Theia's presence at Greystone. They just assumed she was waiting until her plane dried out, which it hadn't. It was nice not to have to lie about why she was here. That would change soon enough. She figured she had a few days' reprieve before she'd have to start flying guests to and from the manor.

Sophie had dropped hints this morning about a sunset tour. She'd also apologized that her brother had drowned Theia's plane. It was obvious Sophie adored her big brother and would probably punch Theia in the nose if she said anything nasty about him. She didn't. She'd forgiven Tall, Dark, and Irresistible. At least for the day she landed in Harmony Harbor. She wasn't happy he continued hijacking her dreams.

And distracting her from what was going on around her, she thought when Daphne said, "Where were you just now?"

Rolling around on the beach with Marco DiRossi. "Playing a game of solitaire in my mind."

Daphne laughed. "You're weird, you know."

"So I've been told. What can I do for you?" She glanced at her phone and stood up. Daniel was five minutes late.

"You know that red halter dress you bought?"

"You mean the one you forced me to buy?"

"Yeah, that one." She fluttered her long eyelashes. "Can I borrow it Saturday night? I have a hot date."

"Sure."

"Aren't you going to ask who with?"

"Am I supposed to?"

"You haven't had many girlfriends, have you?"

"Who are you going out with, Daphne?"

"Guess."

"No."

She rolled her eyes and then grabbed Theia by the hands, moving them up and down. "I'm going out with

Marco. Marco DiRossi. The amazingly sexy firefighter with the hot body."

"I know who you mean." Okay, so probably not the reaction Daphne was hoping for. Theia forced a smile and copied the up-and-down movement with her hands. Now what was she supposed to say? Clearly not her initial reaction which was, *Hey, I saw him first.* "Lucky, lucky you."

It looked like Theia had stumbled on exactly the right thing to say.

"I know, right?" Daphne grinned.

Ten minutes later, as Theia trudged through the woods to Daniel's house, she realized how off her game she was. Daphne dating Marco was almost as bad as the two sisters being forced to remain at the manor for a month. If Daphne fell in love with Marco, they'd never get the woman to leave. Worse, they'd never get her to sell her shares because Marco's sister was manager of the manor. And the Gallaghers and DiRossis were as thick as thieves.

There was only one thing for her to do. She had to crash their date. A happy flutter in her stomach accompanied the thought. She frowned and looked down. What was that all about?

"Careful," said a familiar deep voice from behind her.

She walked into a tree.

Chapter Eight

♥

Theia staggered backward after walking into the tree. Her *ow* almost turned to an *aw* when she backed into a broad-chested, hard body whose tanned, muscular arms went around her. She might have rested there for a few minutes, savoring the feel of Marco DiRossi holding her close, but that wasn't her style. That was something Daphne would do. Theia thought she could learn a thing or two from the other woman because this was awfully nice.

For her, but maybe not for him. Marco stepped back and turned her to face him. A much nicer view than the tree, she decided, looking into his warm caramel-colored eyes. Her gaze dropped to his mouth. He hadn't shaved, and the scruffy look suited him. So did the smile he appeared to be fighting.

"Are you laughing at me?"

The question got her a flash of white teeth. "You walked into a tree." He lifted his hand and moved her bangs aside. "You must be getting used to me. You didn't jump this time. No blood either. Wound's still closed."

"I must have led with my nose and not my forehead."
She liked the feel of his blunt-tipped fingers on her face a
little too much. She was afraid she'd start purring and rubbing her cheek against his palm if he didn't soon stop.

Just as she was about to step back, he gently trailed his
finger down her nose. "Still cute, and it's not broken."

The words *It would feel better if you kissed it* hovered on
her lips. She saw clearly how it would unfold. He'd bend
down and touch his lips to her nose, and then she'd tip her
head back and his beautiful mouth would end up on hers.
And then he'd kiss her, and it would be the most incredible
kiss of her…Good Lord, what was she doing?

"Are you okay?" His gaze roamed her face. "Come on.
My sister's place is just over here. I'll get you an ice pack."

He took her by the hand. His was big and warm.
Something about him made her feel small and feminine.
Which was odd because Caine never did, and he was
about two inches taller and at least fifteen pounds heavier
than Marco.

Feeling delicate and feminine was a completely unexpected reaction, and it threw her for a loop. From the time
she was twelve, her entire focus had been proving to her
uncle that she was as strong as her cousins. That whatever they could do she could do better. It had been the
same when she enlisted. She'd spent the past twenty years
competing with men and proving she was as mentally and
physically strong as they were.

"Ow." He laughed, pulling his hand away. "You have
quite the grip."

"Sorry. Bad habit." She'd done it on purpose. She hadn't
wanted to appear rude or make him think he'd done something wrong by pulling her hand away, but she didn't like
how it made her feel. He made her nervous. When it came

to dating, she stayed far away from men like Marco. She preferred nerds.

Only she hadn't dated in the past two years. And it wasn't because Caine acted like an annoying big brother, scaring off all the offers. If she wanted to date, she would. But she couldn't think of having fun when Holden's wife and son were still mired in their grief.

"I hear you asked Daphne out." He wouldn't have to worry about *her* squishing his fingers.

He glanced at Theia as he placed his hand lightly at her back to guide her across the dirt road. "My grandmother did."

She laughed, wincing at how relieved she not only felt but sounded. "Sorry. I shouldn't have laughed. It's just that you don't seem like the type of guy who needs his grandmother to set him up."

He smiled. "I don't. But that's never stopped her in the past, and I guarantee it won't stop her in the future."

"She'll have to stop when you get married."

"That's a long way off." He lifted his chin at a white stucco house across the road. It had a gabled roof with two chimneys and a low stone wall with a white picket gate. "What about you? No significant other in your life?"

"No." She didn't want to talk about her dating life with him, or his, for that matter. She didn't have time to be distracted. She had a job to do. "I think I'll pass on the ice pack. Thanks for the offer though."

"You sure you're okay?"

"Yeah." She gestured at the cottage down the road. "I have to do Jasper a favor and drag Daniel away from his lady friend. He's late for his dinner with his daughters."

"Daniel's dating someone?"

"Yeah, Perky Boobs," she said, using the name she'd

christened the woman with. "I'm not sure if they're *dating*, but they're definitely having a good time. And I don't think it's because Daniel has joined Perky's yoga classes. The massage sessions though? I can see him enjoying those."

Marco stared at her.

"Is something wrong?" she asked, going back over what she'd said in her head. She made a face. The drawback of hanging out with mostly men was she tended to talk like them.

"Perky Boobs is my mother."

* * *

Marco had spent the rest of yesterday and all of this morning trying to wipe Theia's nickname for his mother out of his head, along with the idea of Tina and Daniel getting it on. Which, given Theia's disgusted expression when she stalked past Sophie and Liam's last night without Daniel, they had been.

"Lieutenant, can you help me with this?" A teenage girl stood in front of Marco wearing her Air-Pak breathing apparatus the wrong way. He was the supervisor at Camp FFIT—Female Firefighter in Training—today. The camp ran for the first two weeks in July and was open to girls fifteen to nineteen who were interested in becoming firefighters.

The chief had started the camp ten years earlier in honor of his seven-year-old daughter, Riley, who'd wanted to be a firefighter when she grew up. Riley and the chief's wife had died ten years ago this November. They'd been killed by a drunk driver in a motor vehicle accident.

Marco had been volunteering on his days off since the camp's inception. Technically, he wasn't supposed to be *off* today, but after his near drowning yesterday, the chief had insisted. And you didn't argue with the chief.

"How about we do it together instead?" Marco suggested to the teen, who was in full turnout gear while Marco wore a pair of khaki shorts and a navy HHFD T-shirt.

"Can't you just do it? I promise I won't tell."

Sam was a sweet kid, and Marco would love to help her, but he wouldn't be doing her any favors if he did. This was her third year at camp, and there was nothing she wanted more than to be a firefighter. Only Marco was afraid she wanted it more for her father than she did for herself. Her dad used to be with HHFD until he was sidelined by an injury. Her brother was a probie—a recruit.

Marco's answer was to help her out of the pack. He laid it on the grass. "Okay, now don't rush. Take it one step at a time."

She looked to where family and friends had begun to gather for today's demonstration. The event was well attended by the HHFD, who were all supportive of the program. Two of their recent hires had graduated from Camp FFIT two years before.

"You know what, I can't do this today. I just got my"—she lowered her voice—"period, and my cramps are really bad."

He'd been wondering what her excuse would be this year. Last year she'd pretended to sprain her ankle. The year before that she supposedly had heatstroke. Looked like she was pulling out the big one this year. Because everyone knew the last thing a man wanted to talk about was periods. She had no idea that growing up with Rosa had ensured Marco could handle just about anything a woman threw at him without making him blush, stammer, or give in.

"Lisa can help you out with that. She's always got extra pads and Midol. You'll be fine, kiddo. You've been practicing all week."

"Yeah, but not in front of my family," she said glumly.

He was surprised they still came. "Look, it's nice that your family wants to support you, but"—she interrupted him with a snort—"this is really just an exercise for you to see how much you've learned and how much you've improved over last year. Forget about competing with anyone else but yourself. You...Oof." Marco was tackled from behind. He glanced over his shoulder to see who'd taken him down. Penelope Gallagher's twins.

He lay there for a second in the grass, trying to catch his breath. He almost lost it again when a pair of long, lean golden-brown legs showed up in his peripheral vision and the owner of the sexy legs laughed. He pushed himself to his knees, the boys still attached to his back, and turned his head to look up at Theia. "As a former fighter pilot, I'd have thought you'd have better control of your charges."

"I might if they were mine. Terror one, terror two, get off the man," she ordered.

Marco laughed. "Their mother and great-grandmother can't be around if you're calling—"

"Weston, William, you apologize to Mr. DiRossi right this minute." Penelope Gallagher hurried over, wearing a long blue skirt and a white T-shirt. She was a beautiful woman, and Marco wasn't at all surprised to see her arrival had caused a stir among the single members of HHFD, who were now looking their way.

"Call me Marco, and don't worry about it. I'm good. They were just happy to see me, weren't you, guys?"

"Yeah," the twins yelled, and then threw themselves at his legs.

"William, Weston, you let Mr....Marco go. He's busy." She gave him an apologetic smile and nodded at the attractive older woman making her way across the training field. "I'm sorry. My grandmother insisted we come."

"You gotta watch those grandmas," Theia murmured, giving him a pointed look.

His smile faltered. She couldn't be insinuating that Kitty Gallagher was trying to set him up with Penelope, could she? He angled his body toward Theia and pointed at himself, then widened his eyes. She smiled and fluttered her eyelashes. The overtly feminine action seemed so out of character that he almost laughed. He might have if he hadn't begun to think about the consequences of dueling matchmaking grandmothers.

Kitty apparently wanted him to date Penelope, and there was no doubt Rosa wanted him to date Daphne. All Marco wanted was to keep the peace. Rosa and Kitty had been best friends since grade school, and the last thing he wanted was to be responsible for their falling out.

He hadn't even factored in his best friend's feelings. But what if he unintentionally hurt Liam's cousins? His best friend was a protective guy. They were closer than brothers. Nothing had ever come between them. He prayed Theia had misread the situation.

As proven by the first words out of Kitty's mouth when she reached them, his prayer went unanswered. "Marco DiRossi, why you're not married with babies of your own, I'll never know. You're all the boys talk about." She nudged her granddaughter with a twinkle in her blue eyes. "It's a good thing for you he isn't spoken for, Penelope."

His jaw dropped. Kitty couldn't be more blatant about her intentions. He was in big trouble. He shot a *help me out* look at Theia.

She laughed. Then obviously taking pity on him, or maybe on Sam, who was standing forlornly nearby, she turned to the teenager and stuck out her hand. "Hi, I'm Theia. You're taking part in the demonstration today?"

"Sam," she introduced herself, while casting a hopeful glance at Marco. "I'm not sure if I am. I'm kind of under the weather."

Theia looked from Marco to Sam. "It doesn't matter. You have to do it. You have to push through. Trust me, you'll regret it if you don't. What you're doing here is amazing. You girls are the bomb."

"Really? You think so?"

"Ah, yeah, we need more young women like you. It's the twenty-first century, and the percentage of women in law enforcement, the military, and fire services is still depressingly low. You guys are trailblazers."

"My dad and brother don't think so. They don't think women belong in any of those professions." She glanced to the chairs slowly filling up with family and friends.

Okay. This was news to Marco. All along he'd thought Sam was trying to make her family proud. Instead, she was trying to prove them wrong.

Sam turned back to Theia. "The lieutenant said you're a fighter pilot. Is that true?"

"I was." A shadow crossed Theia's face, but she erased it with a smile. The smile was forced, and he wondered why. "My uncle and cousins felt the same as your dad and brother, and I proved them wrong. You will too."

"I'm not that good."

"Doesn't matter. If you want it bad enough, you'll work at it. You'll become good, and then you'll keep working and you'll become better, until you become the best."

"Were you the best?"

Theia looked like she'd taken a physical blow. Something had happened to her, and whatever it was, it had been bad. "I thought…" She shoved her hands in the pockets of her shorts, then looked at Sam and slowly nodded. "I was. For a time, I was the very best I could be."

"Hurry up, Sam! We're starting in five minutes." A group of teenagers in bunker gear waved her over. They were a good bunch of girls. Always cheering one another on no matter what.

Marco put on Sam's pack and tightened the straps. He gave her shoulder a light squeeze. "Good luck, kiddo."

"Just give it all you've got, Sam."

"I will. I'll do it. I'll show my dad and brother."

"Don't worry about them. You do it for you. Make yourself proud." Theia held up a fist. "Girl power."

"Thanks." Sam smiled and gave Theia a quick hug before running off pumping her fist and yelling, "Girl power!"

"I can't believe it. She's actually going to do it," Marco said as he watched Sam join the other girls. He turned to explain to Theia what a big deal it was, but she was already striding across the field. While Theia had been giving Sam a pep talk, the twins had taken off, and both their great-grandmother and mother were chasing them down. A couple of firefighters had joined in, probably to get in Penelope's good graces.

Looking like a drill sergeant with her mirrored shades now covering her eyes, her wide-legged stance, and her poker-straight back, Theia put her fingers between her lips and whistled. It was loud enough that people on the other side of the field turned their way.

She raised her hand. "T1, T2, get your baby butts over here now."

The firefighters who'd been chasing the twins stopped

and turned to stare. He knew exactly how they felt. Penelope might be a yummy mommy and Daphne super-model hot, but they had nothing on Theia and her voice.

The twins circled their mother and great-grandmother and headed back the drill sergeant's way. "Drop and give me ten," she said when they reached her.

Marco laughed when the two little boys dropped to the ground, counting their push-ups along with her. "Theia Lawson, you're the bomb," he murmured.

But not low enough apparently because she looked over her shoulder and said, "You're not so bad yourself, DiRossi. And I'm sorry I called you a sexist. You're absolutely not."

And the way she said it made him think that was a pretty big deal in her book. He suspected it had something to do with her uncle and cousins. That was a story he wanted to hear. Just like he wanted to know what had put the haunted look in her eyes.

"She was a fighter pilot, you know," Kitty was saying to the two firefighters walking at her side. "Theia darling, come and meet these lovely men."

Theia looked over her shoulder and gave Marco a *what the hell* look. He sympathized and would very much have liked to help her out, but Kitty wasn't finished with him.

"Marco, be a dear and help Penelope get the boys settled in the chairs for the demonstration. Not in the front though."

"In the fire engine! In the fire engine!"

"Theia, darling, you can sit with me. You're welcome to join us, boys," she told the two men.

Marco sat in a chair three rows from the front, his gaze going to the back row every few minutes. He was too dis-tracted to enjoy the demonstration as much as he usually did. Surprisingly, Penelope's sons weren't responsible for his distraction. The twins remained glued to their seats throughout the simulated car and kitchen fires and the aerial ladder climb competition, clearly fascinated by fire. Something their therapist mother might want to keep an eye on.

Marco wasn't distracted by Penelope either, which his sister would find amusing because the twins' mother looked a lot like Callie.

No, the person responsible for Marco's distraction was none other than Theia Lawson. Theia and her voice. She kept calling to the girls, cheering them on throughout the entire event. He wasn't the only one distracted by her. Several of the single guys at HHFD were eyeing her with interest, which he found distracting too.

As the siren went off, declaring the competition over, Sam and the girls whooped and began peeling off their equipment before running toward him. He stood with a smile. Everyone knew he was their favorite instructor, and they were good for his ego. "Ladies, you were—" He frowned as they ran past him.

"Theia! Come meet my friends," Sam called out.

Well, that put him in his place, he thought with a laugh. His laughter faded when Sam's father and brother joined the group of girls crowding around Theia.

"Are you okay here on your own with the boys, Penelope? I have to take care of something," he said, keeping Theia in his line of sight. He couldn't make out the conversation, but words were definitely being exchanged as Theia pushed her mirrored shades on top of her head to stare down Sam's dad.

"Is everything all right?" Penelope asked, craning her neck to see past the people standing behind her.

"I'm sure it'll be—" He was about to assure her that it would fine when one of the guys from HHFD signaled for him. By the time Marco made his way to where they were standing, the gauntlet had been thrown down. He had no doubt Theia would pick it up.

"You think women can do anything a man can do, prove it," Sam's father said, clapping his six-foot-three son on his broad-shouldered back. "Eric will take you on."

"You bet I will." The twenty-year-old laughed, gesturing to the five-story tower. "We'll have our own version of Firefighters Combat Challenge."

"Tell me when, and I'll be there," Theia said, because she clearly didn't have a clue what the challenge entailed.

"Theia, the combat—"

Eric cut Marco off with a cocky "Here and now works for me."

"Okay. Let's do this," she said.

Marco took Theia by the arm, pulling her out of earshot. "You have no idea what you're getting yourself into. You'll be wearing a hundred pounds of equipment while you drag a hose five stories, and then you have to carry a hundred-and-seventy-five-pound dummy all the way back down. It's a grueling challenge."

She looked over at the tower and then glanced at the girls. She lifted a shoulder. "I can't back down now."

"Of course you can." He turned to tell Sam's dad the challenge was off.

Theia grabbed his arm. "No, I can't. Sam, girls, come help me get ready. You can give me tips while you do."

The teenagers cheered, shrieking "Girl power" with delight while Sam's dad rolled his eyes.

Marco walked over to him as the girls led Theia away. "You wanna explain something to me?"

"Don't give me grief. She accepted the challenge. I didn't twist her arm."

"She's a vet. A former navy fighter pilot. So I have no doubt she can hold her own." Though he was worried she'd kill herself trying. "But that's not what I wanted you to explain to me. You love your daughter, don't you?"

"What the hell is that supposed to mean? Of course I do."

"Okay. Then maybe you want to tell me why you make her feel like she hasn't got what it takes to do this."

"I'm her father. It's my job to protect her. Before you judge me, wait until you have a daughter of your own, DiRossi. See how you feel having your heart walking outside your body. I have a hard time letting her leave for school every morning, let alone fighting a house fire. I promised her mama I'd look after her, and that's what I'm gonna do."

Marco briefly closed his eyes. Sam's mom had died of an aneurysm four years before. He reached over to give the big man's shoulder a squeeze. "You're right. I'm sorry. Sam's a great kid. You should be proud of her."

"I am."

"Let her know that, okay?" He went to walk away but then turned back. "And when Theia beats Eric in the challenge, make sure you tell him you're proud of him too."

Sam's dad guffawed. "Put your money where your mouth is, DiRossi. A hundred bucks."

"You're on."

Fifteen minutes later, the horn went off, and the two competitors took off up the stairs pulling their hoses. Eric left Theia in the dust. There hadn't been enough time for her to practice moving in the equipment or dragging the hose. She was having to figure it out as she went.

By the time Eric hit the third story, Theia had barely cleared the first. She caught a lucky break when the kid's foot got tangled in the hose. When he reached the fifth story, Theia was only ten steps behind him.

The crowd, who'd mostly been holding their breath until then, began to cheer. Once Eric got to the top, it appeared he was having trouble with the dummy. It kept sliding off his shoulder. Theia, on the other hand, got the *victim* over her shoulder in one smooth move. Then her knees buckled under the weight. She glanced at Eric, who was less than a story ahead of her now.

With the win in her sights, she quickened her pace, pushing hard. As though feeling her coming on, Eric pushed harder. The crowd went wild as Theia closed the distance between them and then moved ahead of Eric with only one flight of stairs to go. But Marco could see that she didn't have anything left. With a sudden burst of speed, Eric shot past her on the last four steps to win.

Marco ran across the blacktop, catching Theia before she collapsed. He lowered her to the ground and then quickly got off her breathing apparatus and helmet. She was red-faced and sweating, her hair plastered to her head. "I think I'm going to die."

"Back up and give her some space," he told the crowd as he continued stripping off her gear.

Sam's dad leaned over and tucked a hundred-dollar bill in the pocket of Marco's T-shirt. "Put it toward Camp FFIT."

"You bet against me?" Theia wheezed.

"Never." Marco smiled and then went to help her to her feet. "Let's get you rehydrated."

She ignored his hand to stretch out on the blacktop. "Just pour it in." She opened her mouth.

Once she'd recovered enough to greet her fans, Theia was swarmed. Not just by the campers but by their families too, including Sam's father and brother. Several members of HHFD also joined the crowd.

Kitty stood nearby with a smile on her face, clearly pleased with the attention Theia was receiving from the single members of HHFD. No doubt calculating how many dates would come Theia's way today. Marco didn't have time to wonder why that ticked him off because Kitty then turned her matchmaking sights on him.

She came over and tucked her arm through his. "Marco, I just had the most marvelous idea. Now that Camp FFIT is over, you'll have some free time, and there's no one I trust more to teach my great-grandsons to swim than you. What do you say? A couple days a week, maybe?"

Chapter Nine

♥

At seven in the morning, the manor was just coming awake, but not Theia Lawson. The girl appeared to be on a scouting mission for Caine Elliot, Colleen's nemesis. Although it appeared unlikely Theia would reach her destination. She was having a difficult time climbing the spiral staircase to the tower where the family suites were housed, groaning at each step.

Colleen had climbed the stairs faster in her nineties than this one did in her thirties. It wasn't until her hundredth birthday that Colleen began taking the elevator to her suite of rooms on the right. Her daughter-in-law Kitty's were to the left of the staircase.

"Look at the way she keeps glancing over her shoulder all spy-like. Mark my words, Simon, she's up to no good," Colleen said to the black cat padding along behind her.

Startled when he suddenly bounded to the top of the staircase, Colleen yelped, "Simon, what on earth has gotten into you!"

He, of course, did not respond. Though she sometimes suspected it wasn't beyond the realm of possibility that he would, or could, or had in a previous lifetime. As she'd come to learn, Simon was no ordinary cat.

In fact, over the past year, she'd come to believe that Simon, who'd been known to act like the lord of the manor, actually was William Gallagher. If someone had shared those same suspicions with Colleen when she'd been living, she would have thought they were touched in the head. But given her current circumstances, she knew life could be stranger than fiction.

All that to say, there was a good possibility Simon had come to the same conclusion as Colleen about her nemesis Caine Elliot. The lad had proven to be as canny as her, a worthy opponent, one they may be unable to beat. Especially when he had Theia to do his evil bidding.

Simon darted past the girl. She gasped, grabbing the wrought-iron handrail to keep from falling. "Only a cat, not some big hairy rat," she murmured to herself.

Simon gave her the side-eye before parking himself in front of the door to Colleen's old room.

Colleen smiled at her boon companion. "Now, isn't that a fine thing, you playing security guard. But as much as I appreciate the effort, laddie, I'm afraid it won't stop this one. That'll be up to me, and she's exactly where I need her to be for that to happen."

There was something special about Colleen's old room. It sometimes acted as a conduit to the spirit world. She'd learned not long after she'd become a ghost of her former self that occupants of her suite were able to hear her. She'd used the ability to much effect over the past two years. She couldn't do it all the time, mind. It took an enormous amount of energy and drained her quickly of her abilities to do much of anything else for a time. Now she used the ability only if it proved absolutely necessary.

"Let's see what she's up to first." Colleen joined the girl at the door.

"Okay, kitty cat, you need to vamoose. No cats allowed. Shoo." Theia fake-whimpered. "Please don't make me bend down and pick you up."

Simon didn't budge. And if cats could grin, he did.

"You must have been Colleen's cat. I hear she was stubborn too. Oh Lord." Theia groaned as she bent over. "Take it from me, being stubborn can be a pain and being competitive might kill you. So do not challenge me, Mr. Cat. I have a lock on the title for most stubborn and competitive, which I proved yesterday."

Colleen recalled the conversation she'd overheard about the firefighter challenge and chuckled. "From what I hear, you dazzled everyone with your physical prowess even if you did lose." She watched as Theia carefully picked up Simon and moved him aside. "Though you're not all that impressive this morning."

Theia continued. "And now I'm talking to a cat, who has either had a stroke or is laughing at me. Be a good kitty and stay there. Now the fun part." She placed a hand at her lower back, grimacing as inch by inch she straightened.

"It might be best that you don't come in and risk getting locked inside," Colleen said to Simon, who looked like he planned to mess with Theia. "I may have need of Jasper's assistance, and you're the only one who can get his attention for me."

By the time Colleen returned her attention to Theia, the girl was already in the room and on the phone. She shut the door on Colleen, who walked through it without so much as a shiver. More proof that she'd come a long way in this ghost gig. She would have popped her head through the door to share the news with Simon if Theia's conversation didn't garner her rapt attention.

"Okay, I'm in Colleen's suite. What does this memoir look like?" she asked as she walked to the wall of white wooden bookshelves at the far end of the room.

Colleen damned Daniel to hell and back as she rushed for the door. They were looking for *The Secret Keeper of Harmony Harbor*. And the only reason Caine Elliot knew about it was because her rapscallion grandson had confided in the man last year.

Colleen stuck her head through the door. "Off with you now, Simon. She's after my book, and for the sake of the family and everyone in Harmony Harbor, we can't let it fall into Caine Elliot's hands."

The book was locked in the safe in Kitty's suite, but the fact Theia was hunting for it at her boss's behest sent Colleen into a panic. If only Jasper would look as deep into Theia's employment as he was her genes. Perhaps he would once he discovered her in the tower room.

Theia placed the phone on the back of the sofa, pressing the speaker button before turning to the bookshelves with her hands on her hips.

"I don't understand how a book can help us identify the man your grandmother hired."

Holy Mother of God and all the saints, there are more than the two of them involved! Feeling a mite faint, Colleen stretched out on the sofa, resting her head against a throw pillow.

Caine's voice came through the phone. "When I reminded her how badly things had gotten out of hand the last time she got involved, she accused me of not having the stomach to get things done. She says she found someone who will. According to her, the man she hired hates the Gallaghers almost as much as she does. And unlike me, he won't stop until the job is done."

Colleen shot upright as a name immediately came to mind. It couldn't be. But she was afraid that it was. It wasn't that her inclination to stick her nose in other people's business hadn't gotten her in hot water and ticked off a fair number of the good citizens of Harmony Harbor over the years. It was just that no one in recent memory stood out more than Ryan Wilson.

Her head abuzz with nerves, she could barely make out what else Caine had to say.

"That's where the book comes in," he told Theia. "Back in October, when I was down in the tunnels with Daniel, he said his grandmother had written a book in which she recorded everyone's secrets: friends, family, the people in town. So it only stands to reason that she'd write about whoever hated the family that much. At least I hope it does because we need to figure this out before…" He trailed off, clearly not wanting to share the worst of it.

Theia slowly turned to look at the phone. Colleen didn't have to. She couldn't take her eyes off it. She willed Caine to say something to prove her wrong. The last person she wanted going after the family was Ryan Wilson.

The former police officer had partial evidence in a case that Colleen thought she'd buried. To do so, she'd ensured that Ryan's grandfather, a detective with HHPD decades before, had been kicked off the force when he'd gotten too close to the truth in the disappearance of Antonio DiRossi, Rosa's husband. The last thing any of them needed was Ryan digging up what happened that rainy summer night on the rocks.

"Before what, Caine? What are you keeping from me?"

"I'd wager a lot, girlie," Colleen said. "Don't let his dev- ilish good looks and that velvet-smooth voice fool you. He's not a man you can trust."

"Whoever is doing my grandmother's dirty work won't stop with Daniel's daughters. If I'm not mistaken, they're the second in line on his list. I haven't had a lot of time to look into it, but I'm fairly certain, with some help from my grandmother, he's going after the one person who could afford to bail out the manor should there be a finan- cial crisis."

"Olivia," Theia said at almost the same time Colleen whispered her great-granddaughter-in-law's name. Olivia had inherited shares in the Davenport family fortune. But she'd reinvested her portion in the charitable arm of Davenport International.

"Yes. The man is looking for a way to bring the com- pany down. Yesterday, thirty percent of the stock's value disappeared. He's started a whisper campaign. Investors are jumpy. I'm going to see what I can do to put a stop to it without my grandmother knowing."

Colleen blinked, confused. He was trying to protect them from both his grandmother and her hired hand? Colleen had been so panicked that she didn't grasp it at first. Now that she did, she didn't know what to make of it, or him.

"Go to the board, Caine. Tell them what she's doing. It's crazy. You can stop her."

"I'll stop the man she hired. But I won't go to the board. She built Wicklow Developments, and I won't betray her. She's my grandmother. I owe her, and I made her a promise a long time ago. I mean to keep it. I'll give her Greystone Manor before she dies, and then my debt will be paid."

He'd protect them to a point, it seemed.

"Look, I know you don't—"

"We don't have time for this, T. I won't change my mind. One day you'll understand why I had to do this. But right now we have to figure out who this man is."

"Did you ask Daniel?"

"No. He's not taking my calls. And if I had to guess, it's because he no longer needs us. He's changed sides."

"Or he's too afraid to face his daughters and his family knowing what he's done. He didn't show for either his lunch or his dinner with his daughters," Theia said.

Caine muttered something on the other end of the line. Colleen couldn't be sure, but she suspected it was a derogatory term directed at Daniel. "You give the man too much bloody credit, T. He's motivated by money. Just like the guy my grandmother hired. He gets a generous bonus if he can get this done. He'll want us out of the way."

"I spent more time with Daniel than you, Caine. There's a decent man under all that self-serving bravado. He's broke, alone…Okay, maybe not alone, but he has no relationship with his daughters to speak of and his professional reputation is pretty much shot. And you know what? Despite what it looks like, he loves his family. All he needs is someone to help him figure it out."

"I take it that someone is you."

Colleen picked up on the resignation in his voice, and she thought a hint of worry too. Why? she wondered. Why would Caine Elliot be worried about Theia spending time with Daniel…unless he'd known all along that Theia was Daniel's daughter.

"The blackguard," she muttered. "The canny, canny blackguard."

The enemies were closing in at the manor's gate, and the people she loved were in more danger than she could ever have anticipated. But in all the bad, she'd discovered something that gave her hope. Theia might be in league with the devil and her grandson, but the girl was inherently good, as her plea to Caine and her decision to help Daniel proved.

In the end, Colleen believed Theia would stand up for them and for the manor. All that was left to be seen was if she could hold her own against the invading forces. But of course she could; she was a veteran, a warrior and, Colleen believed, a Gallagher. Except no warrior should fight on their own. She needed someone at her back.

At the distinctive *beep* of the key card in the door, Theia ended the call and stuffed her phone in her pocket, putting on a sheepish smile when Jasper walked into the room, followed by Simon.

"You caught me," Theia said. "I'd heard the room was haunted and wanted to check it out."

"You're more than welcome to stay here, Ms. Lawson."

Colleen smiled. Leave it to her dear friend to come up with the perfect solution. Jasper had just provided her with the means and opportunity to help Theia protect the manor and the family.

"Really? I thought the room was reserved for family."

"Yes, but at the moment none of them wishes to stay here. It's on account of the rumor you just mentioned. People believe the suite is haunted."

"Great. I'd love to stay here. Maybe I can exorcise the ghost for you."

Jasper chuckled. "Good luck with that. If rumors are to be believed, Madam is as unshakable in the afterlife as she was when she ran the manor."

* * *

Daniel Gallagher arrived at the manor for his lunch with his daughters just as Theia had predicted he would.

"He's here," Theia said from where she stood half-hidden behind the atrium just off the lobby. The outer wall of the atrium was made of frosted glass cubes; its interior wall of windows faced Kismet Cove. Sunshine poured through the floor-to-ceiling windows, warming up the room as she talked to her boss on the phone.

After their conversation this morning in the tower room, she was determined to prove Caine wrong about Daniel. Something about the older man got to her. Maybe it was knowing he'd spent his life competing with his brothers and never felt like he measured up.

They had that in common. Only she had cousins, not brothers. She also didn't want to believe Caine's dire summation of the situation. They had to find out who Emily's minion was before it was too late. Theia believed Daniel was their best bet to achieve that goal.

After she'd accepted Jasper's offer to move into Colleen Gallagher's luxurious suite, she'd left Daniel a message on his phone and sent him a text, offering him the one thing money couldn't buy—the opportunity to repair his relationship with his daughters. Something she should have thought to do earlier instead of threatening to expose him to the Greek government. Her mother always told her you catch more flies with honey than vinegar.

"You were right and I was wrong, T. Just more proof that I need you handling this for me at the manor. Let me know if you find out anything from Daniel about our mystery man. Good luck with your lunch."

She rolled her eyes at the note of skepticism in Caine's voice. He clearly thought luck wouldn't help her cause. He'd already told her what he thought about Project Daddy

Do-Over. He'd decided Daniel was a deadbeat dad, and there'd be no changing his mind. She wasn't surprised. As much as she loved Caine, he was a black-and-white kind of guy. He wasn't easy or forgiving either.

From where she stood, she watched Daniel walk across the lobby toward the dining room. He was a big man, with powerful arms and legs that were on display in the navy shorts and white polo shirt he wore. Sporting a tan, he looked remarkably healthy for someone who'd supposedly been on his deathbed not more than two weeks before.

Theia scanned the lobby to be sure he wasn't followed. He didn't appear to be, and he wasn't acting like a man who'd been in hiding as Caine suspected. No, she thought as she stepped from behind the atrium wall, he looked like a man trying to talk himself into jumping off a cliff. His pace had slowed as he reached the stairs leading to the dining room. He scratched his neck and looked around.

She knew the moment he spotted her; relief relaxed the stress lines on his handsome face. A change from last year when he panicked every time she came near. This was much better. She'd have an easier time getting information from him and keeping him in line.

"Daniel." She put out her hand to greet him.

He pulled her in for a hug instead. "Thank the good Lord and the Holy Ghost you're here. I was worried I'd be meeting with my daughters on my own." His thick Irish brogue made it difficult to understand him. Or maybe it was the emotion in his voice garbling the words.

She grimaced as he pulled back to give her shoulder a squeeze. Every muscle in her body was protesting yesterday's punishing workout. She'd discovered muscles where she hadn't known muscles existed.

She didn't remember ever being this sore. Even those

first days of training in the navy couldn't compare to this. Then again, that was more than a decade before. It didn't matter that she still trained every day; she was older. Though definitely not wiser, as evidenced by her inability to refuse a challenge.

Maybe in the end that was a good thing, she thought when she caught sight of Penelope and Daphne making their way down the grand staircase. Because clearly repairing the rift between father and daughters wouldn't be easy.

Penelope, in a pretty floral sundress, looked like Theia imagined she did when she counseled clients in their therapy sessions, which might have boded well for the meeting if she'd brought her sons along. Even though it was probably for the best that she hadn't, it seemed to indicate that Penelope believed things might get heated. But the real challenge would no doubt be Daphne, who had on her lawyerly face and a red power sheath dress.

Theia grabbed Daniel's hand and dragged him behind the atrium wall. She wanted a few minutes alone with him before he faced his daughters.

"What's this about? You were pulling one over on me, weren't you? You had no intention of helping me make amends to my girls. It was all just a ploy to—"

"No. I just wanted a few minutes with you so we could go over what you're going to say."

"We may need more than a few minutes, lass. I don't have a clue what to say to them. Do you have any ideas?" he asked her hopefully.

"As a matter of fact, I do." She'd spent the past couple of nights Googling father-and-daughter relationships and had not only stockpiled some good advice, but the information was revealing. "How long has it been since you last saw Penelope and Daphne?"

He scratched his neck. "A birthday, I'm thinking. Just can't remember which one." He smiled and held up a finger. "I remember now. I surprised each of them on their sixteenth birthdays. It's the most important birthday in a young woman's life. A good time for a father to share some advice. About the birds and the bees, you know."

"And how did that go?" she asked, trying to keep the *Are you freaking kidding me?* out of her voice.

"Not all that well, if you must know. But now that I'm thinking about it, I also made it to both their graduations for high school and college. And up until we lost touch, I always sent a Christmas present and birthday card with a bit of green."

"So you haven't seen or spoken to either of them since Penelope moved to California and Daphne to New York?"

"That's where they're living now, is it?" At her nod, he sighed and looked over his shoulder at the dining room. "I'm not sure this is a good idea, lass."

"It'll be fine. It's just the first step on a long road. Don't put too much pressure on yourself or Penelope and Daphne to fix everything today. They're here for a month. You have lots of time." She thought it wise to take her own advice. Daniel needed a day or two to get to know her better and see he could trust her before she questioned him about Emily's right-hand man in Harmony Harbor.

"All right, that takes off a bit of the pressure. I'll just be my charming self. Regale them with stories of my adventures. The women always like that."

So he was one of those. You give him an inch, and he takes it to the next county. "You can do that. But if you do, don't be surprised when they dump their water glasses on your head and storm out."

"What would you have me do, then?"

"Tell them that you know your lack of involvement in their lives has hurt them deeply."

"But it wasn't all my fault. Their mothers—"

"It doesn't matter. This is about your relationship with them. Take the blame. Take full responsibility. Tell them how sorry you are. You are sorry, aren't you?"

"Of course I am. I know it doesn't look like it from where you're standing, but I love my girls. I always have."

"Tell them that. It's a great place to start." She smiled. "Let's go have lunch with your daughters."

He grabbed her hand. "You'll stay with me, won't you? My mother's looking after the twins and can't join us. I thought about asking Jasper, but he's not particularly pleased with me at the moment."

"Sure." She knew Penelope and Daphne wouldn't mind. They'd both asked that she stay when she set up the lunch date. Although since he'd skipped his previous lunch and dinner dates with them, neither seemed to have great expectations that this one would take place, as evidenced by their wide eyes when Daniel and Theia met them at the stairs to the dining room.

Daniel gave them a weak smile, the emotion in his voice causing it to tremble as he reached for the girls. "Penelope, Daphne." Noting their closed-off expressions, he lowered his hands and stepped back. "I know you don't have much use for me, and I canna say I blame you. I've not been the father either of you deserved. For most of my life, I went about things the wrong way. Putting the most important things on the back burner while I chased my dreams. You girls were the most important things, and I made a hash of it. I'm sorry for the hurt I caused. If you can find it in your hearts to give me a second chance, I'll do better this time. I can promise you that."

"You've always been good at pretty speeches, Daniel. But you suck at the follow-through," Daphne said.

Penelope glanced at her sister, then offered Daniel a small smile. She went up on her toes to kiss his cheek. "Thank you. I know that wasn't easy."

"Let's grab a table on the patio, and the three of you can catch up," Theia said, ushering an emotional Daniel down the stairs. "Just let me clear it of sharp objects and grab us a couple bottles of wine and a keg of beer first."

Daniel and Daphne snorted an identical laugh while Penelope looked relieved. She reached over and gave Theia's hand a grateful squeeze.

Two hours later, they were still sitting at the table. Theia was pumped with how well the father and daughters' lunch had gone. She was much better at this Daddy Do-Over stuff than she'd expected to be. Of course, it wasn't all rainbows and unicorns. But no one was left battered and bruised on the inside or outside. And they were still speaking.

Even better, the two women were beginning to act like sisters instead of mere strangers. In Daphne's case, strangers who didn't like each other. With a little time and some subtle nudging in the right direction, Theia thought the family had a good chance of reconciling. It made her happy to think she'd have a hand in bringing them back together. Even if her motivation was on the shady side.

She felt someone looking at her and glanced over to see Jasper standing by the patio doors. *Well done*, he mouthed with a smile.

His praise warmed her. She had a feeling he didn't offer it easily. She went to smile back, but he'd moved aside to let someone pass. Someone who had both Gallagher girls lifting their cutlery to check their teeth. Theia barely managed to stifle an aggravated groan at the sight of Tall, Dark, and Irresistible.

Marco DiRossi was responsible for practically every bad thing that had happened to her since she'd landed in Harmony Harbor four days before, and there was every indication from the way the Gallagher girls had just turned to frown at each other that he'd ruined the progress Penelope and Daphne had made.

Chapter Ten

♥

Forty-five minutes after Marco broke up the Gallagher-family reunion with the news he was there for the twins' swimming lesson, Theia shuffled behind them on the boardwalk. A couple yards ahead of her, Marco, wearing navy board shorts and a white T-shirt, walked between Penelope and Daphne, who wore cover-ups over their swimsuits and carried floats under their arms.

His head moving from right to left like a Ping-Pong ball being batted around by a couple of seasoned pros, Marco tried to keep up with their conversation. He was as oblivious to their flirtatious attempts as he was to Theia shooting mental darts at his back. The fast-paced walk was murder on her muscles, but she'd rather drop dead in the middle of the boardwalk than admit she was in pain.

The twins, who were walking with their grandfather, weren't helping matters. They jumped on every single board as they bounded along the boardwalk to the beach for their first swimming lesson with Marco the Magnificent. Each bounce vibrated through the soles of Theia's flip-flops to the top of her head, causing eight hundred and forty muscles to contract in response.

She dragged herself to the rail and leaned against it while her party continued on without her. Evidently, they'd forgotten about her. Not surprising since she'd tagged along uninvited. But she didn't have a choice. She was their self-appointed chaperone. The primary focus of today's op was to keep the sisters' recently established relationship from blowing up due to their mutual fascination with Tall, Dark, and Irresistible.

She hung her head, holding back a whimper as her neck and shoulder muscles stretched, her arms hanging loosely over the rails. Two mosquitoes dive-bombed her, and she didn't have the energy to wave them off.

"You okay?" asked an irritatingly familiar voice.

In her opinion, God had unfairly blessed Marco DiRossi. No one who looked that good should also be kind and caring…and willing to run into danger when everyone else was running out.

It was his heroic characteristics that got to her. That was why she stayed away from men like him. The possibility she'd fall head over heels was too great. She knew only too well that relationships based on passion led to pain and heartache. When she finally settled into a relationship, it would be quiet and companionable, no crazy highs and lows.

"You want some help getting back to the manor?"

He didn't just say that! Did he forget who he was talking to? She slowly turned her head. "I'm good, thanks. I just stopped to look at the flowers." She returned her head to its previous position. There were no wildflowers. "Over there," she muttered, turning her head to the right, to where a clump of white flowers was barely visible in the trees' shadows.

He had the nerve to laugh. "Just admit it. You're in pain. I promise, no one is going to laugh or think any less of you because you're a little sore."

"You just did."

"No, I'm laughing at your excuse. It was cute, and pathetic. Here. You need to drink." He handed her a black stainless-steel water bottle.

"Thanks. And just FYI, if I were a *little* sore, I wouldn't be walking like I'm ninety. I think I might have torn my ACL. Maybe pulled a couple of tendons." She flattened her lips at the amusement in his eyes. "What's so funny?"

"You are. I bet you're an annoying patient." He crouched beside her and gently rotated her foot and then moved his strong fingers over her calf. It felt too good to protest, and then it didn't. She pulled her leg away when he began to dig those incredibly strong fingers into her muscles. "What did I ever do to you? That hurt."

"No pain, no gain. It'd be better if I had some warm oil. Come on, I'm sure we can snag a bottle at the beach. I'll have your muscles loosened up in no time."

She stared at him. "You want to rub oil over my body on a crowded beach?" Warmth gathered low in her belly, the muscles in her legs loosening while other muscles tightened with desire. She hadn't thought about or used those neglected muscles in a couple of years. And if that wasn't proof Marco was dangerous, a head-over-heels kind of guy, she didn't know what was.

"Uh, that's not exactly what I was suggesting, but—"

Of course it wasn't. He'd been offering to give her an impersonal deep-tissue massage, and the simple touch of his hands on her leg muddled her brain and tangled up her tongue.

At least she hadn't sounded flirty or hopeful or like she

was begging him to have sex on the beach. She hadn't, had she? No, she answered her own ridiculous question firmly in her head. If anything, she sounded shocked. Because as much as he wasn't her type, she definitely wasn't his.

"I knew that," she said, her flight response kicking in. She pushed off the rail and began walking (hobbling) toward the stairs to the beach.

"Yeah? So if I said we'll find a less crowded beach after the twins' swimming lesson, you wouldn't be interested?"

"I…" She narrowed her eyes on his ridiculously handsome face. A face that had no doubt launched a thousand women's fantasies, including beautiful women like Penelope and Daphne. "You're teasing me, aren't you?"

"Yeah…" His gaze roamed her face, and then he frowned. "No, I don't think I am."

"Of course you are." She punched him in the arm. She'd meant to give him a playful punch but ended up giving him a real one instead. At least as real as her aching muscles permitted.

"Ow." He rubbed his arm. "What was that for? A simple 'I'm not interested' would have sufficed."

She didn't know why she'd punched him. She was angry at him for teasing her and terrified that he might not be. Possibly a little hopeful too.

She shrugged in response to his question. "I grew up with three male cousins who lived to tease me. Or at least that's how it seemed. They didn't respond to tears or pleas, so I learned to punch. Sometimes it worked. Did I hurt you?" She kind of hoped she did. She didn't want him to think she had a girlie punch.

"Of course you didn't hurt me. You're…" He trailed off.

She stopped hobbling to look at him. "You were going to say a girl, weren't you?"

"Actually, I was going to say 'woman.'" He laughed and held up his hands. "I'm joking."

"You must have been an annoying brother."

"Probably. You'd have to ask Sophie. But I guarantee I was a lot nicer than your cousins."

"You're setting the bar low."

"That bad?"

"It wasn't fun. But in fairness to them, they were in their early teens when I moved in. The youngest had to give up his room for me and move in with his brother. My aunt was my mother's only sister. She kind of doted on me. She always wanted a daughter, and the boys grew to resent me."

"At least you had your aunt. Your cousins sound like little shits."

"They grew into even bigger ones. Funny thing though, as much as I loved my aunt and appreciated how good she was to me, it was my uncle's attention I craved." Whoa, where had that come from? Obviously, she'd been reading too many advice blogs about absentee fathers and the effect it had on their daughters. Whatever the reason, she'd just totally overshared with a man who had no interest in her life story.

"So I'm taking it he didn't make your life easy. Did it get any better when you got older? He must have been proud of you. I don't imagine there are a lot of female fighter pilots."

Her aunt always told her he was. The colonel wasn't the talkative sort. Although he had lots to say after the accident. None of it good. Her aunt didn't even try to smooth it over. She knew Theia was too old to fool. She rarely spoke to them anymore.

"I guess," she said in response to Marco's question,

adding a shrug so he'd know she didn't care. She wasn't sure she fooled either of them. "You don't have to wait for me, you know. I'll get there eventually. Penelope and Daphne are probably wondering where you are."

Speak of the devil, she thought, when Daphne, red-faced and sweaty, arrived at the top of the stairs that led to the beach. Her out-of-breath sister arrived seconds later. From where they leaned on opposite rails, they shot each other peeved looks. Then they glanced Theia's way, and she became the recipient of their combined enmity.

Faced with the evidence that she was back at square one with the sisters, thanks to Marco, she pushed him in their direction. It was a light push because sore arms, you know. But he stumbled so she must have caught him off guard.

"Theia!" both women cried, rushing to his aid.

"What? The way you two raced up here I figured it was an emergency. I wasn't going to be much help with my torn ACL, so I gave you the next best thing, Marco." *Hooyah*. She was getting better at the spur-of-the-moment comebacks. There wasn't much they could say to that, now, was there? Better yet, she wouldn't be caught in the middle of the jealous sisters' act.

"You guys get going and deal with whatever it is you have to deal with. Don't worry about me." She inched forward with an exaggerated limp. "I should make it down there in half an hour."

"No way. We can't leave you alone, not with a *torn ACL*," Marco said as he crouched in front of her. "Hop on. You shouldn't be walking."

"I'm not getting on your back." She glanced at Penelope and Daphne, who were watching their exchange through narrowed eyes. They'd probably accept his offer in a nanosecond. "I mean, I appreciate the offer, but my legs can't stretch that wide."

Marco made a strangled sound, and Penelope's and Daphne's eyebrows shot skyward.

"Of course my legs can normally spread that wide, but along with the torn ACL, I've pulled a few other muscles—oomph." Marco put her in a fireman's carry. "I can't believe you just did that! Put me down."

"It's your own fault. Torn ACL," he scoffed, taking the stairs to the beach two at a time, with her bouncing along on his back. "And don't think I didn't catch the *next best thing* line."

"Sorry, I didn't realize you were so sensitive." She would never admit it to him, but it felt so good not to have to walk that she could have kissed him. She lifted her head to see Penelope and Daphne exchanging words as they made their way down the stairs. It hit her then that the twins weren't with them.

"I'm not sensitive. I just…Ow, why did you slap my ass? If that's your way of proving I'm sensitive, you—"

"I slapped your butt because I can't slap Penelope." She lifted her head to look for the twins.

"You do know it's not politically correct to go around slapping men on the ass, right?"

"Says the man who threw me over his shoulder. Twice. Now stop talking and start looking for the twins. What was Penelope thinking, leaving Daniel alone with them?"

"That he's their grandfather," he said sardonically.

She snorted. "He met the boys for the first time an hour ago, Marco. He doesn't have a clue what they could get up to."

"Right. I forgot. Liam told me he was estranged from his daughters. Found them. They're to the left of the lifeguard stand, playing in the sand."

"Great. As much as I appreciate the ride, you can put me down."

"Don't worry. I plan to. I've got just the cure for your sore muscles." She bounced harder on his back as he began to jog.

"Trust me, it's not working, so you can stop jogging," she said, her voice vibrating in and out. Beneath brightly colored beach umbrellas, children stopped playing in the sand to look at her. She gave them a weak wave. "Marco, I look like an idiot and so do you, running around with me on your back. So put me down. Now." He ignored her. "Look, if this is your way of proving you're the best thing, you can stop. There's not a chance I could carry you around on my back, let alone run with you…Hey, we're in the water. What…Marco, don't you dare! Don't you dare…"

He dumped her in the ocean. The very cold ocean.

*　　*　　*

Theia sat beside Daniel on a beach towel, her hair drying in the midafternoon sun. Her waterlogged denim shorts were drying nearby. She'd been wearing them over her black racer-back one-piece when Marco dunked her in the water. He wouldn't let her out until she swam for twenty minutes. She'd joined the twins for the first half of their lesson, along with their mother and aunt. Which, though she was loath to admit it, had done a world of good for her muscles. The cold water and light swimming, not Penelope and Daphne. They were just annoying.

"You have a crush on the DiRossi boy too, do you?"

Their father was annoying too. "No. Why would you think that?"

"You haven't taken your eyes off him."

"I'm watching the kids horsing around this side of the first buoy. They're out too far, and the lifeguard is too busy flirting with the group of girls hanging around his chair to notice."

Which was mostly true. Every once in a while, her eyes may have strayed in Marco's direction. She might be ticked at him, but that didn't interfere with her ability to admire his incredible physique. The way the water glistened on his bronzed chest or the way his pecs and biceps flexed when he lifted the boys. He was also pretty great with kids. Patient and fun. It was no wonder they loved the guy.

Out of the corner of her eye, she caught Daniel's smirk. She put her fingers to her lips and blew a shrill whistle. "Hey, you up on the chair! Stop flirting and do your job." She pointed to the kids near the buoy, earning her glares from lifeguard's fan club and a smile from Marco. It wasn't her fault he happened to be between her and the kids near the buoy.

Beside her, Daniel sighed as he watched his daughters vie for Marco's attention. Daphne wore a sexy purple bathing suit with strategically placed mesh inserts while her sister wore a crocheted pink bikini, which was modest compared to Daphne's swimsuit. The sisters lay on their backs on their floats. They looked like they were catching a few z's and enjoying the rays. But if you focused on their hands and feet, every few minutes one of them would push off the other's float or kick it away to get a lock on the prime real estate, which was directly in Marco's line of sight.

Daphne obviously had had enough and shoved her sister's flamingo float off with her foot. Due to the strength of her shapely runner's leg, she had enough power behind the kick to send Penelope careening into several swimmers, who were not particularly pleased to be run over by a pink flamingo. Which meant the bird received a few well-placed shoves and overturned, its occupant shrieking that she didn't know how to swim as she went under.

How a woman who lived in California never learned to swim was beyond Theia. As far as she and Daniel were from shore, there wasn't much she could do to help, so she sat back and watched Marco expertly handle the situation.

Be still my heart. Okay. Those were four words she'd never thought to utter, even if they were in her head. She gave herself a pass because watching Marco in action was a breath-stealing sight. He had the situation under control within two minutes. His calm and confident manner as he ensured the boys remained safe on the air mattress while he rescued their mother guaranteed the twins weren't traumatized. Penelope was another story. She clung to Marco as he deposited her on the righted flamingo, thanking him for saving her life.

"Two sisters going after the same lad never ends well in my experience," Daniel said, nodding at his daughters. "They've only just set their sights on him and look what's happened. Mark my words, it'll get worse."

He was right. They needed a plan. A better one than Theia crashing Daphne and Marco's date. "I have an idea."

"So do I. You run interference. The lad seems to like you, and you like him." He held up a hand when she opened her mouth to argue. "Don't bother trying to kid a kidder. I see what I see. So do us both a favor, ask the lad out. It won't do either me or your boss any good if the girls are fighting. They're liable to do the opposite of each other when the month is out."

"You're still onboard with Caine's plan, then? You haven't changed sides?"

"What are you talking about? I haven't changed my mind. My situation hasn't improved, as you well know. You threatened me with exposure not two days ago. And while I may be living here for free, my ex, Tara, she's coming after me to pay for Clio's schooling. Not to mention the bill collectors nipping at my heels."

"All right, calm down. Caine said he'd help, and he will. But you've been ignoring both of us for the past couple of days, so you shouldn't be surprised that we thought you bailed."

"I was afraid the girls would turn me away and couldn't face another rejection. By then I'd heard about Granny's codicil and knew I had some time to work up the courage to face them." He smiled out at the sea. "Marco's mom, Tina, she's been helping me with that. She's been good for me."

Theia grimaced, remembering talking about Perky Boobs to Marco. It hadn't been her finest moment. She'd had a lot of those kind of moments in Harmony Harbor, and Marco had borne witness to each and every one. Which meant Daniel's plan wouldn't work. Despite his teasing, Marco wouldn't want to date her.

She ignored the tiny pinch in her chest at the thought, focusing on Daniel instead. "I'm glad to hear we're good, and you're good, but just how much have you told Tina?"

He rubbed his earlobe between his thumb and forefinger. "I may have inadvertently told her everything."

"What were you thinking? You—"

"It wasn't my fault. I'm telling you, the woman has magic hands. She did this thing, Reiki, I think she called it. She had me bawling like a baby one minute and confessing all my sins the next."

She was just about to ask if he'd confessed hers when he answered her question. With the one answer she didn't want to hear.

"You don't have to worry about her blowing your cover. She wouldn't hurt me. She loves me."

Chapter Eleven

♥

Marco crouched by a tree at the far end of the park to ensure the inflatable movie screen was well secured. He usually enjoyed movie night, but he couldn't wait for this one to be over. He had visions of Daphne and Penelope Gallagher having a cat fight in the middle of the movie, their hair-pulling shadows illuminated on the big screen for everyone to see.

Despite what some people thought, guys did not get off on a girl-on-girl brawl. He thought about a couple of firefighter friends. Okay, so *he* didn't get off on women fighting. Especially when it was over him and the women involved were related to his best friend. He had no idea how he'd gotten himself into this mess.

"Hey, Marco," a familiar voice called from behind, reminding Marco exactly why he'd agreed to the date with Daphne.

He stood, taking a second to rearrange his face into a smile before turning.

With his arm wrapped possessively across Callie's shoulders, Johnny looked around. "Where's your date?"

"On her way. I volunteered with the setup and had to come an hour early. Not much fun for her to hang out on her own." *Total overshare, DiRossi.* He couldn't help himself. He was nervous around the couple, afraid he'd do or say something wrong.

He glanced at Callie, unable to stop his gaze from dropping to her stomach. The jean jacket she wore over her sundress made it difficult to tell if she had a baby bump. No help solving his dilemma of whether or not to offer his congratulations. He wasn't sure if they'd shared the news about the baby with their family and friends or if Johnny had blurted it out in a fit of jealousy.

He decided it was safer not to mention it. "Hey, Cal. How's it going?"

"Not bad." Her smile was off. "So, who's the lucky girl?"

He didn't have to look at Johnny to know he wasn't happy with his wife's question. Marco could probably take care of that by joking that he appeared to be dating two women at the same time, sisters at that, and wasn't sure which one would arrive. He'd be relegated to dog status in Callie's eyes, and Johnny would be happy. So would Marco. He didn't like to think Callie still had feelings for him and clung to some misguided notion that one day they'd get back together.

Johnny must have been thinking the same thing because he said, "Yeah, tell us who it is. Inquiring minds want to know." He smiled down at his wife. "He's the talk of the station. He's got the chief's nieces on the hook and the woman I told you about, the fighter pilot who took the probie on in the challenge." Johnny shook his head. "You always were a dog, DiRossi."

The guy was taking it a bit too far. Especially after the crap he'd pulled with the disconnect valve and the joint off-shore drill. But since Marco had been thinking of saying something along the same lines, and it was more believable coming from her husband, he let it go.

The anger that was directed at himself was harder to release. He'd been so concerned dating one of Liam's cousins would put a strain on their friendship if things blew up (which, come on, was an absolute given) that he'd completely overlooked the fact that Daphne and Penelope were also his boss's nieces.

The last thing Marco wanted was to jeopardize the promotion he had in his sights. Even if his recent screwups were orchestrated by Johnny, they didn't look good for him. Mainly because he'd let the guy off the hook and took the blame. But the higher up the chain of command he climbed, the more his interpersonal relationships with his fellow firefighters came into play. Punching Johnny in the face could come back to bite him.

What he needed was a way out of this that would keep everyone happy: Johnny, Liam, the chief, and Kitty and Rosa—especially Rosa. So that meant he needed to date someone who wasn't related to the Gallaghers. Someone who wouldn't get the wrong idea and want more than some summer fun. There was one problem with the idea. That was basically Marco's previous dating strategy in a nutshell, and look where that had gotten him. He needed to hire someone to play his girlfriend, or better yet, get someone to volunteer.

He glanced at the silent couple in front of him. Apparently, while he'd been figuring out his dating dilemma, Callie and Johnny had been arguing with their eyes.

It looked like the silent thing wasn't working out

because Callie huffed, "You guys are worse than a bunch of old ladies. You better not let Mrs. DiRossi hear you talk about Marco like that, or she won't sell you a slice tonight, Johnny. And since I'm married to you, she probably won't sell me one either."

Last spring, Marco had finally given in to years of Liam's constant prodding to open a pizza shop. But a pizza shop on Marco's terms. He liked making both money and pizza, and he was great at the latter, but he didn't want the headaches of operating another year-round business. He already had that with the family deli he helped Rosa run.

So he bought a food truck and got himself a permit and sold pizza at every event in Harmony Harbor. He opened up for the Flower Festival in May and shut down after the Turkey Run in November. He'd made some good coin last year, and business was already up over last. For obvious reasons, Rosa had been only too happy to take his shift tonight, and Mia was more than happy to help out. Though her father had grumbled about child labor laws.

And Callie was clearly not happy about the prospect of no pizza at the movies.

"I'll put in a good word for you, Cal. Ma always liked you." And clearly Marco was clueless in situations like this, because that's not what either Callie or Johnny wanted to hear, as evidenced by the regretful expression on Callie's face and the resentful one on her husband's.

He was drowning and needed help, which might have been why, when he caught sight of the woman coming through the trees on the path, he broke into a wide *thank God* smile.

Theia Lawson was exactly the person to help him out of this mess. She was decisive, dependable, confident, and no drama. Okay, so she could be a little dramatic. But not in an irritating way. She was cute and funny, even a little awkward. He liked that about her. She was also no BS, and he liked that even more.

He didn't have to worry about her getting the wrong idea. She'd be up for a good time…well, any good time that involved a physical challenge or a competition. He liked the same, and he really liked her sexy voice and the way she looked in the faded denim shorts and the gray sweatshirt she wore.

She frowned at him from across the green, then looked behind her. A second later, she shrugged and then self-consciously returned his smile as if still not convinced it was meant for her.

He grinned. That pretty much settled it for him. Theia Lawson would make the perfect fake girlfriend. Now he had to convince her.

Feeling better and more relaxed, he had just opened his mouth to smooth over the situation with Johnny and Callie when Daphne and Penelope caught up to Theia on the path.

"If it isn't Charlie's Angels," Johnny said with a smirk. "You're a better man than me, DiRossi. I couldn't handle more than one woman at a time." Callie elbowed him. "What? That's a good thing, isn't it? Babe, what did I say wrong?" he called after Callie, who'd walked away with a disgusted expression on her face. Whether it was reserved for Johnny or for him, Marco couldn't be sure. Probably both.

Johnny didn't seem to care though. He gave Marco a friendly slap on the back. "I owe you, bro. Thanks for not outing me about the baby. Callie doesn't want to say anything until she's in the second trimester." He grinned as the Gallagher sisters and Theia approached. "Good luck. It looks like you'll need it."

Theia strolled his way, glancing back at Daphne and Penelope, who'd stopped in the middle of the path to argue. He had a good idea who they were arguing about and muttered, "Thanks" to Johnny. The guy was getting on his nerves.

Johnny nodded at Theia, then turned to waggle his eyebrows at Marco. In his head, Marco flipped him off.

Theia looked from Johnny's retreating back to Marco. "Not your best friend?"

"Not exactly. He's my ex's new husband." If he was going ahead with this, he might as well go all in and give her the lay of the land.

"Ah, I see," she said as she watched Johnny catch up with his still-annoyed wife. Callie said something to her husband before glancing Marco's way, her eyes narrowing on Theia.

Now's as good a time as any, he thought, and stepped closer to the woman he hoped would agree to fake date him. He smiled down at her and went to brush the hair from her eyes. A gesture Callie would assume was intimate.

Theia's forehead creased, and she took a step back, glancing at Liam's cousins, who were still arguing. It looked like Daphne was trying to convince Penelope to leave.

Even if she did, Marco was still committed to his plan. But if he wasn't careful, he was going to scare off his plus one. "Sorry. You had a caterpillar in your hair." He shouldn't have said that. It wouldn't help his cause if she ran away from him screaming at the thought of a creepy-crawly in her hair. "Not a caterpillar, definitely not a caterpillar," he quickly added. "A twig. From the trees. The ones you walked under."

"Um, okay," she said, looking at him like he was an idiot.

He was an idiot. The woman was a navy vet, a former fighter pilot. Probably nothing scared her.

She held out the blanket she'd been carrying under her arm. "Here. You're going to need this more than me. I hope you brought a chair for Daphne though. She's not exactly a casual-night-at-the-park date. Penelope is, so you'll be okay on that end." She laughed, a laugh as raspy as her voice, and he wondered what he had to do to make her laugh some more. "I don't know what will be more entertaining, watching you three or the movie." She turned to walk away…laughing.

Good to know her laugh didn't always make him picture her naked and tangled up in his sheets. Still, no way was he letting her get away. "Wait. You have to stay. I didn't invite Penelope. I can't go on a date with two women."

"So, what, going on a date with three women is better?" She made a face. "You don't want to date me. You want me to chaperone. I knew that."

She couldn't have given him a better segue if she tried. "Actually, now that you mention it, the dating thing wouldn't be a bad…" He trailed off, turning to follow her gaze.

Arms crossed, she stared at a guy in a dark-blue uniform a few yards away, checking out Penelope and Daphne. "Who is he?"

"One of the security guards."

She arched an eyebrow.

"Oh, you mean do I know him?" All he could see was a hint of the guy's profile beneath the navy ball cap. Marco leaned forward. "Looks like it might be Ryan Wilson. Why?"

"I don't know. Just something about the way he's looking at Penelope and Daphne seems off."

He was going to say the sisters were the type of women who drew attention, but then he saw what Theia did. The guy wasn't just checking them out. He was studying the two women intently. Just then he remembered Wilson's name coming up in a conversation with Liam. "Something happened last summer, and Ryan got kicked off the force. Supposedly he blames the Gallaghers and has named them in his suit against HHPD. So obviously he's not a fan of Harmony Harbor's founding family."

As though he sensed them watching him, Ryan glanced their way. Tugging the bill of his cap lower, he set off across the green toward the bandstand, where a group of teenagers had congregated.

"Why would someone hire a cop who was kicked off the force to act as a security guard?"

"I'm not exactly sure. But whatever the charges against him were, he denies them. I guess that was good enough for Night Moves. They're the company that operates Movie Night in the Park. Not everyone in town is a fan of the Gallaghers. They have their fair share of people who'd like to see them brought down a notch."

"So, what you're telling me is this Ryan Wilson is just one of many who have a problem with the Gallagher family?"

"You make it sound like they have a boatload, and that's not the case. It's more like a handful...maybe two handfuls. There's a lot of Gallaghers, you know," he said in an attempt to tease the serious expression from her face and get the conversation back on track. The track where she immediately agreed to be his fake girlfriend.

"That's great. You probably know everyone who has a problem with them and could write them down if I asked."

"You don't actually mean you want me to write down

everyone in Harmony Harbor who has a grudge against the Gallaghers, do you?"

"That would be helpful, thanks."

"Why? What reason could you possibly have—" he began, breaking off as Daphne and Penelope fast-walked toward them. Daphne was in the lead, which was surprising given her sky-high heels and tight siren-red dress. He'd thought Penelope, who wore ballet slippers and a long, flowy skirt and pink top and sweater, would easily beat her sister, but someone had caught her attention. If he wasn't mistaken, that someone was Ryan Wilson, which didn't escape Theia's notice.

"Sorry about that, Marco. My sister *somehow*"—Daphne gave Theia a tight-lipped look—"got the mistaken impression you'd invited her to join us for movie night."

"Um, does anyone else smell that?" Theia asked, sniffing the air. Marco caught a whiff of pizza and cotton candy, but he had a sneaking suspicion Theia just wanted an excuse to get out of there after Daphne's not-too-subtle reveal that she'd been behind his awkward double date with the Gallagher sisters.

It bore looking into, but not then, because Theia took off with a muttered, "I'm starved."

Except she didn't head in the direction of the three food trucks lined up on the edge of the park. She strode toward Penelope, who was sending a flirtatious smile and a small wave in Ryan Wilson's direction. But before she made it to Penelope, Theia was waylaid by two determined firefighters.

He heard her say, "I had no idea Kitty had arranged for you guys to join me here tonight. That was so *thoughtful* of her."

She appeared about as happy with Kitty's matchmaking

as he was with Rosa's. He watched as Theia walked away between the two men, who did seem happy with Kitty's matchmaking and planned to take full advantage of the opportunity. Which ticked Marco off…on Theia's behalf, of course.

But as much as he didn't like the idea of her hanging out with the two men whose reputations preceded them, this might be exactly what he needed to get Theia onboard with his plan to outsmart the matchmaking grandmothers.

Chapter Twelve

♥

Theia sat on the blanket, bookended by the broad-shouldered firefighters Kitty had chosen for her to date tonight. They seemed nice enough, but she was preoccupied with keeping an eye on how Marco's date with the Gallagher sisters was going five blankets over, at the same time Googling Ryan Wilson. Every now and again, she caught the security guard looking Penelope's way from where he leaned against a tree.

The problem was, Theia didn't know if it was because he found Penelope attractive or because he was Caine's grandmother's henchman. The local newspaper was about as helpful as Marco had been.

She grimaced as she recalled her earlier conversation with him. Her interest in learning the names of the Gallagher family's enemies had aroused Marco's suspicions. Daphne had unwittingly timed her interruption well, though Theia had a feeling the gorgeous divorce attorney wasn't done with her. Penelope had obviously spilled the beans that

Theia had encouraged her to attend movie night. As Theia knew, Daphne was the type who practiced payback.

But at that moment, paying back Theia appeared to be the last thing on the other woman's mind. Flipping her long locks over her shoulder, Daphne leaned in to whisper in Marco's ear. Penelope glanced over, saw what her sister was up to, and did the same.

Theia huffed a disgruntled sigh. This was not how the night was supposed to go. The plan was for the sisters to get tired of sharing Marco and flounce off. In opposite directions. She'd weighed the risks and decided it was best to bring the matter to a head sooner rather than later. Theia should have known their double date wouldn't go according to plan. She was kind of clueless when it came to how a woman's mind worked, other than her own, of course.

But as she'd learned over the years, her responses weren't exactly the norm. Which might be why her supposed dates were way more interested in the movie than in her. Or maybe it was because the movie was *Backdraft* and her dates had been critiquing every second of every firefighting scene.

"Ah, come on, the guy would be dead if he did that," date number one said.

"Him? Look at this idiot." Date number two pointed at the big screen. "They don't have a clue."

Theia's stomach growled, almost as loud as the fire on the screen. The two men were so intent on the action, they didn't look her way. She scooted backward while they continued pointing out everything that was wrong with the scene. They didn't notice when she got to her feet and walked away.

The smell of pizza called to her. Even the sight of the attractive older woman in the window of the red, white, and green truck didn't deter her. Rosa DiRossi had once been as determined to fix Theia up with her grandson as Kitty was to match her with the firefighters.

Since the logo painted on the side of the truck read THE PIE GUY, Theia assumed this must be Marco's venture. It appeared business was good.

She turned while she waited at the end of the line, stuffing her hands in her pockets and looking up at the night sky. It was a pleasant change from lying on the roof of her apartment building, trying to locate the stars through the glare of the city lights. Here they were clearly visible, glittering high above the crowded, tree-lined park.

Everywhere you looked, people were sprawled on blankets and chairs. The roar of the fire on the movie screen was drowned out by the low drone of conversation and parents calling out to bored children who were running among the audience. The ocean breeze had cooled off the day's heat, but it was warmer here by the food trucks with their ovens blasting and compressors humming.

Other than the matchmaking fiascos, it was a nice night. She wasn't used to events like this, at least not for the past few years. When she wasn't working, she didn't venture much farther than the two blocks around her building. Her interactions with people were limited to the guy at the dry cleaner, the owner of the corner market, and the bartender at the local pub.

"Theia. Theia Lawson, is that you?" a heavily accented voice called to her.

She turned with a smile, surprised the older woman remembered her. "Hi, Mrs. DiRossi. How are you?" she asked as Marco's grandmother handed the couple ahead of Theia their order.

"Rosa, remember? I'm good. Better now that my grandson

is dating." She waved at the movie screen and dramatically covered her eyes. "You tella me, how am I supposed to watch this? Eh, Mia, don't look. You'll have nightmares," she told the pretty young girl, who stuck her head out the window.

"It's just a movie, *Nonna*. Daddy and *Zio* don't fight high-rise fires." The girl smiled at Theia. "Do you want a slice?"

"I'd love one." She leaned back to look at the extensive menu. "Meat lover's, please. And a Coke."

Mia nodded, waving off her grandmother when she moved toward the cash register. "I can do it, *Nonna*. Five dollars, please."

Theia dug in her pocket and pulled out a five-dollar bill, handing it to the young girl, who went to get her soda while her grandmother slid a slice of pizza in the oven.

Theia leaned against the truck, enjoying the appetizing scent of garlic, tomato sauce, and melting cheese. "Smells great," she said.

"A DiRossi secret recipe." Rosa smiled over her shoulder at Theia. "We get the olive oil and olives right from Italy. My son lives there with his new family."

That made it sound like he'd replaced his old family with a new one. She wondered how that made Marco and Sophie feel. "Do you get over often to see them?"

"We do, but my *nonna* and *Zio* Marco won't go," Mia answered for her grandmother. "They're afraid to fly," the young girl added when she handed Theia her soda.

"If we were meant to fly, God would have given us wings," Rosa said.

Mia rolled her eyes. "You grew up in Italy, *Nonna*. You had to fly here when you immigrated."

"No. I came on a boat," Rosa said before serving another customer.

"My mom says you're a pilot and have a really nice plane." Mia continued talking to Theia while getting the man his soda. "Maybe you can take my *nonna* and *zio* for a ride?"

"Sure. I'd love to." Theia grinned, thinking that would be the perfect payback for the man who'd effectively grounded her.

Rosa would be a different story, as Theia soon discovered through her back-and-forth with the older woman and Mia. Two slices of pizza and a cannoli later, Rosa gave her head an adamant shake. "You offer me a million dollars, and I still won't get in the metal coffin." The older woman smiled past her. "Eh, *mio bel ragazzo,* you should see this one eat. Not like those skinny girls you bring home." She pinched Theia's cheek.

"Ma, don't pinch her cheek. You're too rough," Marco said as he joined them.

Rosa lifted a shoulder. "So what? She's tough." She stuck her head out the window. "How's your date? I did good, eh? She's *bellissima.* Smart too."

"Yeah, they both are." He gave Theia a pointed look.

"Both. Whatdaya mean *both*?" Her hand shot out as though to swat Marco, but he'd stepped out of reach. "You can't date two women at the same time."

"You should tell that to Theia."

"You're dating two women?"

"No, Ma. She's the one who—"

"I'm dating two men." She interrupted Marco before he outed her. The last thing she wanted was to be in Rosa DiRossi's bad books. Theia turned to point at her dates, only to discover the two men were on their way over. She groaned. So did Marco. Daphne and Penelope were also race-walking their way.

Marco's jaw set in a determined line, and he threw an arm around her shoulders. "Just go along with everything I say," he said out of the side of his mouth before raising his voice. "I thought I could do it, babe. But I'm no good at keeping secrets, especially from my *nonna*."

"What? What are you keeping from me?"

Theia looked around. He was calling her *babe*. And now he was holding her closer and rocking her against his body. A body she had bounced against and maybe had considered rocking against too, if she was honest. But not in front of his grandmother and the approaching Gallagher sisters.

"We're dating, Ma. We met last year when Theia was here. You talked about her nonstop after the parade, and I decided I had to meet her. We've kept in touch ever since. Although she's been a little ticked at me since I drowned her plane. You forgive me now, don't you, *cara*?"

Theia stared at him. She tried to talk, but nothing came out.

His niece was jumping up and down in the food truck, shouting, "Yay! We're going to have a wedding and cousins! The wish papers worked, *Nonna*."

Theia let out a panicked yelp and then opened her mouth to clear up any thoughts of a wedding or children. But just as she was about to, Marco swooped in for a kiss. It was the worse kiss she'd ever had, and she'd had some stinkers. Their noses collided, and her teeth bashed against his. But when she finally pulled away with a palm pressed to her face, she realized her wishes for the night had come true. The Gallagher sisters flounced off in different directions, while Theia's dates returned to the blanket to no doubt continue critiquing the movie.

*   *   *

"I think you broke my nose. Some warning would have been nice." Theia scowled up at Marco.

It wasn't his finest moment. He took her by the hand, drawing her away from his grandmother and niece, who'd had their celebratory dance interrupted by customers. "Sorry about that," he said as he leaned in to look at Theia's nose in the light from the streetlamp. "It might be a little swollen in the morning, but otherwise you're good."

"No, I'm not good. You just told everyone we're dating."

He rubbed the back of his neck. "Yeah, I meant to talk to you about it before springing it on you like that, but then I saw Daphne and Penelope coming my way…" He lifted a shoulder. "I was afraid I might lose my cool and say something that offended them. I can't risk upsetting them."

"Well, that plan just went out the window. You kissed another woman when you were supposed to be on a date with them. How do you think they're going to feel? And it won't matter to them that it was a terrible kiss."

"It wasn't that bad," he said, slightly offended.

She touched her nose. "Trust me, it was bad."

He looked into her brilliant blue eyes, which were sparkling with irritation—it sure as heck wasn't passion—and then his gaze dropped to her slightly parted pink lips, and all he wanted to do was kiss her and prove her wrong.

It wasn't the first time he'd wanted to kiss her tonight. When he'd glanced back to see her smiling at the idiots she'd been on a date with, he'd barely resisted the urge to go over and grab her face between his hands and stake his claim with a bone-melting kiss, not the teeth-cracking one he'd just given her.

She waved her hand in front of his face. "Hello. Are you going to tell me what that was all about?"

"Yeah," he said as he tried to process his reaction to her.

It worried him. But despite all of these unsettling thoughts and feelings that were coming out of left field, he was confident his fake-dating idea was not only the best way to protect his relationship with his boss and best friend but also to save his summer.

"Look, I'm sorry I kissed you and sprang the dating thing on you without asking. But unless you want to spend the rest of the summer hiding from the men Kitty tries to match you with, pretending we're in a relationship is the best way to—"

"A little warning would have been nice, but you're right. It's a good plan."

His jaw dropped. He couldn't believe she'd capitulated so easily. He closed his mouth and swallowed at least ten minutes' worth of arguments in defense of them fake dating, then said, "It's a good plan?"

"Yeah. A really good plan. Why? Don't you think so anymore?"

Hearing a hint of vulnerability in her voice and seeing it in her downcast eyes, he was overcome with a sudden need to know everything about her, to take away the pain she'd suffered at the hands of her uncle and cousins.

And right then he knew this was a terrible idea. One of the worst ideas he'd ever had, and he'd had quite a few in his thirty-three years. "I…" He was trying to figure out a way to back out without hurting her when he saw Callie walking toward the food truck. She was alone.

"Hi, Rosa. Have you seen Marco?" he heard her ask his grandmother.

"At the back of the food truck, *cara*." Rosa had always liked Callie.

Marco stepped in to Theia and raised his hands to frame her face. "It's the best idea I've had in a long time."

"You're going to kiss me again, aren't you? Is that your ex coming this way?"

"Yes to both," he said. "You good with that?"

She nodded. "We could use the practice." She went up on her toes at the same time he lowered his head, and their foreheads collided.

He drew his hand from the side of her face to rub his forehead. "You have a hard head."

"So I've been told." She put her arms around his neck, a smile playing on her lips. "Maybe you better let me handle this."

"Yeah?" He put his hands on her waist, drawing her close, satisfied with the small gasp she tried to hide but couldn't.

"Mm-hm. How about we go on the count of three?"

"One." He raised his hand to cup the back of her head, her silky black hair sliding through his fingers.

"Two," she said, her raspy voice igniting a fire inside him, but nothing like when she pressed against him.

"Three," he said, his voice rough. He lost all train of thought once his mouth smoothly closed over hers. There were no bashed teeth or bumped noses this time. Just her soft lips and her warm mouth. He could taste the sweet vanilla of the cannoli and hear her sexy whimpers and needy moans.

The gasp wasn't hers though. It belonged to Callie. He'd accomplished what he'd set out to with the kiss. He should stop now. It had already gone too far. But he couldn't make himself tear his lips from the woman in his arms. Instead, he steered her out of the view of curious onlookers.

He pressed her back against the truck and kissed her long and deep. A kiss she'd remember. But he'd forgotten the woman was competitive. She gave as good as she got.

Better. He would have stayed there all night if not for some-one on a loudspeaker announcing the movie for next week.

His legs were weak as he reluctantly pulled away. "Better?"

The tip of her tongue touched her kiss-swollen lips, and then she nodded. "Better."

He smiled. Her eyes had gone from ocean blue to mid-night black, her face flushed. The kiss hit *better* out of the park. "We'll need to practice."

Her teeth worried her bottom lip, and then she gave him a small nod before looking over her shoulder. "I, um, should go."

"It's late. Let me drive you. I just have to take care of a couple things and then—"

"I'm good. Thanks for the offer though." She'd regained her balance. They were on equal footing now.

"I'm on duty for the next two days, but drop by the art festival Tuesday. It's on the waterfront. I'll feed you," he added when he thought she might refuse. They had to spend time together if this was going to work, he told himself.

"'Kay. See you then." She looked like she was talking to herself as she turned to walk away. Her murmured words floated back to him on the night breeze. "Pretend. It's just pretend."

He rubbed his hand along his stubbled jaw. It wasn't a good sign that she was already having to remind herself they were in a fake relationship. He considered calling her back, telling her it was a stupid idea and they should call it off. His jaw remained stubbornly locked. As though his subconscious knew what he needed and wasn't about to let him screw it up.

Chapter Thirteen

♥

Colleen sat on the couch in her old suite of rooms in the tower with Simon curled up beside her. The cat had Theia properly trained. She responded to his demanding meows better than any other member of the family now. Colleen had a feeling Theia was fast becoming his favorite. She wondered if perhaps Simon sensed, like she did, a deep-held hurt in the girl.

"Don't worry, my boy. We'll uncover her secrets before she leaves the manor. Truth be told, I'm hoping she'll stay when she discovers she's one of us. She is, you know. One of us. I feel it down to my bones. She reminds me a bit of myself in my younger days."

Simon lifted his head and raised a white-whiskered brow.

"I suppose you're right. It might have been better if she'd fallen a little farther from the proverbial tree. She's a bit too good at all this skulking about and hiding the truth, if you ask me." She looked to where Theia pulled a large whiteboard from the closet, dragging it across the hardwood floor to rest against the bookshelves.

Colleen's smile broadened as she took in the photos, notes, and arrows on the board. "Yes indeed, she's truly like me. She might be doing the devil's dirty work, but she's trying to do good while she's at it. And not an easy task she's chosen at that. Though it appears she's making some headway in her Daddy Do-Over project. My husband would say she's playing God like I used to. But her heart's in the right place. Just like mine was. Though some people might not agree, I suppose."

There was a knock on the door. Theia grabbed a blanket off the couch to cover the board and then went to answer.

"Oh ho, look who it is, Simon. I never thought Daniel would visit my room again. It appears he's brought reinforcements. Marco's mother, Tina, no less. I wonder what Theia thinks about that. Rumor among the waitstaff is that she and Marco are an item. I'm not sure if the credit goes to Rosa or Kitty, but whoever matched the pair deserves a gold star. They'll be perfect together. Which should help in our bid to keep her around, Simon." She was about to rub her hands together in glee when she remembered why Theia was here. Gallagher or no Gallagher, the girl was consorting with the enemy. And not just Colleen's enemy. The entire town's. If Marco discovered what she was really up to, Colleen could kiss any hope she had for the couple goodbye.

"Granny, I'm just stopping by for a quick visit. So begone with you while I'm here," Daniel said, peeking his head into the room.

"Don't be ridiculous. There's only me and Simon in the room," Theia said.

"You think that's a cat, do you? Well, let me tell you, if

that's a cat, I'll eat my hat. He's Granny's familiar. Does her bidding, he does."

Theia's lips twitched. "I'll have to remember that when I need a late-night snack. Now, get in here before you draw attention." She pulled Daniel inside, offering his companion an awkward smile. "Hi. You must be Per—ah, Tina."

Tina DiRossi (although Colleen suspected she was going by her maiden name these days) looked more like a woman in her early forties than in her midfifties. She had on neon-purple spandex shorts and a top that bared a strip of tanned skin, showing off her flat stomach. Her pink-streaked blond hair was pulled up in a high ponytail, her pretty face glowing and makeup free.

"I am, and you're the woman who's going to help me win back the love of my son." She hugged Theia, holding up a small white ceramic bowl to the side as she did. "I can't tell you how grateful I am that you would do that for me, a perfect stranger."

"I'm not sure what—" Theia said, looking a little panicked before Daniel cut her off.

"You go about your cleansing business, love." Putting an arm around Theia's shoulders, Daniel walked her to the French doors that led onto the balcony. Theia had them open, a warm ocean breeze causing the heavy brocade curtains to billow and the papers on Colleen's old desk to rustle.

"Daniel, how could you promise her that? I'm not the relationship expert; your daughter is," Theia whispered.

"And a lot of good that did her. She's getting a divorce." He smiled at Tina, who'd just set a match to whatever she had in her bowl. "No. Best she puts her faith in you. Look at the fine job you're doing with me and my daughters."

"Daniel, you're the reason Penelope is getting a divorce.

And her divorce is the reason she's thinking of closing her practice."

"So you're putting all the blame on me now?"

"Pretty much. According to the experts, there's a direct correlation between a woman's sense of self-worth and her relationship with her father."

"There's a lot of pressure being a parent. Had I known, I might have gone and gotten myself snipped."

"Thanks for sharing, but that isn't something I needed or wanted to know." She pointed at Tina, who was fanning a sweet-smelling smoke about the room. "That's not weed, is it?"

Daniel chuckled. "No. It's sage. She's cleansing the room of spirits." He made the same sweeping motion with his hands as Tina did. "Go to the light, Granny. It's time for you to join Granda and Da."

"I'll cleanse the room of you if you're not careful, laddie." Colleen got up and slammed one of the French doors shut, chuckling when Daniel practically jumped into Theia's arms.

"You dig up bones for a living. How can you be afraid of a little ghost?" Theia asked.

"You've seen her, then, have you? I knew it! I knew I wasn't imagining things. And don't let her fool you. She might be the size of a leprechaun, but she has the will of a giant."

"I'm four eleven, I'll have you know. But I'll grant you the will of a giant." Colleen smirked.

"I haven't seen her, Daniel," Theia said as if not completely sure that was the truth.

"You haven't seen me, but you've heard me. Of that I'm certain. I've been warning you about Ryan Wilson every chance I get."

"But…?" Daniel said, picking up on the lass's uncertainty. He always was a canny lad. Too bad he was a Judas as well.

"It's nothing. Just some nights I wake up thinking someone is whispering in my ear."

"I'm not whispering. I'm yelling. And I'll keep it up until you clue in." She went to stand by Theia and shouted, "Ryan Wilson!"

Theia rubbed her ear. "Daniel, do you know someone by the name of Ryan Wilson?"

He went gray beneath his tan. "It doesn't ring a bell. Why do you ask?"

"He's a security guard for Movie Night in the Park. He was there Saturday. I didn't like the way he was looking at Penelope and Daphne. Marco said he had a grudge against the Gallaghers, but that's all he knew. I couldn't find out much about him."

"Are you thinking he might be the one working for Caine's granny?"

"Yes, but from what Marco said, he's not the only one who has a problem with the Gallaghers. I need to find Colleen's memoir. Caine said you mentioned something about the book. Do you have any idea where it might be?"

"You don't need the book. You just need Daniel to tell the truth." Colleen went to slap her grandson upside the head for withholding important information from Theia, but her hand went through him. Still, he jumped, his gaze darting nervously about the room. "I'm right here you, lug nut. And you'd best start telling the truth."

"Jasper would be the one to ask about the book. He might know something about this Ryan character too," Daniel said.

Colleen blew the papers off her desk, and he yelped. "Okay, okay. I know the man, and he's as bad as they come.

But don't go telling him I told you so or telling Caine so he shares it with his granny. Wilson has it in for me. I reneged on a deal. He's got a past with my family too. Of that I'm certain. With Granny, no doubt. She was always putting her nose where it didn't belong." He looked up and around the room and practically shouted, "And don't you—"

In response to Daniel's raised voice, Tina hurried from the bathroom to rush to his side. "Oh my." She shivered. "The spirit of Mrs. Gallagher must be here. It's freezing." She stroked Daniel's arm. "Don't get yourself worked up. It's not good for your blood pressure, Danny. Come with me." She led him to the canopy bed and patted the red and gold comforter. "Sit."

He did as he was told, and she climbed in behind him. "There. Isn't that better?" she asked, massaging his temples while rubbing herself against his back. "Ohm." She hummed, and he joined in.

Theia went to slump on the couch beside Simon. "Caine can't pay me enough for this job."

"Now, on that you and I agree, lass. I wonder how you'll feel when you learn you're one of us." She sighed when Tina and Daniel's *ohms* got a little lusty sounding. "And that *he's* your father." Colleen was just about to remind the pair they had an audience when the fire alarm went off.

Tina giggled. "We're so hot we set off the fire alarm, Danny."

"All right, you two. It's probably a false alarm, but you know the drill." Theia got up and walked to the door, holding it open. "And next time you want to make out, get a room. Preferably one without me in it."

"We'd best hope it's a false alarm like Theia believes, Simon. The fire at the carriage house two years past was no accident, as you well know. We'd best be on our guard."

Chapter Fourteen

♥

Theia shut the door to Colleen's suite and glanced at the elevator doors. She always took the stairs, but today she was willing to make an exception in order to get rid of Daniel and Tina faster. As the couple made their way down the spiral staircase, Theia weighed the odds of the fire being a false alarm or getting stuck in the elevator if it wasn't.

"Theia, quit your woolgathering and get a move on." Daniel waved at her from halfway down the stairs. "Can you not hear Jasper? It's no false alarm, lass."

She sighed and took the stairs. Because of the way the floors were laid out, she could hear Jasper calmly directing the guests to the exits. It was a beautiful morning, so many of them had already set off on their tours.

The couple waited for her at the bottom of the staircase on the second floor. A family rushed past them with anxious expressions on their faces. "You two go ahead," she said, waving Tina and Daniel on. "I'm going to make sure everyone's out of their rooms."

"You know, I think the universe may have had a hand in this," Marco's mother said.

Theia bit back another sigh as she ushered them to the stairs. "Why is that, Tina?"

"Well, you just agreed to help me repair my relationship with my son, and the universe is about to deliver him to your door."

She was right about one thing. Marco was on the job, so he might very well be arriving at the manor any minute now. She looked down at what she had on and, in what she could describe only as a moment of temporary insanity, wondered if she should change out of her shorts and sleeveless T-shirt into one of the sundresses Daphne had insisted she buy at Merci Beaucoup.

But even more terrifying than the idea that she was actually contemplating dressing up to see the man she'd agreed to fake date was the memory of the dancing-on-the-moon feelings she'd had when he'd kissed her. A kiss she hadn't wanted to end. A kiss that felt all too real and all too wonderful.

She looked up to see Tina staring at her with a hopeful expression on her face while Daniel was giving her an encouraging nod. Maybe Tina was right. Maybe this was the universe's way of balancing the scales of justice. If helping Daniel rebuild his relationship with his daughters was her retribution for lying and spying on the Gallaghers, then helping Tina rebuild her relationship with Marco would be Theia's penance for lying to the DiRossi family.

"Look, I'm not promising anything, Tina. But I'll see what I can do. Now, get going." The beeping of the fire alarms throughout the manor hadn't subsided and were now joined by the sound of sirens.

"Thank you, Theia. Thank you. If you can get him to speak to me, that would be a miracle."

Whoa, she'd had no idea their relationship was that bad. Although there had been something about his reaction to her *Perky Boobs* comment that indicated it wasn't great. Theia didn't bother responding. She leaned over the rail. Jasper stood at the bottom of the grand staircase, cautioning people not to run.

"Jasper, I'm going to make sure everyone is out of their rooms on this floor. Any idea how the fire started?"

"*Fires*, miss. There's one in an office and one in the study. They appear to be mostly contained behind the paneling. We have no idea how they started at the moment, but the sprinkler system has been activated in both rooms."

"Okay. I shouldn't be long." She ran down the corridors, banging on doors. They were all empty but two. A family of three who were looking for their son's pet lizard and an older man with a walker. Theia insisted the family leave, reassuring the crying boy his pet would be fine.

"Are you up for a piggyback, sir?"

"That's the best offer I've had in a long time, miss," the man said with a twinkle in his eye.

"You need to get out more. I hear the Widows Club meets in the dining room on Wednesday night for wings. You definitely want to check that out if you'll still be here."

"I just arrived yesterday for a ten-day stay."

"Great. I'll have Penelope get in touch with you once the excitement is over for the day."

She'd suggested to Jasper that Penelope be put in charge of guest services to fulfill her mandated work experience at the manor. She thought it would help rebuild her confidence in herself. A lonely older man in need of some social interaction would fit the bill.

It didn't escape Theia that up until a few days ago, people might have said she was a lonely woman in need of some interaction. She'd certainly made up for lost time, she thought when one incredibly hot fireman strode purposefully across the lobby with his eyes locked on her.

Her knees wobbled, and her heart picked up speed. And no matter how much she'd like to blame her reaction on the physical exertion required to carry the little old guy on her back, she couldn't. And that right there was the reason she did not date serve-and-protect men, especially handsome men like Marco. He'd looked great in his jeans and his black Henley the other night, but right now, in his turnout gear, he was to die for.

To die for, really? Since when did she say stuff like *to die for*? All she needed now was to faint at his feet. She frowned. Her legs didn't exactly feel steady.

"You doing my job for me now?" Tall, Dark, and Irresistible asked with a smile that didn't help with her wobbly knees.

"Yes, I…" She cleared her throat. "I checked the rooms on the second floor."

"You can put me down now, miss."

She briefly closed her eyes. She'd forgotten her passenger. Forgotten him because her mind and eyes were filled with Marco DiRossi. She felt like dying when Marco took the walker from her hands, his lips twitching as if he held back a grin.

And if she had any doubt that was the case, she heard the amusement in his voice. "Let me help you down, sir."

After thanking Theia and Marco, the older man made his way across the lobby, barely avoiding the firemen who were coming in and out of the rooms. "I should probably go help him," she said.

Marco nodded. "I have to get going too. I'll see you—"

She frowned as he began walking toward the back of the grand staircase. "Where are you going?"

"Down into the tunnels." He frowned and came back to her.

She'd been down there once before, and it wasn't an experience she wanted to repeat. Images of the dark, dank tunnels with their narrow openings, the sound of the ocean pounding against the outer walls, of gas leaks and explosions, filled her mind with worry. Worry for him. She swallowed past her suddenly dry throat. "Let someone else go. Someone who knows the layout. Someone—"

He lifted a gloved hand to her cheek, interrupting her babbling. "Hey, you don't have to worry about me, okay? I know the tunnels as well as the Gallaghers do. This place is like my second home."

Listen to her. She barely recognized herself around him. She cared what he thought about her looks, what she wore, how she kissed. She had this odd compulsion to make him smile, to make him laugh. She wanted to please him, protect him. She didn't scare easily, but these feelings terrified her.

Her greatest fear had been that she'd lose herself to love like her mother. That one day a man would come along who would turn her emotions inside out and upside down, and she'd never recover. She'd spend the rest of her life trying to recapture feelings that only a once-in-a-lifetime love can evoke. A love that breaks your heart and your spirit and shatters your soul. A love that consumes you every second of every day and makes you forget to take care of yourself and your daughter. A love that no child can compete with.

She had to stop the charade before it was too late. "Right. I don't know what I was thinking. But, Marco, we—"

Can't fake date was cut off by Penelope, who ran across the lobby, crying, "My babies! My babies are missing!"

Theia, who was trained to deal with life-and-death situations in a calm and decisive manner, went to take control of the situation, but Marco beat her to it.

"Penelope, look at me. Take a couple of deep breaths. That's right," Marco said when she did as he directed. "Where was the last place you saw the boys?"

"Beside…They were beside me," she said on a desperate sob.

"Okay, that's good. Now, can you give us an idea where you were standing?"

"With everyone on the front lawn. Near the bench under the tree. I remember because I helped an older woman…" Her face crumpled. "They must have run off then."

"We'll find them. They'll be okay," Marco said in a confident, reassuring voice, his gloved hand resting on her shoulder.

Her eyes fixed trustingly on him, Penelope nodded. He even had Theia convinced, and she wasn't nearly as gullible as the other woman.

As he spoke into his radio, alerting everyone to the situation, Marco held Theia's gaze and then lifted his chin at the door. She nodded her understanding. She'd start searching outside.

She gave Penelope's arm a reassuring squeeze and headed across the lobby as Marco waved over a couple of firefighters, instructing them on what to look for in the tunnels. Jasper and Daniel were hurrying inside as she ran out. She was heartened to see the genuine concern on Daniel's face. He was worried about his grandsons and his daughter. He loved them; she was convinced of that. Now they just had to convince his daughters.

She made her way through a crowd of people who were being organized into search parties by two firemen. Theia worked better alone and headed for the man sitting with his walker under the shade tree in hopes he might have useful information. She was steps away from him when a shout rang out.

"I found them!"

Everyone turned toward the voice, including Theia. Her eyes narrowed at the sight of the man holding each twin by a hand. Ryan Wilson. She didn't believe in coincidences. He had something to do with the twins going missing, and no one would convince her otherwise. She was positive she'd just discovered the identity of the person working for Emily. Now she had to let Caine know before the stakes went even higher.

"Weston! William!" Penelope raced down the stone steps and across the front lawn to gather her sons in her arms. Once she had assured herself they were fine, she hugged and thanked Ryan Wilson, the man Theia was certain had lured them away. But her attention was immediately captured by Marco, who'd crouched to talk to the boys.

If Ryan had thought to win over Penelope by playing hero, he hadn't counted on her attraction to Marco DiRossi. A man who didn't have to fake at being a hero. It was who he was.

Daphne ran to them, hugging her nephews and then her sister. It was the first sign of real affection between the women that Theia had witnessed. At least something good had come of the situation.

At the sound of an alert on her phone, Theia pulled it from her pocket. She had a Google Alert set to activate whenever Holden's family was mentioned.

His son and his wife, who lived in a small town in

Nevada, had been featured in their local newspaper. They were celebrating the boy's unexpected good fortune. He'd received a call from the college he couldn't afford to attend. It seemed his scholarship letter had been sent to the wrong address, and they were giving him an extension on his acceptance. They didn't have to. He said yes right there and then. Theia already knew he had. She'd heard from the head of administration and had sent in the first of three payments.

A flash of movement drew her attention to Daniel, who stepped over the bed of pink roses to reach her. "You know what Wilson's about, don't you, lass? You have to do something about him. Talk to that boss of yours."

"I was just about to." She held up her cell phone.

He cast a worried glance at his daughters, who vied for Marco's attention as he carried the boys to the fire engine. "Look at the two of them. The crisis brought them closer, but their crush on Marco will tear them apart again. You have to intervene. Just ask the man out."

There was more at stake here than her heart. As the Google Alert had reminded her, she still had a debt to repay.

"Relax, Daniel. Marco and I are dating." But considering how Penelope and Daphne were still throwing themselves at the guy, they hadn't been convincing enough. She folded her arms across her stomach. They'd have to up their game.

"Glad to hear it. I'll tell Tina. She's been trying to get the lad's attention, but he won't have anything to do with her. This will give her a little hope. Cheer her up a bit." He patted Theia's shoulder and walked to where Tina watched her son.

Theia had almost forgotten she'd been enlisted to reunite mother and son. The idea of her as Harmony Harbor's resident family fixer was laughable. But before she did anything else, she needed to have a private conversation with her boss, away from the prying ears and eyes of Colleen Gallagher's ghost.

The thought made her laugh. She'd never been the superstitious sort or had an opinion of any kind on life after death. But there'd been enough odd goings-on in the tower room for her to believe the Gallagher matriarch had yet to leave the building.

Theia's cell rang.

"T, are you okay?" Caine asked before she got out a *hello*.

Obviously his source in Harmony Harbor had told him about the fire. She'd always known he had someone in town feeding him information. But despite how close they were, Caine refused to divulge the name(s) of the person or persons who were providing him with information. No matter how often she asked. In some ways, he was more untrusting and isolated than her. She blamed Emily for that.

Still, she was angry the fire might have been connected to the company she worked for, which in her mind made her culpable. "I'm fine, and so is the manor."

Caine sighed. "I know what you're insinuating, but from the information I have, the fire was a result of faulty wiring. The electrical needs a complete overhaul, but because of the expense and the revenue they'd lose from having to close for renovations, the Gallaghers have been doing piecemeal repairs."

"You know better than me, but this wouldn't be the first time a Wicklow operative used fire as a means to get the Gallaghers to sell."

Before Theia had come to work for Caine, his personal assistant had been responsible for the day-to-day management of the Greystone Manor project. What Caine hadn't known at the time was that the man was reporting his every move to Emily, who didn't care what means were used to acquire the manor, including the first harmless attempt to smoke out the Gallaghers.

"I realize that, T. But I convinced my grandmother that the possibility of a fire devaluing the property as well as putting the town in harm's way was too high."

"Not to mention the lives of innocent people," she said dryly.

"You know me better than that. I've done everything in my power to ensure no one is harmed by the takeover. The offer for the estate is so high above market value, my accountants and lawyers were positive an alien had invaded my body."

"I know. I get it. But I also know your grandmother, and you said yourself, she's desperate to get this done before she dies." Theia blew out an exasperated breath, mad at herself for reminding him about Emily's impending death. No matter how much Theia despised the older woman, she was Caine's grandmother and, as misguided as it may seem, he loved her.

"Look," she continued, "you don't have all the facts. There's a reason I was concerned the fire might be arson. I'm pretty sure I know who's working for your grandmother in Harmony Harbor, Caine. His name is Ryan Wilson. You need to do whatever you can to get this guy off her payroll. I have a bad feeling about him." She filled him in on what had taken place with the twins, what she'd observed at Movie Night at the Park, and what Daniel had said.

"All right. I'll look into it. I have to go. Take care of yourself, T."

She frowned at the screen, surprised his reaction wasn't stronger. Unless he'd known all along it was Ryan…And the man didn't work for Emily; he worked for Caine.

Chapter Fifteen

♥

It was two days after the fire, and Theia had just returned from flying three women from New York City to Harmony Harbor. The women were staying at the manor for the week leading up to their best friend's wedding this Saturday. Although if you went by the number of bags they brought, it looked like they were staying a month. Theia helped Jasper fit the last of their luggage in the trunk of the limo.

"I appreciated the help, miss. It was more luggage than I had prepared for. You did an excellent job fitting it all in," Jasper said with a satisfied smile when the trunk stayed shut.

"We moved around a lot when I was younger. I learned quickly that if I couldn't fit it into the trunk, it stayed on the curb." It was the truth but one she should have kept to herself, she thought at the sympathetic look he sent over the roof of the old-school black limousine.

The Gallaghers and the staff at the manor were very good at taking something destined for the garbage and giving it a second chance. Case in point, the manor's entire electrical system. The study and office were now undergoing major and costly repairs to the scorched and water-damaged walls and floors.

"Nice chauffeur's hat," she said in hopes of avoiding a walk down memory lane with the man sliding behind the wheel of the car.

There was something about Jasper that made her want to tell him the truth. A feeling that he already knew more about her than he let on. Or maybe it was the feeling that he had secrets of his own and wouldn't judge her for hers. There'd been times over the past couple of days that she'd wanted to test her theory. But it always came back to her loyalty to Caine. The last thing she'd ever do was betray him.

Jasper touched the brim of the black cap as though he'd forgotten he wore it. He made a face. "Kitty's idea. The limo drivers for the hotel in Bridgeport wear them, so she insisted I do the same. They're a major competitor of ours."

Oh, she was well aware of that. Caine owned the hotel in Bridgeport. It had been his second salvo in the war against the Gallaghers.

"I suppose I shouldn't complain. You probably wear a uniform for the same reason. It inspires faith in your passengers that you're a professional."

She wasn't a fan of her black pilot's uniform and hat, but she supposed he had a point. Though she was positive Caine had initially meant the uniform as a joke. Then again, it may have been Emily's idea. The older woman wasn't a fan of hers. She didn't like that Theia and her grandson were friends. No doubt she'd see the uniform as a way to put Theia in her place.

"My uniform doesn't always inspire confidence in my passengers. I wish it did." A sex change would probably do a better job than a mere uniform. It still amazed her that in this day and age there were people who assumed just because she was a woman, she wasn't as good a pilot as a man. And it wasn't just male passengers who felt that way. "At least I don't have to worry about what to wear."

"Quite." Jasper agreed with a half smile and then lifted his eyes to the rearview mirror before turning off the airport road. The clear, soundproof privacy partition was no match for the passengers in the back. "It seems we have a lively bunch."

"They started the party on the plane."

"They didn't give you any trouble, did they?"

"My flight with Penelope, Daphne, and the boys set the bar pretty high. They didn't come close."

He snorted a laugh. "I'm glad to hear it. I noticed you had a different co-pilot this flight. I hope you didn't lose an employee because of the girls and the twins."

"No. He's more of a friend than an employee." And boss. A boss who was at that moment in Ireland visiting Wicklow's home office. "He was doing me a favor until my regular co-pilot returned from vacation."

"Good. I wouldn't want to think we'd cost you an employee."

"Not at all. But speaking of employees, how are Penelope and Daphne working out in their new positions?" she asked as Jasper turned onto the road to the manor.

"I'm afraid Sophie had to fire Daphne this morning."

"Really? I thought she'd be perfect as the wedding planner's assistant. She has a such great eye, and she's so stylish." All true, but that was not why Theia had suggested her for the job.

Mixing one bitter divorce attorney with happy, stars-in-their-eyes brides was a recipe for disaster. What Theia didn't understand was why on earth Kitty and Jasper had listened to her suggestion. For some odd reason, they took every opportunity to pull her into situations that had nothing to do with her. Then again, they seemed to like and trust her, which was nice, but it also made her feel guiltier than she already did. The sooner she could leave Harmony Harbor the better.

"Why did Sophie have to fire her?" she asked, crossing her fingers that, whatever the reason, it had obliterated Daphne's nostalgic feelings for the resort by the sea. Even better, if Daphne, Penelope, and the twins created enough problems for the manor, Theia hoped the Gallaghers would turn a blind eye to the stipulation in Colleen's will and let the girls leave before the month was up.

"She insisted the brides sign a prenuptial agreement before they could marry at the manor. She can be rather forceful, you know."

Ha. That was the understatement of the year. "That's too bad. But you know, Daphne has great organizational skills, and touring with a group requires a forceful personality at times. Why don't you switch her to guest services and Penelope to wedding planning?" Theia suggested, fighting to keep the laughter from her voice.

Daphne would last about a day and alienate two-thirds of the guests before she quit. And surely Penelope would remember her own wedding while planning someone else's and be reminded of how much she loved her husband and how much she missed him.

"That might just work. I'll pass along your suggestion to Sophie," Jasper said as he drove the limo under the stone arch and into the manor's parking lot.

Penelope stood beside a white twelve-seat passenger van holding a walker while Daniel helped Theia's piggyback friend up the steps. Daphne, with her nephews' hands in hers, walked down the path toward the van. She'd been playing the doting aunt since the day the boys went missing.

Jasper pulled in a few parking spots over from the van. "We're most grateful for all the help you've given us these past few days, Theia. Especially where Daniel and the girls are concerned. Without your efforts, I highly doubt we would have gotten the three of them to even speak. And now look at them. They're acting like a family."

She glanced to where the three of them were now talking and laughing outside the van and felt a small measure of pride. But there was something else, too, just under the surface, an emotion she couldn't name. Though she had a feeling she wouldn't like it if she could.

She looked away from Daniel and his daughters. "I'll give you a hand with the luggage."

"No need, miss. It appears Daniel wants you to join them on the tour." Jasper rolled down the window as Daniel motioned him to.

"Tell Theia to hurry up. We can't leave without her."

Theia leaned across the console. "You're going to have to. I'm still in my uniform."

"That works. You're driving the bus." Maybe because he saw the irritated expression on Theia's face, he jogged over and leaned in the window. "The van is a bit of a bugger to drive. I don't want to entrust our lives to Penelope. She needs glasses and won't admit to it. And Daphne hasn't driven in seven years. I'd do it, but I'm used to driving on the other side of the road."

Theia cast a hopeful glance at Jasper.

"I'm expecting an important package within the next hour and need to be here to sign for it. But you don't want to miss out on the art festival. People come from all around to attend," Jasper said as he waved Daniel out of the window.

The art festival she'd promised Marco she'd attend on Tuesday. Which was today. Maybe this wasn't such a bad idea after all, she told herself despite a sudden case of nerves. She'd have an excuse to hang out with him for only a few minutes. Surely she could keep from making a fool of herself in that short amount of time.

"I've come up with a plan to get Penelope back with her man," Daniel said out of the side of his mouth as they walked toward the waiting van. "I'm going to give him a call, chat him up a bit, see if he loves her and the boys. Make sure Caine's man was right and the rumors that her husband was seeing the talk show host were unfounded. If he passes my sniff test, I'll invite him for the weekend. What do you think?"

"It's a great idea. I couldn't have come up with a better plan myself."

"I hope it works. I don't like to think she didn't trust her husband because of the poor example I set."

"I shouldn't have said that, Daniel. Penelope says she was burned out. I'm sure that played into her meltdown on the talk show."

"I appreciate you saying so, but I have to own up to the pain I've caused my girls. I'm trying to make it right now."

"I know you are. And it looks like it's paying off," she said when the twins yelled for their granddad to get on the bus.

"At least I know the terrors love me." He smiled, gesturing for her to go ahead. Once onboard, he introduced her. "Theia will take care of the driving, and I'll take care of the tour guiding," he said, taking the seat beside her.

Theia said hello to her passengers, ignored Daphne's

raised-eyebrow look, and shrugged off her jacket. She'd barely removed her hat when it was slapped back on her head by Daphne, who sat in the seat behind her. "Keep it on. You have hat hair."

"Now I have hot head, which is worse," Theia said, tossing the hat onto the dashboard, out of the other woman's reach. "I don't care what my hair looks like."

"Obviously," Daphne said, and leaned over to shove her fingers in Theia's hair to fluff it. "It's bad enough you have on your uniform. The least you can do is have half-decent hair in case you run into your boyfriend." Her eyes met Theia's in the rearview mirror. "Yes, I know all about you and Hottie DiRossi. I thought you threw yourself at him to mess with me at movie night, but for some reason, the man's fallen for you."

Daniel glanced from Daphne to Theia, doing his best to suppress a grin.

"He hasn't fallen for me. We're just…dating."

"Well, if you want to continue dating him, you'd better keep an eye on my sister. She's not as willing to step aside as I am." She glanced over her shoulder to where Penelope sat in the back row of seats with the boys and then lowered her voice. "It's the twins' fault. She feels bad they're missing their papa."

Daniel reached back to pat Daphne's knee. "Don't you worry. I've got a plan to reunite the family."

"You'd better hurry. She's asked me to file for her divorce."

"Who's getting a divorce?" the older woman beside Daphne asked.

Worried Penelope would overhear them, Theia said, "So, Daniel, when exactly did William Gallagher land in Harmony Harbor?" The storyteller in him couldn't resist, and he had Theia driving slower than anyone else on the road so he could point out places of interest.

"Santa! I want to see Santa," one of the twins cried, pointing to a window display in a redbrick building on Main Street. Holiday House was the town's year-round Christmas store.

Several passengers echoed the twin's demand, and Theia found a parking spot a few doors down from Holiday House.

Daniel gave the passengers twenty minutes to check out the Christmas shop, adding ten more for the two older women who'd spotted Truly Scrumptious, the local bakery they wanted to visit. Theia was last out of the van, grabbing her hat as an afterthought. If she wasn't careful, she'd become as appearance conscious as Daphne.

The sight of temporary fencing distracted her from wondering just how bad her hair looked. The fencing blocked off the three vacant lots that were the future site of Wicklow Developments' office tower. Theia pulled out her phone and took a couple of pictures for Caine.

A few weeks before, they'd received word that the fence had been covered with signs encouraging residents and tourists alike to call the mayor's office and vote for the proposed Heritage Park over the office tower. Caine would be happy to see the fence had been cleared and remained signage free.

"It's an eyesore, isn't it?" a woman walking toward her said. She carried a basket of cookies that smelled like Christmas. She smiled and offered one to Theia. "I know it's only July, but I own a holiday shop." She nodded at the redbrick building beside the empty lots, which Theia's passengers had crowded into. "Come in and check it out. You can sign the petition while you're at it."

"Petition?" She had a feeling she'd just met the leader of Caine's opposition. Although she wasn't exactly the unreasonable shrew Caine had made her out to be. She actually seemed reasonable and friendly…Until she started talking about Wicklow Developments' ogre of a CEO, whose office building would not only destroy the charm of Main Street but would decimate the mom-and-pop shops in town.

The woman then went on to talk passionately and at great length about the park she'd proposed to Harmony Harbor's town council. A plan that supposedly had the support of one of the mayors. There were two, a husband-and-wife team, Connor and Arianna Gallagher. Marco was right; there were a lot of Gallaghers.

"I've talked your ear off and haven't even introduced myself. I'm Evangeline Christmas. My friends call me Evie."

"And you own a holiday shop," Theia said, unable to keep the amusement from her voice.

"I know." She laughed. "I recently inherited it from my aunt. It's been in the family for generations." She scowled at the KEEP OUT sign on the fence. "And if Caine Elliot gets his way, I'll be the one to lose it."

Feeling like she should be defending her best friend and boss, Theia said, "You know, it could actually be good for your business. There've been studies—"

Apparently Evie didn't want to hear about studies and opened the door. Instead of chimes, they were greeted by the voice of Santa welcoming them to Holiday House with a *ho, ho, ho*.

Twenty minutes, three cookies, and a quick tour of the three-story house later, Theia had heard some pretty convincing arguments as to why the worst thing that could happen to Harmony Harbor and Evie Christmas was Wicklow Developments' office tower.

She left the shop to call her boss. She gave him the good news first and then… "You signed her petition?" he practically yelled into the phone.

"I didn't know what else to do. She gave me cookies, and she's really nice. I actually think you'd like her if you gave—"

"No, I wouldn't. I've spoken to her, and she's an unreasonable harpy. She's costing me a small fortune with the delays."

"Yeah, about those delays. I wouldn't count on breaking ground in September like you hoped. She got the council to agree to push the meeting back to early October."

"How in the bloody hell did she accomplish that?"

"Well, it seems she got Holiday House designated a historical landmark, and she claims the construction of the office tower will damage the structure. She's asked that the meeting be delayed until she's consulted with an engineer who specializes in historic buildings."

"I can't believe…I've got a phone call to make. If you see Daniel, tell him to call me immediately or I'll cut him off. He was supposed to stay on top of this."

"You know, my mother always said you catch more flies with honey than you do with vinegar."

"Theia," he grumbled.

"It's true. Evie's single, you know. And beautiful. Smart too. Exactly your type."

"I'm sorry. Is this the Theia Lawson I know and love?"

"Shut up," she said without heat.

"Do me a favor, stop drinking the water and hanging out with the Widows Club. And stay away from Evangeline Christmas." He muttered something about the woman's ridiculous name as he hung up.

He might be right. Not about Evie's name, but about

Theia not being herself. She'd been thinking the same thing more or less for the past few days. Somehow, she'd gotten sucked into the matchmaking madness of Harmony Harbor. A town where love was on everyone's mind. Except she hadn't felt that way the last time she was here. Maybe the blame lay on the hedonistic feelings invoked by the sun on your bare skin and the sand between your toes.

Or maybe it was Marco DiRossi, she thought when she spotted his food truck parked in a prime location down by the wharf. The art fair attendees would have to pass his truck coming or going.

She walked over to where Daniel stood waiting patiently for his daughters and grandsons beside the van. "I just got off the phone with Caine, and he's not happy you didn't tell him about the historical designation Holiday House received. He wants you to call him ASAP. If you want the money train to continue"—she gave the Holiday House bags he carried a pointed look—"I suggest you do as he asked."

"If he thinks it's easy dealing with Evie Christmas, tell him to give it a try. Don't let all that sweetness and light fool you. She's as stubborn as my old granny, and what's worse, she knows what you're about before you do. She was a therapist of some sort. Reads you like an open book, she does. And I don't want to be read. By anyone. You shouldn't either, so stay far away from the lass."

"You're letting your guilty conscience get the better of you. It's no secret you want the office tower to go through. You ran your campaign on it, and your nephew the mayor agrees with you."

"I'm not so sure he does anymore. Arianna is thick as thieves with Evie, and my poor nephew is head-over-heels in love with his wife. He couldn't tell her no if he wanted to, especially now that she's given him a son." He angled his head as the owner of Holiday House said goodbye to her customers. "Other than being a pain in the arse, she's a beautiful woman, with all that lovely dark hair and dark eyes."

"Don't even go there, mister. You'd ruin all the progress you're making with your daughters if you date a woman half your age, especially when you're apparently in a relationship with Tina."

"What are you going on about? I meant for Caine. The man has a one-track mind, and it'd be a nice change if he was focused on something other than me. He's a wee bit scary, you know."

"He's goal-oriented. He goes after what he wants and doesn't let anything get in his way."

"Right now that lass is standing in his way."

"Yes, she is." God help her.

"She doesn't stand a chance. He'll squash her like a bug," Daniel said, and then gave Theia an impish grin. "Unless you and I do something about it."

Clearly, Daniel had been spending too much time with the Widows Club, but he had a point. Her best friend needed someone in his life. The beautiful heiresses and actresses he was frequently photographed with didn't stick around long enough to make him happy. She wanted him to be happy, just like he wanted her to be happy. He needed someone who was more important to him than accumulating property and wealth. Someone who was more important to him than revenge.

"What exactly did you have in mind?"

Chapter Sixteen

♥

"Put your eyes back in your head, Sully," Marco said to the man who tripped in a rut while trying to get a look at Daphne Gallagher.

"Aw, come on, DiRossi. You have to leave some women for the rest of us," the commander of the Coast Guard said as he walked toward Marco's food truck. Sully glanced over his shoulder to get one more look at Daphne and nearly took out an elderly couple.

"You have no game, man. Which is good, because that particular woman is off-limits to guys like you and me."

"What's that supposed to mean?" Sully rested an elbow on the small take-out counter while angling his body toward the row of brightly colored fisherman shacks Daphne was headed for. Artisans with higher-end wares paid top dollar to display them in the fisherman shacks, whereas crafters and locals typically rented out the white tents set up across from them at a lower rate.

"It means she's a Gallagher. Liam and Griffin's cousin,"

he added when Sully didn't seem to get what the problem was. "You know, your best friend, Griffin. The guy who'd kill you if you broke his cousin's heart."

Sully laughed. "I don't think that would be a problem. She's more likely to break mine."

"Whatever. It's an unwritten rule. You don't date a member of your best friend's family."

"It's unwritten for a reason." Sully waggled his eyebrows and then ordered his usual.

Marco turned to put a slice of meat lover's pizza in the oven and then grabbed him a bottle of water, setting it in front of him. "Don't say I didn't warn you."

"You're not interested though, are you? Because that's one rule I don't break."

"No. I'm already dating someone. Theia Lawson." He wondered why the lie rolled so easily off his tongue. Maybe because it kinda felt like the truth.

"And why am I just hearing about this now?"

"We've only been dating for a few days. She's…" He caught sight of his *girlfriend* and smiled. She was with Daniel and the twins, whose chocolate ice cream cones were dripping all over them. Daniel grabbed one and handed it to Theia and then took the other one and began to lick the cone. Theia made a face and tried to hand hers back to Daniel, giving in when one of the twins started to cry.

"Theia," Marco yelled in an effort to be heard above the crowd. She turned his way. He went to hold up some napkins and a cup with a spoon but got a little distracted by the sight of her licking the cone and fumbled the cup.

Sully looked from Theia to Marco and raised an eyebrow. "Someone's got it bad."

"I always have that effect on women," he said in an

effort to convince himself those odd sensations in his chest meant nothing.

Sully laughed. "I didn't mean her. I meant you."

Marco stared at the other man. To his relief, the oven timer dinged, saving him from having to respond. He couldn't be falling for the woman. Sure, he admired her, liked being around her, wanted to spend more time with her, wanted to know who had broken her heart and why she got that haunted look in her eyes sometimes. It didn't mean he was falling for her just because he liked the look of her, the feel of her in his arms, the taste of her…No, no way.

"Hey, how's it going? I'm Sully."

"Hi. Theia. Theia Lawson."

Marco inwardly groaned as his body reacted to her voice with heat and need. He wanted her, and he wanted her bad. His head came up. That was good. His panic subsided as he realized he'd overreacted. Lust was fine. Great, actually. He was in lust with Theia, not love. What was he thinking? No one falls in love in a matter of days.

When he turned to give Sully his slice, his eyes met Theia's. He couldn't tear his gaze from hers. *Lust*, he reminded himself, and thrust the slice at Sully without looking at him, barely registering the other man's laughter or the pizza disappearing from his hands. Theia's eyebrows went up, no doubt as a result of him staring at her like an idiot.

He let his gaze drop to her lips. There was a ring of chocolate around her mouth. He reached for a napkin before he gave in to the urge to curve his hand around the back of her head, drawing her close enough for him to kiss the sticky sweetness from her lips. But instead of letting her do it like a normal person or a fake boyfriend would, he leaned out the window, cupped her chin with one hand, and wiped the chocolate from around her mouth.

Theia and Sully stared at him—Sully with the pizza stalled halfway to his mouth.

"What?" Marco said. "She wouldn't have been able to get it all on her own." He turned to Theia. "You wouldn't have." His gaze followed hers to the chocolate splatters on her white shirt. "Come inside the truck. I've got something that'll get the stains out."

Sully laughed. "You sound like the big bad wolf."

"Eat your pizza." His tone translated to *Shut it, or you won't get another slice*.

"I should probably go. I'm driving the tour bus for the manor. They'll be ready to leave soon," she said, sounding more hopeful than disappointed as she pulled more napkins from the dispenser.

He didn't want her to go. He wanted to explain why he was acting like an idiot. And how was he supposed to do that without looking like a bigger one? He should just keep his mouth shut and…

Crap, Johnny and Callie were walking their way, and they looked like they were arguing again.

Marco returned his gaze to Theia. "If Penelope and Daphne are on the tour with you, you have some time to kill." He nodded at the two women who were stopped in front of a blue fisherman's shack, haggling with the vendor over a watercolor. Just down from them, Daniel chatted up the owner of the local art gallery while the twins painted a mural with a couple of seniors.

Theia looked like she was about to come up with another excuse to leave when Johnny and Callie arrived. "Hey, how's it going?" Johnny said.

Theia gave Marco a look and muttered, "Fine," and then walked around to the side door. He wasn't sure if the *fine* was for him or for Johnny, but for his sake, he was relieved to see her come inside. Funny when a few minutes ago the last thing he wanted was her in the close confines of the food truck.

"I'd love to hang out all day and watch you make a complete fool of yourself over that woman, but there's a gorgeous brunette dying to meet me," Sully said.

"Trust me, it's you who'll be dying. Don't say I didn't warn you," he called after Sully, who gave him a two-finger salute as he walked toward the Gallagher sisters. "Hey, Johnny, Cal, I'll be right with you." He turned tò Theia. "Do you want me—"

She stepped in to him and shut him up with a kiss. Once again, there were no gnashed teeth or bumped noses, just a deep kiss with a little bit of tongue and a whole lot of heat. She pulled back, and he went to dip his head for more when he remembered where they were.

"That's what you wanted, wasn't it?" she said with a pointed look at Callie and Johnny.

"Right. Absolutely." He'd totally forgotten they were fake dating and why. She was obviously much better at pretending than him. "Okay, what can I get you guys?"

"Hey, don't let us interrupt. We know what it's like not to be able to keep your hands off each other, don't we, babe? We used to be just like you…" He grimaced and tried to dig himself out of the hole. "I can't keep my hands off my baby mama either."

Behind Marco, Theia sucked in air and then nudged him out of the way to stick her head out the window. "Just so we're clear, I'm not his baby mama. But that's great that you are. Congrats." She looked from the couple to him. "What? Oh no. I didn't mean your baby is Marco's. It's not, right?"

Marco swore in his head, loudly but silently.

Johnny didn't have the same level of control. "What the hell? What the hell does she mean by that?"

"Relax. Theia's just a little unsure of herself. Aren't you, babe?" He put his arm around her. "But I've told you this before, *cara*. You don't have to be jealous of every woman I've dated. I never felt about any of them like I do you." He kissed the top of her head, murmuring sweet nothings in Italian. *"Sono a di te. Sei la donna dei miei sogni, amore mio."*

"You love her? We dated for more than a year, and you never told me you loved me." As though just remembering she was married and her husband was standing beside her, Callie said to Theia, "Congratulations. You've done what no other woman in Harmony Harbor has been able to. You brought Marco DiRossi to his knees. How does it feel, Marco?"

"Ah, not very good when you put it like that, thanks."

Callie snorted a laugh, and her husband almost sagged with relief beside her.

"What can I get you guys? I promise Theia won't spit in your food. Right, babe?"

She rolled her eyes and went back to dabbing water on her shirt. He made small talk with Johnny and Callie, trying to get things back on an even keel. Theia got their drinks and took their money while he got their pizza ready. So they seemed to be good too, although he had a feeling she was going to pay him back when the couple walked away. In his book, that kiss was enough payback.

"See you two at the wedding next weekend," Johnny said.

"Wedding?" Theia asked after they'd walked away.

"Yeah. I'm a groomsman. It should be fun. You wanna come? It's at the manor."

"Sure. I owe you after my slipup." She glanced at him.

He sighed at the look in her eyes. "No, Theia. There isn't a chance I'm Callie's baby's daddy."

"Would you like to be?"

He didn't even have to think about it. "Would I like to be a father one day? Of course. But not the father of Callie's baby." He also didn't want to be the third person in their marriage. Which was why, even though his feelings for Theia were making him nervous, he didn't put an end to their charade.

Out of the corner of his eye, he saw Jasper hurrying after Rosa and Kitty with an envelope in his hand. He caught up to them at the yellow fisherman shack. Probably because the crowds and the life-size mermaid display rack slowed the two women down.

He wondered what they'd gotten up to now. Whatever it was, Kitty seemed to be agreeing with Jasper, nodding solemnly. No surprise, Rosa was arguing with the man.

Jasper pointed to someone or something in the crowd, looked like he'd demanded a promise from them both, and then strode off in the opposite direction. Rosa perused the iridescent swimsuits hanging off the mermaid's arm until Jasper was out of sight, and then she grabbed Kitty by the hand.

"What's going on?" Theia asked, coming to lean beside him in the window.

"I think we're about to find out," he said as his grandmother dragged Kitty to the food truck. "Hey, ladies, what can I get you today?"

His grandmother went up on her toes, reaching out with both hands to pinch Marco's left cheek and Theia's right. "Look at them. Look how cute they are together, Kitty."

"Ma, let go. You're too rough." He glanced at Theia. "You okay?"

"Yeah, I—"

Rosa talked right over Theia. "Tell them, Kitty."

Both hands pressed one over the other against her chest, Kitty smiled softly at them and then shook her head. "I can't. I promised Jasper I'd wait. He says—"

"Oh, don't listen to the bag of bones. Who better to share the wonderful news with her than her own grandmother?"

Theia jerked out of the window, banging the back of her head on the edge. Reaching around to rub her skull, she glanced at Marco. "She wasn't looking at me when she said that, was she?"

"Yeah. Yeah, she was," he said, staring into Theia's distinctive sapphire eyes. Gallagher-blue eyes. He should have known. But how could he when she didn't know herself. Or did she? "This is a surprise? You had no idea?"

"None. None at all." She shook her head. "It can't be true. He would have told me."

"Who? Who would have told you?"

"Oh God." She buried her face in her hands. "Of course he knew. He knew from the moment he saw me. He's been using me all along."

"Do you mean Daniel knew and didn't tell you?"

Her head came up. Her eyes filled with hurt and betrayal. "Daniel? Is that who my father is?"

The door opened, and Kitty and Rosa crowded into the food truck. Kitty elbowed Rosa aside and then turned on her. "You see, Jasper was right. This wasn't the time or the place." Kitty reached out to touch Theia's arm. "I'm so sorry, dear. You shouldn't have heard the news this way. Jasper's gone to get Daniel."

Marco shot his grandmother a disappointed look. She avoided his gaze, instead picking up a dish towel to mop up an imaginary spill on the counter.

"Daniel's my father?"

"Yes. I'd begun to have my suspicions when you were here last fall. Your story about how your mother and father met seemed familiar, and then there were your eyes and your voice. It's beautiful, just like your father's. There's also your name. Daniel's girls were all named after Greek goddesses."

"I'm sorry, but I think you've made a mistake. My father never knew about me. You can't just assume I'm his daughter because of my eyes, my voice, and my name."

"We didn't, dear. We—"

Theia touched the back of her head. "The day I arrived, Jasper pulled out some of my hair, didn't he? The important package he was waiting for today. That was the results from the DNA test you ran, wasn't it?"

"Yes. I'm sorry we went behind your back. We didn't want to say anything until we were certain."

Marco felt bad for Kitty, who'd obviously seen this playing out differently. Maybe she thought Theia would be glad to finally know the identity of her father or belong to a family as loving as the Gallaghers. But the majority of his sympathy went to the woman standing beside him. She was pale, clearly in shock.

"Did he know?" Her voice was barely a whisper, and she cleared her throat. "Did Daniel know?"

"No, of course not, dear. Whatever his faults, that's not one of them. He would have told us, told you had he known. He always owned up to his mistakes." She clapped a hand to her mouth, her eyes filling with tears. "That's not what I meant. We don't think of you as a mistake. We already love you, and we barely know you. Please, give us a chance."

Rosa put a protective arm around Kitty. "Don't blame

her. It was my fault. I was excited and let myself get carried away by the moment."

"Theia needs a minute, Ma. This is a lot for her to take in. Let's get out of here. It's crowded and hot."

Theia nodded, and he placed his hand at her lower back to gently guide her to the door. "Ma, take over for me. I'll get one of the girls to relieve you." When she didn't argue, he knew she felt genuinely bad for what she'd done.

He gave Kitty's arm a comforting squeeze as she moved out of the way. "Everything's going to be okay, Mrs. Gallagher."

"You'll take care of her? Make sure she's all right?" she asked, wringing her hands as she looked at Theia.

"Of course. I'll bring her back to the manor in a couple—"

Daniel threw open the door to the food truck, his face as stricken as Theia's had been moments before. "I didn't know, lass. I swear to you. I had no idea you were mine." He dipped his head, his cheeks ruddy, then he raised his gaze to meet hers. "I canna lie to you. I don't know who your mother is."

She lifted her chin. "Aislinn. Aislinn Kelly. My aunt and uncle adopted me when she died."

He briefly closed his eyes, swallowing hard before saying, "Aye, I remember her. I remember her well. I…I'm sorry. I'm sorry she's gone."

"She looked for you. Every summer. She dragged me from Dublin to Cork to Galway. We hit every pub where you supposedly sang for your supper. No one had ever heard of the Mick O'Shea we were looking for."

He winced. "I'd gotten myself in a bit of a jam. I was running with a bad crowd and changed my name. Left Ireland for England not long after your mother and I were together." His gaze moved over all of them as if trying to gauge their reactions before returning to Theia. "I need a moment with you in private. Please." When she tried to move past him, he reached for her. "It's important."

She looked at him, then nodded. He led her to a tree behind the food truck.

Jasper came to stand beside Marco. "I should have kept the results to myself until later this evening," the older man said.

"Rosa was at the manor with Kitty when you got them?" Marco guessed.

"Yes, and of course Kitty had to share the news with your grandmother. They were gone before I knew what they were up to. They took the limo. I had to borrow Sophie's car."

"She and Liam know anything about this?"

"No, but it's only a matter of time before everyone in Harmony Harbor does. Kitty and I thought we'd organize a small welcome-to-the-family party tomorrow evening, but I think it might be too soon."

"Yeah, I think that might be pushing it." He glanced over his shoulder at the sound of familiar voices heading their way. Sully was walking with Daphne, while Penelope and the twins trailed behind. This had the potential to go from bad to worse.

He jogged to Sully. "Hi, ladies, boys. Sully, can I talk to you for a minute?"

"Marco, have you seen our dad?" Penelope asked. "Someone said they saw him run this way and that he looked upset."

"Yeah. I'd give him a minute. He's okay, though. Just, ah…" What was he supposed to say? "Give me a minute. Sully." He motioned for the other man to follow. "I need a favor. Can you give me the keys to your boat? I've gotta get Theia away from here for a bit."

"Sure." He dug in his pocket and pulled out a set of keys. "Tank's full, and the fridge is stocked. Anything else I can do?"

"Yeah. Keep Daphne and Penelope away from here for another ten, fifteen minutes."

"You got it, but what's going on?"

He filled him in.

"Wow, all right. I'll, um." He started to laugh and then put up a hand. "I'm sorry. I know it's not funny, but c'mon. You just warned me away from Daphne and—"

"Shut up, Sully."

Chapter Seventeen

♥

Hey, you okay?" Marco asked from where he sat beside Theia in the white leather captain's chair.

It's the first he'd spoken to her since they'd boarded the boat. He'd given her time to process all that had happened. Comfortable to leave her to her thoughts, comfortable with the silence. She appreciated that, appreciated him. He knew better than she did what she'd needed after learning she was Daniel's daughter, a member of Harmony Harbor's first family, heir to the Gallagher family estate and Greystone Manor.

What he didn't know was that she'd been betrayed by Caine, a man who'd been the best friend she'd ever had. A man she thought of as family. A man who she was a hundred percent certain had known exactly who she was the day he sat beside her at the bar in Dublin more than two years before.

The warm, humid ocean air blew her hair around her face, and she held it back with her hand to respond to the handsome man beside her. Instead of lying out loud, she nodded. She wasn't okay. The hurt of Caine's betrayal went soul deep. But that wasn't what Marco was talking about. He didn't know about her involvement in Wicklow Developments' plan to buy the estate out from under the Gallaghers. From herself, ironically. If Daniel had his way, Marco would never find out. No one would.

Part of her wanted to break her promise to Daniel. To rip the bandage off and get everything out in the open. She imagined Kitty and Jasper and the rest of the family wouldn't be so interested in having her stick around if they knew. But she couldn't do that to Daniel, or to his daughters. Her half sisters. Imagine that.

No, she wouldn't do that to the man who was her father. It wasn't like he'd knowingly abandoned her and her mother. He didn't really have anything to make up to her. Penelope and Daphne were a different story. If they learned he'd brought them here just to get them to sell their shares to Caine, he might lose them for good. She wouldn't be the reason he did.

She felt the weight of Marco's gaze and looked up from her lap. "Thank you for this. I couldn't face all of them. I didn't know what to do. Where to go."

"I thought you might take off in your plane and we'd never see you again."

Only it wasn't her plane. She hadn't just lost her best friend, she'd lost a job she mostly loved and her ability to cover tuition and expenses for Holden's son. She turned her head so Marco wouldn't see the tears she couldn't keep from falling. As she wiped at her eyes, he powered down the boat, bringing it to a stop in the middle of the ocean. The anchor made a whizzing sound as he released it.

"You don't have to stop. I'm okay," she said, her voice and nose clogged with tears.

He didn't respond. Just got up from the chair and gave her neck a gentle squeeze with his warm hand before making his way down to the starboard cockpit.

The wind had died down now, and the boat gently rocked in the wake of the other speedboats. They were out in the middle of nowhere. Nothing for miles. She shivered, reminding herself she trusted Marco before nerves got the better of her. Marco and the sleek, powerful boat he expertly captained. She wondered if there was anything he didn't do well. Crying women, it seemed.

He proved her wrong seconds later when he returned, handing her a box of tissues, a chocolate bar, and a bottle of water. Then he sat, turning to face her. "Don't try not to cry because of me. You've met Rosa. Tears don't scare me."

She took a tissue, wiped her eyes, and then blew her nose. "I'm fine, really."

"You're forgetting, I lived with Rosa. Kinda still do."

"You live—"

He motioned for her to drink the water. "The bottom half of our house is the deli, the upper half family apartments. She has a key to mine and comes and goes as she pleases. Now, back to the point I was making before you tried to distract me. I have a sister, and I've dated a few women. *Fine* never means fine."

"You're forgetting your mother."

"It won't work, you know. Ask anyone, I'm a determined guy. I don't give up until I get the truth. Now, are you going to come clean, or do I have to badger you until you do? Again, I'll remind you: Rosa."

She swallowed. She didn't want him to know the truth about her after all. She opened the bottle and took a sip of water before answering, "How about I don't ask you about your relationship with your mother and you let me pretend I'm fine?"

"One condition. You talk to me if you need to. When you're ready to. No judgment. I'll just listen. I've been told I'm a pretty decent listener. It might be one of the reasons I've been a groomsman in sixteen weddings."

She smiled, thinking that despite being off-the-charts gorgeous and no doubt a bit of a player in his day, he was a good guy. "That's a lot of weddings."

"Tell me about it. I could have had a hefty down payment on a house for what I've spent on being a groomsman and best man." He took her hand, caressing her palm with his thumb. "Seriously though. I'm here for you. Whatever you say stays with me."

And looking into his eyes, she believed him, which might have been why she told him a truth she'd never told anyone else. "Would you mind if we went closer to shore?" Her cheeks warmed as she admitted, "I get nervous this far out."

"Of course. You should have said something sooner."

She liked that he didn't try to talk her out of her nerves or make her feel bad for having them. Her uncle's and cousins' merciless teasing over the years had ensured that she never admitted her fears. "Actually, I'm scared spitless this far from shore."

He sighed. "*Cara*, do you even like being on the boat?"

She smiled at his reaction, but her own disturbed her. She had an overwhelming urge to throw herself into his arms and kiss him. "Yes. I love it." A more honest answer would have been that she loved being with him as much as she loved the wind and the sun on her face, the adrenaline rush, the sense of freedom and adventure. "It's just being out this far. The water's so dark and deep." She shivered once again as the memories of the accident returned.

"I'm sorry. I thought…" He gave his head a slight shake. "There's a life jacket under your seat. Put it on."

"You're not taking me back to Harmony Harbor, are you?" she asked as she reached under her seat, even though she knew Marco made her feel safer than a life jacket would.

He looked around, twisting his lips to the side. "How do you feel about a private island? Great white sand beach with a view of the harbor."

"Sounds perfect. Do you know the owners?"

"Yeah, you." He winked, then made a face. "Sorry. It's probably too soon to be teasing you about your new family."

"Don't worry about it. I'm used to being teased." Although this was hardly the same.

"The cousins again. I'd really like to meet those guys."

"And beat them up for me?" Maybe because she sensed he respected her and knew she could handle herself if she had to, she didn't get defensive at the idea of him wanting to fight her battles. Instead it made her feel a little warm inside.

"Yeah. And word of advice, you might not want to share with your new cousins what the Lawson boys put you through growing up. They'll track them down, and it won't be pretty."

"I don't know what's worse."

"Look, I get that you're overwhelmed right now and still coming to terms with everything, but the Gallaghers are great. You couldn't have picked a better family to be born into. They'll follow your lead, you know. If you need some space, all you have to do is tell them."

"There's a lot of them," she murmured, her mind circling back to her secret. Even if she wanted to be a part of the family, and deep down she thought it might be nice, she couldn't.

It didn't matter that she no longer worked for Wicklow Developments. She'd emailed her resignation to Caine before boarding the boat—no explanation other than *I know*—and then she shut off her phone. She'd played a role, no matter how small, in trying to bring the family down. And now, because of her promise to Daniel, indirectly she still was.

"You have that look on your face again. You might feel better if you got whatever's bothering you off your chest."

She leaned back against the seat as she got a glimpse of a small cluster of islands in the distance. The sailboats were still so far away that they looked like whitecaps on the waves. Her head resting against the seat, she looked at him. "I'd like to rewind the day to a few minutes before your grandmother delivered the news."

His eyes lowered to her mouth. "Works for me."

Reminded of what she'd done minutes before the older women arrived at the food truck, she nibbled on her bottom lip. "Uh, yeah, about that kiss."

"It was nice."

"Nice?"

His amused gaze met hers. "Really nice."

"Maybe we should practice some more so, you know, Callie and Johnny believe the act."

"Trust me, I think they're pretty convinced we're dating."

"Oh, okay," she said, unable to keep the disappointment from her voice. Kissing Marco earlier had pulled her out of her head. She'd gotten lost in the sensation of his warm, firm lips, the lazy strokes of his tongue, the feel of his hard body pressed against her. She wanted to lose herself completely in him. To shut off all the thoughts about the Gallaghers, her sisters, her father, and Caine.

She'd loved her mother and her aunt. But for very different reasons, she hadn't been able to count on them or trust their love. She'd counted on Caine's completely.

The boat slowed, and she straightened in her seat. They were at least a nautical mile from Harmony Harbor, but she could see a hazy outline of the town's harbor front in the distance and hear the buzz of a motorboat nearby. Marco steered toward a dock about a hundred yards from the heavily wooded island's sandy shore. He powered down and then turned to look at her.

"I probably should have asked this before, but how do you feel about swimming from the dock to the shore? I don't want to damage the motor by bringing her in too close. Sully would kill me if I put so much as a scratch on his baby."

"I'm fine here. It's just out in the ocean I have a problem." She looked down at herself. "I guess I do have a problem. I don't have a bathing suit."

"Not a big deal. There's no one around to see you. Just wear your bra and panties."

"You're not no one," she said while trying to recall what bra and panties she'd put on this morning, and then she remembered. Daphne had not only helped pick out her clothes, she'd picked out her underwear. Theia hadn't put on panties this morning. Underneath her uniform she wore a flesh-colored lacy bra and matching thong. Without thinking, she sighed and said, "I might as well be naked."

"Sure. Works for me." He stood up and tugged his Pie Guy T-shirt from his khaki board shorts.

"I don't think we know each other well enough for that." He waggled his eyebrows. "We're dating."

"Fake dating," she said, a second before she swallowed her tongue when he pulled his T-shirt over his head to reveal an eight-pack of glorious, tanned muscle less than a foot away from her lips. All she had to do was lean in…

"It's beginning to feel like one and the same," he murmured as he crouched in front of her. He raised his hands, and she thought he was going to undo her shirt. Instead he undid her life jacket. She barely managed to swallow a disappointed groan.

She had a feeling he knew how she felt when he took off her life jacket and said, "How about we forget about the fake dating and the Gallaghers and just enjoy the day together? No expectations. Whatever happens, happens."

"Like what happens on the beach stays on the beach?" she said, tempted to throw all caution and hang-ups to the wind. She blamed it on the gentle rocking of the boat, the faint smell of suntan oil, the gorgeous man looking at her with heat in his eyes. She knew what she wanted; he seemed to know too.

"Yeah. Same goes for the water." He remained crouched in front of her, his eyes heavy-lidded as he watched her undo the first button on her shirt and then the next.

"And on the dock?" she said, her voice low and breathy.

"Yeah. What about on the boat?" His gaze held hers as he smoothed his warm palms up her bared stomach.

"Definitely. Definitely on the…" She didn't get *boat* past her lips, the word swallowed in a mind-numbing, toe-curling kiss.

* * *

Theia snuck into the manor at six in the morning, leaning back to wave at Marco, who waited in his truck to make sure she got in all right. He hadn't known if the door would be locked. He'd reminded her to ask for a key before he gave her another one of his toe-curling kisses. Intimating there would be more days and nights like they'd just spent together.

She was onboard with that. She couldn't remember ever enjoying spending time with someone as much as she enjoyed spending it with Marco. But now she was back to reality. It was like she'd had a mini-vacay from her life. She wished it could have lasted a bit longer.

Theia closed the door, a smile lingering on her lips.

"Thank goodness. We've been—"

She jumped, cutting off Jasper with a yelp. She placed a hand over her racing heart. "Sorry. I didn't see you there."

"My apologies. I didn't mean to startle you. Are you all right, Theia? We've been worried about you. Kitty feels terrible about how you heard the news. As do I."

"I know, but really, it would have been a shock no matter how I was told," she said, feeling a little protective of Marco's grandmother.

"I hope you can forgive the part I played. I thought it was best in case you weren't Daniel's daughter as we suspected."

"It's okay, honestly. I'm sorry you were worried. Marco said you knew I was with him."

"Yes, but we expected you back in a few hours, not the next morning." He clasped his hands behind his back and looked down at his polished black shoes. "I suppose it's your father's place to speak to you about—"

"Jasper, I'm thirty-four. My mother gave me the birds and bees talk on my twelfth birthday." The same day she became a *woman*. Five months before her mother died.

"Of course," he said. His cheeks pinked. "But what I wanted to say…What Kitty and I wanted you to know is that the manor is as much your home as any of the children's. In accordance with Madam's will, your share of the estate is equal to that of your cousins and sisters."

"Thank you, but it's not necessary." She wouldn't take it. She couldn't. Not when she'd been deceiving them this entire time.

"Please, promise me you won't make any decisions right away. You are a Gallagher, Theia. As much a member of this family as anyone else."

It seemed so important to him that she said, "I won't. I promise." She glanced around the lobby and spotted the coffeepot on the bar. "I'll just grab a coffee and head up to my room."

"I'll send someone for your uniform. We can have it laundered and ready for your flight this afternoon."

Crap. Now what was she supposed to do? It suddenly dawned on her how dire her situation really was. The last thing she should have been doing yesterday was hanging out with Marco. It made coming back to reality so much harder.

"Okay. Thanks. I'm going to head over to the hangar in a couple of hours. There's a few things I want the mechanics to check out."

"Nothing serious, I hope."

It would be. There was no other way for this to play out. "If we have to make other arrangements for the party, I'll let you know in plenty of time. I can drive to New York and get them if need be."

"Let's hope that won't be necessary. Theia," he called as she walked toward the bar. "Kitty and I were hoping you'd join us for dinner this evening. We'd like to discuss a small get-together to welcome you to the family."

"Dinner with you and Kitty would be nice, but can we hold off on the get-together for a bit?" she said, her previously relaxed muscles knotting with tension. She still hadn't decided if she would stay or go. There was nothing keeping her here now. She didn't owe Caine anything. It was the only positive thing that had come out of this. She no longer had to work behind the scenes undermining the Gallaghers.

So maybe she owed it to herself to stay. She'd always wanted a big family, sisters, a father. Now she had them. She even had nephews. And a fake boyfriend she thought she'd fallen a little in love with last night. A little love was okay. She could handle a little love. It was the dancing-on-the-moon, wishing-upon-a-star kind of love that terrified her.

"My apologies. I can see you're uncomfortable. I don't blame you. Finding out you have thirty new family members can be a lot to take in."

"Thirty?" she croaked.

"Yes, and I believe you'll fit in beautifully. They're going to love you."

She was leery of the pronouncement. She'd heard it before. From her aunt. The only difference was that Jasper looked like he actually believed it. Her aunt never had.

"I'll see you and Kitty tonight." She started to walk away and then turned. "Jasper, do you think Kitty wants me to call her by her name or Granny?"

The corner of his mouth tipped up. "I'm sure she'd be honored if you referred to her as your grandmother. But may I suggest instead of Granny, you call her Grams. It's what most of her grandchildren call her."

"Okay. Good thing I asked."

"Feel free to come to me for anything. At any time. Your father…" He lifted a shoulder. "I suppose I don't have to tell you. You seem to know Daniel as well as any of us do."

She imagined she knew him better than they did. Daniel didn't need to put on a show with her. He bared his soul, warts and all. Which meant it would be difficult for her to see him as a father figure. She had a feeling that's what Jasper was tactfully trying to say, but it didn't really bother her.

"Thanks, Jasper. I appreciate it. I'll see you this evening around…?"

"Would six give you enough time to relax after your flight?"

"Yes. That'll be great. See you then." She grabbed a coffee before heading for her room. On her way up the stairs, she tried to figure out what she'd say when the plane everyone thought she owned vanished. The rate she gave the Gallaghers was ridiculously low because the job was part of her cover. But if she had to rent a small plane to fly the manor's guests from here to New York, she'd either be operating so deep in the red it would turn maroon or charge a fee no one in their right mind would be willing to pay.

She walked into the tower room and nearly had a heart attack. There was a man lying on her bed.

She slammed the door. "What are you doing here?"

Caine jolted upright and then scrubbed his hands over his beard-stubbled face before moving to sit on the edge of the bed. "What do you think I'm doing here? And where the bloody hell have you been? I've been worried sick about you. I thought—"

"Cut the act. You don't have to pretend with me anymore. I know, Caine. I know I'm a Gallagher, and don't pretend you didn't. You used me. Our friendship…None of it was real." She cleared her throat of the emotion threatening to choke her. "But how did I fit in the plan? What was the endgame? How were you going to use me against the Gallaghers? Please, enlighten me. I think I deserve that much at least."

He slowly came to his feet. "It wasn't my idea. It was Emily's."

She held up a hand. "You can only use that excuse so often. You do have a mind of your own. You're not a kid anymore."

"You're right. I do. Which is why I didn't fire you every time my grandmother told me to."

"Because I was a Gallagher. Because we were friends."

"Best friends. And yes, her hatred of the Gallaghers runs deep."

"How can you call yourself my friend when you kept this from me? I was in Ireland looking for my father. You could have ended my search with one word."

"I barely knew you. But once I came to know you, to like and admire you, to know what it was like for you growing up with your uncle and cousins, I wasn't about to tell you Daniel Gallagher was your father. You deserve better than him, T. Look how he's treated his other daughters."

"It was my choice to make, not yours."

"I gave you that choice. Why do you think I sent you here last year? If just once you had said to me, 'That Daniel's a great guy, Caine. He'd make a wonderful father.' If you said anything close to that, I would have told you."

"I trusted you. You were my best friend in the world. You were my family. The one person I could count on. And now…" She turned her head to hide the tears filling her eyes.

"Don't do this. I'm sorry. I made a mistake. A horrible mistake. T, please. Look at me."

He reached for her, and she took a step back. He lowered his hands to his sides. "The thing I feared most was that I'd lose you to them. And now I have."

"You have to go before someone finds you here." He

needed to leave before she broke down in front of him. She couldn't stay strong for much longer.

"I don't care. Out me to the Gallaghers. Out me to the world. The only person I care about is you. The plane's yours. I was going to give it to you after you finished the job, along with the bonus." He drew an envelope from inside his rumpled black jacket and pressed it on her. "Take it."

When she didn't move to take it, he tossed the envelope on the bed.

"They don't deserve you. They don't deserve an ounce of your love and loyalty." He lifted his hand as though to touch her cheek.

She held up her hand. "Don't."

He bowed his head and then squared his shoulders, raising his red-rimmed eyes to hold her gaze. "They aren't who you think they are. Be careful. Promise me that at least," he said, just before walking into the master closet and disappearing from view. That was how he'd gotten in without anyone knowing. There were hidden rooms throughout the manor, most leading down into the tunnels and then out onto Main Street.

Theia sat on the end of the bed and picked up the envelope, emptying its contents onto her lap. There was a check for twenty thousand dollars and the ownership papers for the Cessna. No strings attached. He'd given it to her free and clear. She didn't think he could break her heart again, but he had.

"What did they do to you, Caine? What did Emily do to make you this way?" She thought maybe it wasn't so much what Emily had done to him but what she was holding over him.

Chapter Eighteen

♥

The back door opened, and Marco turned expectantly from where he stood at his sister's stove, frying chicken. He smiled at the woman who pushed mirrored shades on top of her head as she stepped into the kitchen. "Hey, pretty lady. I was getting worried you were going to stand me up."

He'd been checking his watch every five minutes, which wasn't like him. It was also kinda interesting considering his previous concerns about dating a Gallagher. But after spending the day and night together, the only thing he wanted to get out of was the fake part of their arrangement.

Admittedly, he'd felt a little differently the next morning when he'd dropped her off at the manor. Things weren't quite so rosy in the cold light of day. His earlier concerns had been no match against the time they'd spent on the secluded beach, laughing, talking, swimming, and building castles in the sand. And later wrapped in each other's arms. It wasn't until they drove under the manor's stone arch that his worries resurfaced.

He had a feeling Theia had a few doubts of her own. She hadn't exactly brushed him off yesterday, but their conversation via text made it clear she was no longer basking in the afterglow.

"That makes it sound like a date. A date for two, not thirty." She jerked her thumb at the back door as she walked toward him.

"There's not thirty, *cara*. There's fifteen, including us. And we are dating, remember?" At the pop and sizzle of the fat in the cast-iron frying pan, he lowered the temperature on the burner.

"They just sound like thirty people, then." She leaned in and sniffed the chicken. "Smells good. What is it?"

"*Pollo Romano*. It tastes even better than it smells. But you didn't answer my question." His hands were clammy. He didn't remember ever being this nervous waiting for a woman's answer to a question. If he hadn't known how he felt about Theia before, he did now. He was willing to take the risk. He'd talk to Liam. Figure out a way to deal if things went south. But first it seemed he had to convince Theia to take a chance on him.

"You didn't ask me one." She leaned against the counter, arms crossed. She was wearing an off-the-shoulder blue-and-white-checked top with white jeans "So you're not just a pizza guy. You're some kind of chef?"

"No. I'm just a guy who loves food and loves to cook." He rested the tongs on the side of the frying pan and then reached for her. With his hands on her hips, he drew her slowly toward him, giving her a chance to object. When instead she moved closer, resting a hand on his chest, he lowered his head to where her neck and shoulder met and nuzzled her there. "Don't try to change the subject unless you're planning to dump me," he murmured against her soft, sweet-smelling skin. "You smell even better than the *pollo Romano*."

She laughed. "I don't know if that's the worst or the best compliment anyone has ever given me." He gave her a gentle love bite, and her breath hitched. She angled her head to give him better access. "I don't think you can dump someone you're fake dating," she said, her voice husky.

He smiled into her neck and then lifted his head. "I don't want to fake date you anymore. I just want to date you."

"Oh, I..." She worried her bottom lip between her teeth and then nodded. The breath he hadn't known he'd been holding released. He had a feeling Sully had been right the other day. He had it bad. Though from her reaction, he didn't think Theia did. That was a new experience for him. His sister would say it was about time. "We can do that," Theia said.

"Are you sure? Because you don't sound like you are. You don't sound enthusiastic about it either."

She looked up at him, a smile in her eyes. "I'm pretty sure."

"Really? Maybe this will help clarify it for you, then." He bent his head and kissed the tip of her nose and then her cheek, along her jaw and back to the tender place between her neck and shoulder.

"You forgot a spot," she said.

"Just give me time. I'll get there. I—"

"Hey, you can't—" Liam walked into the kitchen carrying a pot. "Sorry about that," he said, not looking sorry at all. "I was going to say you can't hog the guest of honor."

Theia tensed in Marco's arms. He stepped back, giving her shoulder a comforting squeeze. She hadn't wanted the Gallaghers to make a big deal about welcoming her into the family. She hadn't been thrilled about tonight's dinner but had reluctantly agreed when Marco had promised it would only be her immediate family and his. She was about to be less thrilled if the pot Liam had just put on the stove was a contribution from Marco's cousin, as he suspected.

"So, let me guess. A few more family members dropped by unexpectedly?" he said.

Liam held up his hands. "Don't blame me. It was your sister's idea. You know Sophie. She likes a party. We haven't had everyone over this summer, so she figured this would be as good a time as any."

Theia leaned against the counter, her arms once again crossed. "How many?"

"Um, well, just, you know, my brothers and their families." Liam stammered a little in response to Theia's unyielding stare. Marco would have laughed if he wasn't hoping to get lucky tonight. "Maybe a few of the cousins too. All right, I give up. Thirty. There's thirty of us for dinner. Now, don't shoot the messenger." He went to the fridge. "Soph asked when the langoustines would be ready."

Marco lifted the lid on the pot on the back burner. "Ten minutes," he said, then opened the oven to pull out three loaves of golden-brown rustic bread.

Balancing two trays of shrimp in his hand, Liam leaned in and inhaled deeply. "He's a keeper, Theia. If only for his skills in the kitchen. And let me tell you, the guy has mad skills."

"Thirty people," she grumbled as Liam headed outside.

"Look, just forget they're here because of you and enjoy the food and the company. Later, after they all leave, you and I will take a walk on the beach, and I'll continue to convince you that dating me is a great idea."

"Public or private beach?"

"Very, very private." He kissed her bare shoulder. "So

private, you won't need to go back to the manor for your swimsuit."

An hour later, Marco thought he'd be lucky if he could drag her away. She was bonding with the women of the family. He wasn't really surprised. He figured she'd be fine if she just relaxed. Except it might have been better if she wasn't bonding with his cousin Ava, who was worse than his sister when it came to teasing him. At that moment, it sounded like she was regaling Theia with stories of his misspent youth.

A good time for him to take care of coffee and dessert, he thought, and got up from the picnic table. Liam, Griffin, and several of the male cousins followed him inside.

He turned and looked at them. "You can't be serious," he said as they basically surrounded him.

"Hey, we're duty bound as her cousins, and as Gallaghers, to make sure your intentions are honorable," Liam said.

"We're dating, not getting married. Now, would you mind? I have to finish up the dessert. And if you guys harass me, you won't be getting any."

"What did you make?" Griffin asked.

"Lemon panna cotta with raspberry jelly and crema gelato."

There were a couple murmurs and a shuffle of feet as a few of them moved closer to the door, but Griffin stopped the defection. "Don't worry about it. Ava's panna cotta and gelato are just as good as his. I'll have her whip some up for you guys."

"Okay. Do you seriously think that Theia needs or wants your protection? And how did I become the type of guy she needs protection from?"

Griffin glanced around the room. "Who wants to go first?"

"A lot of help you are," Marco said to Liam. And then to

the rest of them, "I haven't been that guy for a long time."
He sighed when they all crossed their arms and stared him
down. "Okay, I get it, and I'm glad you want to protect
Theia. She won't tell you this, but she didn't have it easy
after her mother died. Her aunt was good to her, but her
uncle and cousins weren't. They made her life hell." He
turned on the tap to fill the coffeepot and over the running water said, "She hasn't come out and said it, but I
think she's been looking for a family ever since she lost her
mom. Now she's got herself one. Maybe a little bigger than
she counted on, and I'm not completely sure about Daniel
or her sisters, but I am sure about the rest of you. I trust you
guys and your families to be there for her if she needs you,
and I hope you'll trust me to do the same."

"I'll be damned. Sully was right," Griffin said, and then
gave Marco's shoulder a conciliatory pat. "Boys, I think we
got it wrong. We don't need to worry about Theia getting
her heart broken. We need to worry about Marco."

*   *   *

The dinner had gone better than Theia could have hoped.
The Gallaghers were a wonderful, noisy, welcoming family. And the food...She practically hummed eating the last
spoonful of the lemon panna cotta. It was as delicious as
the man who made it. The man who wanted to date *her*.

He smiled from where he sat beside her. "You ready for
some gelato now?"

"Are you kidding? I won't be able to wear these jeans
again if I do."

"That would be a shame." He leaned in to whisper in her
ear, "But don't forget, we have a date on the beach. You'll
easily burn off the gelato and more."

Heat warmed her cheeks and other parts of her body. "You shouldn't say things like that to me when we're surrounded by family," she whispered back, glancing at the family members crowded around the six picnic tables.

"Babe, take a look at Liam and Griff. What do you think they just whispered in their wives' ears?"

"That's different. They're married."

"Married? Who's getting married?" Rosa, who was sitting across from Marco, put her dessert spoon down.

"No one," Theia and Marco practically shouted at the same time. Possibly because all night everyone had been acting as if all they had left to do was set the date.

Daniel looked over from where he sat with Tina and his brother's family, while Penelope, Daphne, and the twins sat at another table with Jasper and Kitty. To say it was awkward was an understatement. Daniel had been avoiding Theia since the day he found out she was his daughter. Marco barely looked at or spoke to his mother. And Theia's sisters barely spoke to her or their father.

Daniel held Theia's gaze, angling his head at the house.

"I'll be back in a minute. Anyone need anything?" she asked as she picked up her empty dessert dish and Marco's.

He laughed when she received four requests for coffee and two for tea. "Looks like you're just one of the family now, babe."

She smiled even though the requests kept coming. But her smile faded when she entered the kitchen and Daniel said, "What the bloody hell do you think you're doing, leading on Tina's lad that way?"

"Excuse me?" she said as she put the dishes in the sink.

"You can't be cozying up to him like you are. You're giving him the wrong idea. All you have to do is look at his face to know he has feelings for you."

She might have smiled hearing him say Marco's feelings for her were obvious, even if the idea made her heart race a little, but she didn't appreciate his tone. "We're dating, Daniel." She couldn't ever see herself calling him *Dad*. He'd been avoiding her just like he'd avoided Penelope and Daphne. She now had a better understanding of how they felt.

He pulled out a chair and sat down. Resting an elbow on the table, he rubbed his head. "You're angry with me, aren't you? I can't say as I blame you, lass. It's obvious I'm just one big screw-up. I broke your mother's heart. Ruined both your lives with my idiocy. So I realize you're not interested in taking my advice, but step back and have a think on this. How will the lad feel when you sell your shares of Greystone to me and jet off in your plane?"

"At the moment, I don't have plans to fly off anywhere other than for the manor. I'm dating Marco, not marrying him, Daniel. As to my shares in the manor, I won't be selling them to you or anyone else." She was as surprised as Daniel appeared to be. But as soon as she said the words, it felt right. "And once Penelope and Daphne have gotten over their snit that you fathered another daughter, I'll be advising them to vote to keep the manor in the family."

"I might have expected you to turn on me, but never on Caine."

"He knew I was your daughter, knew I was a Gallagher, and had me working against them all this time without telling me. He's not the man I thought he was." It still hurt to think about his betrayal. Despite everything, she missed him. He'd played such a big role in her everyday life for these past two years that she felt like she'd lost a small piece of herself. "I no longer work for Wicklow Developments."

He nodded. "It makes sense why he's been communicating with me about Wilson, then."

"What about Wilson?"

"Why do you care? You've turned on both me and Caine."

"I care because if Ryan Wilson is as dangerous as you make him out to be, not only is he a threat to Daphne, Penelope, and the boys, he's a threat to the entire Gallagher family."

"You can set your mind to rest on that account. It was why Caine was in Ireland. He went to see Emily. Insisted she fire Wilson. Then he flew directly to Harmony Harbor to hunt down the man himself and give him his walking papers."

"You saw Caine?"

"Aye, I did. And now it makes sense why the man looked the way he did. I thought perhaps he'd been burning the candle at both ends for far too long and it had finally caught up with him. But now it seems your betrayal is the reason. I hope you're happy, lass. You destroyed the man."

She placed her palms on the table and leaned in to him. "You have the nerve to lecture me on betrayal? I used to feel sorry for you, but not anymore. Stop playing the victim. Step up and be a man."

"You're going to tell them, aren't you? That's how you'll get back at me."

"No. I don't break my promises, Daniel. Even if you asked when I was at my most vulnerable, still reeling from the news that my best friend—a man who was more my family than you will ever be—betrayed me. What I will do is everything in my power to stop you, Caine, and Emily from getting what you want."

He stared at her. "I'm as good as dead, then."

"Give back the treasure that rightfully belongs to the Greek government—and don't think I don't know that you still have it. It's just too hot to sell, and you're biding your time."

"How am I supposed to get my equipment back from the dig if I do that? I don't have the money the farmer's asking for. Caine barely gives me enough to live on. How am I supposed to pay off my creditors and pay for Clio's education?"

"Come clean with your family and ask them to cosign a loan. Declare bankruptcy and start fresh. Just do something, Daniel. Find a job that doesn't cause you to lie, cheat, and steal."

"You don't like me very much, do you? I canna say I blame you." He rubbed the table with his thumb. "I'm not much of a father. Certainly not the kind little girls dream of."

She thought maybe she owed her uncle a thank-you. He'd cured her of these kinds of dreams a long time ago. "Should I play 'Cry Me a River' in C or D?"

He snorted a laugh. "You're your granny Colleen all over again, you know." He pushed to his feet. "I'll think on what you said, but for now I'll see if I can repair what's left of my relationship with my other two daughters. I talked to Penelope's husband. He's agreed to visit this coming weekend. Do you think you could see yourself clear to flying him here? Maybe I could go along with you. Me and Tina."

"Text me his contact information, and I'll see when I can fit him in." She moved to the coffee urn.

"I'm sorry I'm not the father you were hoping for, Theia," he said quietly, heading for the back door.

Chapter Nineteen

♥

"Leave that," Marco said, taking the tray from Theia. He set it on the picnic table and then took her by the hand. "Let's go for that walk now."

Obviously, from the covert glances being sent their way, everyone had a fairly good idea her father-daughter chat with Daniel hadn't gone well. Worse, as Marco had proved, she'd been the one who gave it away.

She'd tried so hard not to pick apart the conversation with Daniel in her head. She'd focused on preparing the tea and coffee to shut off her thoughts. But her subconscious wouldn't be distracted. It had been busy looking for an indication that beneath Daniel's concern for himself, there'd been a little for her. Maybe even a clue that he could learn to love her.

She was honestly surprised that his obvious lack of fatherly feelings bothered her. She didn't expect to care. She certainly didn't have father-daughter feelings for him. But maybe because it felt like another rejection in a long line of them, Daniel's managed to sneak past her defenses, and she didn't get up her I-don't-give-a-crap mask in time.

It was embarrassing to know the Gallaghers and the DiRossis could tell she'd been hurt. And if she needed further evidence that they did, all she had to do was glance at Marco. He gave her hand a gentle squeeze just before he scowled at Daniel. It wouldn't do much good since her father appeared to find his cup of coffee fascinating. But Marco's mother had caught the angry look her son had sent her boyfriend and lowered her eyes. No doubt she'd pass along to Daniel that he was in Marco's bad books.

Theia doubted he'd care, but he might be concerned that his other daughters were clearly unhappy with him. It wasn't as if Daphne and Penelope had laid out the welcome-to-the-family mat for her, but it looked like they intended to have words with Daniel on her behalf. Except Kitty didn't appear to be onboard with their plan and motioned for them to sit down. Theia understood her reluctance to have her granddaughters cause a scene. Daniel was her son after all, and she barely knew Theia.

But she couldn't help smiling when Jasper shook off Kitty's restraining hand and got up from the picnic table. He walked over to put the squeeze on Daniel. Literally. Theia knew this because Daniel made a face and his shoulder sloped under the weight of Jasper's hand. Clearly under duress, Daniel got up from the table. Noting the direction Marco was leading Theia, Jasper gestured for Daniel to follow him to the other side of the house.

"I thought we were going for a walk," Theia said as Marco let go of her hand to hold open the screen door.

"We are, but I need to grab a couple of things before we go," he said as he closed the door behind them.

It sounded like he'd had a change of heart about their

night on the beach if he was planning to grab a pair of swimming trunks. Even if she'd been a little embarrassed when he'd given her a hint as to what was on the agenda for later that night, she'd very much been onboard with his plans.

He glanced at her as he walked to the fridge and then backtracked. "You okay?"

She sighed and leaned in to him. "I feel like you've been asking me that since the day I landed in Harmony Harbor."

"At least today it's not because of something I've done." He winced and wrapped his arms around her. "I probably shouldn't have said that." Then he brushed his lips across the top of her head. She tipped her head back, expecting more. Instead, he released her and walked to the fridge. "I've got just the thing to make you feel better."

"I thought that's what I was going to get, but you walked away." Even if that's exactly what she'd been thinking, she was surprised she'd said the words out loud.

He laughed as he took a bucket out of the freezer. "Patience, *cara*. I'm saving the best for later." He winked over his shoulder. "Me, in case you're wondering. But my crema gelato comes a close second."

"That's a lot of pressure to put on some frozen milk and sugar. I've never had an ice cream cone come close to giving me an orgasm."

Just as she was about to do a face-plant into the palm of her hand, he turned to look at her, a slow smile curving his lips. "Theia Lawson, I really, really like you."

His smile and his words filled the tiny hole Daniel had made in her heart. Marco was the one good thing that had happened to her since coming to Harmony Harbor. "I'm glad you do. Because I really, really like you too, Marco DiRossi."

She didn't just like him. She'd fallen in love with him. She poked and prodded beneath the warm fuzzy feelings filling her from head to toe, looking for signs of panic and fear just beneath the happy glow. They weren't there. She smiled, feeling free from her past for the first time in years.

For better or worse, she'd found her father. And while it didn't completely assuage her guilt, she'd been able to make Holden's dream for his son come true. Lastly, but even more important when it came to having a relationship with Marco, she'd cut ties with Wicklow Developments.

She pushed away thoughts of Caine. He no longer had a place in her life. His betrayal colored all her good memories. She couldn't think about him without wanting to break something or cry for a week. And right now, she'd rather forget about everything other than her night with Marco.

He handed her a waffle cone with two scoops of straw-colored ice cream. "Don't eat it yet," he said when she dipped her head to do just that. "Humor me. I've been waiting to watch you eat an ice cream cone since the art festival."

"Why? So you can correct my technique?"

"You didn't look like you had much of a technique, babe, but it didn't matter."

She knew it; he was going to ruin her first taste of his gelato for her. So when he turned to scoop more from the container, she licked the cone.

"Watching you—" he continued.

She cut him off with an orgasmic moan, smiling when he turned around. She gave the cone another long lick, closing her eyes as she released a moan to outdo the last. She'd barely gotten her eyes open when he was on her. Taking her face between his hands, he kissed her. Kissed, tasted, licked, and devoured.

Her knees went weak, and the moan that escaped from her this time was far from fake. She felt his kiss all the way to her toes and back to her heart, and she was just about to cry uncle, or whatever he wanted her to cry, and ask him to take her right there on his sister's kitchen floor. She was so far gone that the idea didn't give her pause; neither did the stars exploding behind her eyelids. It was the creak of someone opening the back door.

"My apologies for the intrusion. I wanted to check that you were all right, Theia," Jasper said. "But I see that Marco has the matter well in hand."

She glanced at Marco, who wouldn't meet her eyes, and unlike her, it wasn't from embarrassment that Jasper had caught them kissing. He looked like he found it all highly amusing. But he lost his amused expression when nearly every Gallagher and DiRossi stopped in the kitchen to check on her over the next forty-five minutes. Everyone but her father and sisters.

"I never knew how annoying big families were until now," Marco said when they finally got a chance to slip away. He opened the front gate that led onto the gravel road. "Especially the Gallaghers." He leaned in to lick her cone. Her other one had melted, and then every one of her cousins had wanted a cone, so there had been none left for Marco, which was what she figured had put him in a bad mood.

Seconds later, she learned his bad mood had nothing to do with the ice cream and everything to do with her father. "But at least they checked on you. Unlike your father and your sisters. What is wrong with them? Actually, forget about Penelope and Daphne. They'll come around. It's Daniel who needs someone to clean his clock. Jasper looked like he might. Here's hoping." He glanced at her and then retrieved her hand, bringing it to his lips. "Sorry. I shouldn't be going off on him."

"It's okay. I appreciate you looking out for me. But I'm a big girl. I don't need a father anymore."

"It doesn't matter how old you are. Everyone needs their family."

"As you know, I now have lots of family." She gave his fingers a light squeeze. "I'm not the only one with parent issues. You seem to have one with your mother."

"I wondered how long it would take you to go there," he said, leaning in to take a bite of her cone. "I don't hate my mother. I'm ambivalent." He led Theia across the gravel road and onto a path alongside a small creak. "My mother left when I was twenty. No warning. Everything between her and my dad seemed fine, and then one morning she was gone. She took Sophie with her. A couple of months later, my brother left. Then about a month after that, my dad flew to Italy, got himself a new family, and never came back."

"So basically, your entire family abandoned you in the space of a few months. And you were left behind to look after Rosa and the deli."

"Yeah, that's about it. But I was twenty—not twelve—and my mom was alive and well and living it up in LA. It's not the same as what happened to you." He helped her over a fallen tree. "We're a little off the beaten path, but trust me, it'll be worth it."

"I trust you." She smiled and then got back to the conversation she sensed he'd rather avoid. "You know, just because you were twenty doesn't mean you didn't suffer too." She ducked under the tree branch he held back for her. "But your mom loves you, you know."

"Right, that's why she took off and never looked back."

"She's here now, and she wants to talk to you, Marco.

Why don't you hear her out? You might find it helps to tell her how you felt when she left."

"Okay, I'll make you a deal. You talk to your uncle, and I'll talk to my mother."

"It's not the same thing."

"From where I'm standing, it is. He was the closest thing to a father you had growing up, and you never felt like he loved you or gave you the attention you craved."

"Wow, what an incredible view." He gave her a look. "Well, it is." She held up a tree branch. Green grass and mature trees covered hills of granite boulders that jutted out to sea on either side of the cove, framing a sand beach. But it was the sun sinking into the horizon that gave the view the wow factor.

"Okay. I'll give you that. But I was talking to Sam's dad…Girl power," he said as if to jog her memory.

She smiled. "I remember Sam. What about her dad?"

"I'm thinking her dad and your uncle might have something in common. All along, Sam thought her father didn't think she was good enough to become a firefighter, but it turns out all he wanted to do was protect his little girl." He put an arm around her shoulders. "Men—with the exception of me—aren't that great when it comes to talking about their feelings."

"Okay, Mr. In-Touch-with-His-Feelings, why don't you talk to your mother, then?"

"I've got a better idea," he said as he dropped the overflowing beach bag onto the sand. "First one to the buoy has to have a conversation with their estranged parent." He pointed to a buoy about half a mile from shore. "In your case, you have a choice of two. Your uncle or Daniel."

"Wait. That's not fair. It's not dark enough to go skinnydipping."

"Secluded, remember? But if you're too shy…" He shrugged and then whipped his T-shirt over his head. "I win by default."

"Just because it's secluded doesn't mean someone else hasn't gotten the same idea. It's the perfect night for a swim. Let's wait until dark," she said even as she started shedding her clothes. She got her answer while pulling her top over her head—the sound of someone running into the water. "You cheat!"

She tossed her top, shimmied out of her jeans, and then kicked off her sandals to race into the water wearing her underwear. Her white bra and panties were a little less revealing than the ones she wore the last time they swam together, but to her mind they were sexier since she'd hoped that he'd be undressing her at some point tonight.

With his lead and his powerful strokes cutting through the water, there was no way she'd win. She smiled. Unless she cheated like him. As soon as she hit deep water, she cried out and grabbed her leg.

"Theia, what is it?" he called out, two yards from the buoy.

"Cramp. I've got a cramp." She was impressed with her totally believable, thready, pain-filled voice.

"Hang on. I'll get you back to shore," he said when he reached her.

She sprang into action, pushing him under and leapfrogging over his back. She used his body like a springboard and swam for the buoy, giving it all she had. It struck her a few seconds out that he should at least be yelling or coming after her by now, but it was eerily quiet.

She glanced over her shoulder. There wasn't even a ripple in the water, and she began to get nervous.

She was just about to swim back when strong fingers

latched around her ankle and pulled her underwater. Her eyes popped open to see Marco's blurry, grinning face under the water, just before he used her head to push himself off. And that's how he beat her.

"Two out of three," she wheezed when she reached the buoy minutes behind him.

"Babe, I've got big plans for the night. You might want to conserve your strength. Just admit it. I'm the better swimmer."

"You cheated."

He laughed. "So did you."

Three races later, they lay flat on their backs, half in the water and half out, breathless and gazing up at the stars. Marco turned his head to look at her. "Please tell me you concede and we don't have to do that again."

"I con…I can't. It's not in my DNA to concede. Besides, you—"

He rolled over her, caging her in with his arms and legs, shutting her up with a kiss. When he finally let her up for air, she said, "I concede."

"Thank God. I thought I'd have to." He helped her to her feet. "I want to be there when you talk to your uncle."

"I have a better idea. We'll take your mother's sunrise yoga class on the beach. You'll talk to her, and I'll talk to Daniel."

"Ah, you lost the bet, remember? You conceded."

"Maybe. But it's something we should do. These past couple of weeks, I've done a lot of reading on the subject, and we need to find a way to forgive them so we can move on with our lives."

"If I agree, will you promise to talk to your uncle?"

"Fine."

He laughed and kissed the tip of her nose. "I'm going

to hold you to that, you know," he said, picking up the beach bag.

He emptied the contents onto the sand, standing to shake out a blanket. He'd brought two. He'd also brought two sweatshirts, a bottle of wine and plastic glasses, bottled water, and two small insulated cooler bags. The first one contained fruit, cheese, and his amazing homemade bread. She didn't get to the second bag because something in the sand caught her attention. She held up an unopened box of magnum-size condoms. "You took these from your brother-in-law?"

He gave her a look as he spread out the blanket in the sand. "Don't even. She's my baby sister. They're mine just like everything else in the bag. I forgot a few things when I was house-sitting for them last winter."

"So you thought you'd need the entire box tonight?"

"Yeah, but that was before you wore me out trying to beat me." He winked at her. "We'll probably only need half now."

Much later, she patted the cool sand for the extra sweatshirt Marco had brought for her, found it, and pulled it on. "Cold?" he asked when she returned to snuggle against him.

"Mm-hm. Are you going to warm me up again?"

He laughed. "Don't believe everything you've heard about me. I actually do require a little recovery time." He gave her a quick kiss and then reached for his jeans. "I'll be right back. I'll build us a fire." As though he'd read her mind, he said, "There's a fire pit and hardly any wind to speak of. We're good."

"Great. Too bad we don't have any marshmallows." She couldn't remember the last time she'd roasted marshmallows over a campfire. Though it was possible she'd blocked it out because it would have been not long after her aunt and uncle adopted her.

"Babe, no night at the beach is complete without a bonfire and s'mores. You must have missed the yellow insulated bag."

"Wow. You are good at this, aren't you?"

"Stick with me. You haven't seen anything yet." His cell phone rang. He checked the screen, frowned, and then answered, "Hey, what's up? Yeah. Okay." He nodded as he walked a few feet away. "Sorry. I don't think I heard you right." A short silence followed. Then, "You're sure about this? Tomorrow's edition of the *Gazette*? Yeah. I am too. More than you know."

It looked like he'd been given bad news, and she didn't want to intrude. He stared out at the ocean, the waves splashing lightly as they rolled onto shore. The distant sound of bullfrogs and crickets didn't make the silence any less uncomfortable. Just when she didn't think she could stay quiet any longer, he turned to look at her. "Were you ever going to tell me?"

Chapter Twenty

♥

Marco's eyes always seemed warm, but they were cold now, his expression hard. Theia considered pretending she didn't know what he was talking about, and then she thought about lying. But that would ruin any chance they might have to move past this. He'd eventually discover the truth and see it as one more betrayal. "That I used to work for Wicklow Developments? No. No, I wasn't."

"At least you're honest about it." He didn't look at her as he shoved his phone in the back pocket of his jeans and returned to the blanket. "So how did I fit into your plan?"

"Marco, please, let me explain."

He pulled on his T-shirt. "My sister runs the manor. My best friend is a Gallagher, a member of your family. The family you were working against. Who does that to their own flesh and blood?"

"I had no idea I was a Gallagher. The Elliots used me too, Marco." She held up a hand. "I'm not making excuses.

I was doing my job. But whether you believe me or not, I tried to protect the Gallaghers while I did."

"Right, so if things go the way you and your boss want them to, the Gallaghers will lose the estate. And they won't just lose it. It'll be bulldozed into the ground to make room for condos." He took a step toward her. "Do you have any idea what the people who worked on your company's behalf have done? Do you?"

He didn't give her a chance to respond. "My sister and my niece could have died in the carriage fire. Liam and I nearly did."

The blood rushed from her head, leaving her dizzy. She hadn't known the details. "I didn't have anything to do with that, and neither did Caine."

"So what? That makes you innocent?" He crouched down, shoving the half-empty wine bottle, glasses, and condom box in the bag. "Was I supposed to fall in love with you and then get Liam to vote to sell out his family like your father?"

"No, I...I didn't want you to date Daphne and Penelope. I was afraid they'd fall in love with you and not want to leave Harmony Harbor. They'd vote to keep the manor in the family to make you happy."

He released a harsh laugh. "Looks like the joke's on me. There'll be quite a few people in town who probably think I deserve to be made a fool of, and you sure fooled me."

"I quit working for Wicklow Developments the day I found out I was a Gallagher. None of what I've said or done these past few days has been an act. I really do like you. A lot. I wanted to be with you tonight. I loved our day on the island. I loved being with you today and tonight. I..." She briefly closed her eyes and then opened them to look at him. "Please, I don't want us to be over." It's the closest she'd ever come to begging in her life.

He scrubbed his hand over his face, inhaling deeply and noisily. "I can't be with someone I don't trust. You put my family at risk." He glanced from her to the blanket and then stood up.

If he cared enough about her well-being to leave the sweatshirt, bottled water, and blankets behind…She made one last desperate attempt to save their relationship. "I didn't just quit Wicklow Developments. I told Daniel that I'm planning to keep my shares and convince Penelope and Daphne to do the same. I'm going to work to stop Wicklow. I might be the only one who can."

"Too little too late, *cara*. It was fun while it lasted." Hefting the beach bag over his shoulder, he turned and walked away.

She stared at his back until he disappeared from view, using the blanket she wrapped around herself to wipe away her tears. She'd never cried over a man before. At least not a man she wasn't related to or who felt like family. She had her heart broken before, but this felt different. This felt worse.

She shivered and gripped the blanket tight around her shoulders, glancing at the firepit. It was her only option for staying warm tonight. She had no intention of going back to the manor. They must have learned the truth about her by now. They'd probably changed the locks. Early tomorrow morning, she'd sneak in using the tunnels. She'd be gone before anyone got up.

As painful as it was, she thought back to parts of Marco's conversation on the phone. He'd said tomorrow's edition of the *Gazette*. There was only one person who would have leaked the news to the press, a man who wanted revenge.

She doubted Ryan Wilson had any idea just how well his plan had worked. Emily would probably rehire him and give him a bonus if she knew he'd ruined Theia's chance at a once-in-a-lifetime love with a man who'd made her see stars twice in one night, a man she'd fallen hopelessly, head-over-heels in love with. Maybe she should be thanking the evil duo instead of wishing them both dead.

She wondered how Caine would take the news. She'd never felt more alone in her life than at this moment. Even after blocking Caine and banishing him from her life, she hadn't felt nearly this bad. She picked up the phone and unblocked his number. She couldn't bring herself to call him. Not yet at least. The hurt of losing Marco was too fresh.

Because while she may have initially begun dating Marco to help Caine's and indirectly Emily's cause, that didn't make what she felt for him a lie. They may have been fake dating for a time, but her feelings for him had been real right from the start.

Her cell phone rang, and her pulse quickened. She prayed it was Marco before looking at the screen. It wasn't. It was Caine. She owed him an apology.

"Are you okay?" he asked as soon as she picked up.

"No, but I will be. I'm flying home tomorrow." There was nothing to keep her here. Her father and sisters had made it clear they didn't want her around either.

"Stay, T. Don't run away. You've finally gotten what you always wanted."

With Marco, she got exactly what she didn't want, the thing she'd feared the most. Small comfort to know she'd been right all along. "I've spent my entire life fighting for my place, whether it's in my family or the navy. I'm tired, Caine. I can't do it anymore."

"What about Marco?"

She didn't even bother asking how he knew; it was a small town. No doubt his source had found out they were dating. "His sister manages the manor, and his brother-in-law is a Gallagher. They're family. I'm not. I betrayed them, so in his mind I betrayed him. In some ways he's right, I guess. He doesn't believe my feelings for him were real. That I could separate how I felt about him from the job I was sent here to do."

"You understand only too well how he feels. I made you feel the same."

"I do, and I'm sorry for the way I spoke to you. I'm sorry for cutting you out of my life. That wasn't fair. I should have trusted you. I—"

"No. You had every right to say and feel how you did. You'll never know how much I regret holding out on you. I only wish I'd been wrong about Daniel. He's hurt you, hasn't he?"

"Wow. Your source is well worth whatever you're paying him or her. But it is what it is. Whatever doesn't kill you makes you stronger. Isn't that what they say?"

"You've been hurt enough for three lifetimes. I thought you were finally going to get the happily-ever-after you deserve."

"That doesn't sound like the Caine Elliot I know and love." The silence stretched until it became uncomfortable. She was about to pretend they had a bad connection when his voice came back on the line.

"I can't tell you how relieved I am to hear you say those words. I thought you were gone from my life for good." She heard him drumming his fingers on his desk. Something he did when he was trying to work out a problem. "Would it help if I talked to Marco? I could tell him the truth. You tried to dissuade me at every turn. I basically had to bribe you to do the job."

"I don't think he'd consider the fact I can be bribed a

positive attribute, Caine. It was never going to last anyway. It's better that it ended now before I got in too deep."

"We never used to lie to each other." He cleared his throat. "At least when it came to our romantic life."

This time she was the one who let the silence between them grow. For no other reason than she realized she'd actually believed there was a chance she'd have a true romance in her life.

Caine broke the silence. "If your mind is set on coming home, text me when you log your flight plan. I'll take you out to dinner or we'll order in. I don't want you to be alone."

She saw it clearly. The two of them sitting on the couch in her apartment. They were old, their gray hair blending in with the color scheme of not only her apartment but of her life for the past few years. The only pop of color in the vision was in the crocheted afghans they each wore around their shoulders while they watched television and ate takeout because neither of them liked to cook.

It wasn't a new vision. She'd had it many times before. It used to make her happy…content at least, she corrected, now aware of what happy felt like. At that moment, the vison depressed her and made her sad. And it had nothing to do with Caine.

*   *   *

Sneaking in and out of the manor the next morning had been disappointingly easy and somewhat concerning. She'd mentioned it to Jasper in the note she'd left behind for him and Kitty to find. Theia hadn't been sure at first if she should address it to them both. But if she had a grandfather, she'd want him to be like Jasper.

Other than maybe Sophie and Liam, she didn't know

anyone else in the family as well as she knew him. As she wrote the letter of apology to Kitty and Jasper, she realized out of everyone, it was his forgiveness she most wanted. She hadn't left a note for her father or sisters. She'd call Daphne and Penelope and explain herself then. Eventually she'd talk to Daniel. She'd promised Marco she would, after all.

As she trudged along the dirt road to the airport, she glanced at the two shopping bags she carried. All she had left of her time with Marco were her memories: the starfish he found for her the day they spent at the beach, some sea glass, and his sweatshirt. She'd left the blankets on the end of the bed with a note asking that they please be returned to him.

A tear dripped off her chin. She wiped her cheek on her shoulder, annoyed with herself. It brought back uncomfortable memories of her mother crying in bed over Daniel whenever something or someone reminded her of Ireland or of him. She'd cried a lot.

Theia had grown impatient with her as she got older but never reached the point of telling her to her face. Instead the anger and resentment grew inside her, ensuring she'd wallowed in guilt for years after her mother died. Later, when the information could no longer help her or her mother, Theia's aunt confessed that Aislinn had suffered from depression since her early teens and that it had only gotten worse when Theia was born.

Her aunt never said anything more about it. Theia suspected she'd been monitoring her mental health since they'd adopted her. Or maybe it had been her aunt's way of feeling her out. Letting her know she could come to her if ever she felt overwhelmed with emotion. There'd been only the one time Theia had felt that way.

Days after the accident, she'd gone to them looking for support, and maybe absolution. She hadn't gotten it and took off for Ireland first thing the next morning. She'd drowned her guilt and sorrow in Guinness as she'd traveled the back roads of Ireland in search of her father. And then she'd met Caine. He'd tossed her a lifeline and a job.

Theia wished she'd been able to do the same for her mother. Aislinn had given up on finding Daniel the last summer they'd gone to Ireland. She'd come down with pneumonia a week after they'd returned home. She didn't take her medicine. She didn't fight. She was done with this world, done with being a mother. She'd convinced herself Daniel had died, and they'd be reunited on the other side.

Theia wiped her wet cheek on her forearm. She wouldn't become her mother. It was a thought she'd had many times in the past, though not in this context. But instead of the anger that usually accompanied the thought, there was a small measure of understanding, especially given Aislinn's predisposition to depression. Her mother had known Daniel for months and she'd had his child. Theia had known Marco for a little less than two weeks.

At the sound of an approaching car, she readjusted the bags in her hands and stared straight ahead. The black limo slowed and then pulled onto the shoulder in front of her.

Jasper got out. "There's no need for you to walk. I'll drive you."

Her breath hitched. It might have turned into a sob if she hadn't swallowed it first. Jasper didn't even suggest she stay and they'd work it out. He made everything right for the Gallagher family, but this job was too big for even him. Maybe he was so disgusted with what she had done that he didn't want to try. He probably wanted to yell at her in the privacy of the car.

"Thanks, but I can walk," she said as she went to move past him.

"You're scheduled to take off in twenty minutes. You won't make it in time to do your preboarding check. I promise, I'll get you there on time if you still decide you wish to leave."

Her head came up. "Why would I want to stay? Better yet, why would you want me to? You know who I am. What I've done."

"I do. I know all about you, Theia. I began looking into you as a result of my investigation into…" He cleared his throat, looking like he'd said something he hadn't intended to. "Kitty's suspicions about your parentage."

Just then things began to click into place. Like how Jasper knew she'd left the manor and the exact time her flight was scheduled to leave. "You're him, aren't you? You're Caine's source."

His lips twitched. "I told him you'd eventually figure it out."

She'd never been more disappointed in her life. "How could you? How could you do that to Kitty, to her children and grandchildren? You've been with them forever. They think of you as family."

He looked down his narrow nose at her. "I thought you'd understand. Clearly, you don't know me very well if you believe I would do such a thing."

"What am I supposed to think? You're working for Caine!"

"As were you."

"That's different. I barely knew any of you, and I sure as heck didn't know I was a Gallagher. Besides, I tried to—"

"I'm well aware you were trying to do good to make up

for your involvement with Wicklow Developments. I saw your whiteboard in Madam's closet."

"You were snooping in my room?"

"Yes. And your taking offense is rather hypocritical when you've been snooping too."

"That's not the point. You owe the Gallaghers your loyalty. I don't. Well, I didn't."

He sighed. "Theia, have you ever heard the phrase 'Keep your friends close and your enemies—'"

"Closer," she finished for him with a smile. "I can't tell you how relieved I am to hear you're not a bad guy, Jasper." The smile she gave him faded. But now she had to lie to Caine. She would have made a horrible spy. "Caine isn't either, you know. A bad guy," she clarified. "He's let his loyalty to his grandmother and the company color his perception of what's right and wrong. He'd never hurt anyone."

"I'm well aware what drives Master Caine and plan to use it to my advantage. Although, as I've learned, he's a canny lad. I worry that he's one step ahead of me in this game of chess we're playing. Emily is another story. But I believe once the truth comes out…" He gave his head a small shake. "Come, we have much to do today."

"Wait. What truth are you talking about?"

"We'll save that for another time. Right now we need to find you a job at the manor so you can fulfill the stipulation in Madam's will."

"I already am. I'm flying guests to and from the manor."

"I checked with the family's attorney, and he says it doesn't meet the criteria as stipulated in the will. I thought perhaps you can help the wedding planner. As a matter of fact, I think we'll move Daphne back to wedding planning from guest services." He smiled. "With your experience in the military and as the oldest sister, I have every faith you can keep both girls in line."

"You're enjoying this, aren't you?"

He chuckled. "Quite."

"Okay, now that we've settled that, tell me what truth you were talking about. What are you keeping from me?"

"Nothing to be concerned about," he said as he opened the car door.

But as she went to get in the passenger side, she was almost certain she heard him murmur, "Everything will come out whether we want it to or not."

Chapter Twenty-One

♥

There was a lot to be said for living in a big city where no one knew your name or your business, Theia thought as she walked through the dining room with her head down. She was almost certain that the wedding planner had a hidden agenda when she'd asked her to talk to the chef about the menu for Saturday's wedding. The woman made it obvious she wasn't Theia's number one fan.

Since the wedding planner also made it clear she didn't like her sisters much either, Theia didn't feel quite so bad. She might have felt better if she could commiserate with Daphne and Penelope, but they didn't appear ready to welcome her into the fold. They were no longer ignoring her. She just didn't get the warm fuzzies, especially from Daphne. Not surprising really.

Theia had confessed everything. There'd been no sense holding anything back to protect Daniel. The exposé in the *Harmony Harbor Gazette* hadn't only outed her, it had outed him. She'd tried to soften some of the harsher things Ryan had said in the article about Daniel and his motives.

At the sound of several older women talking at a table to her left, one with a distinctly Italian accent, Theia kept her eye on the prize, the swinging door to the kitchen. Leave it to the wedding planner to decide five o'clock on Wednesday Wing Night was the perfect time to talk to the chef.

"You should be ashamed of yourself for selling out your family," a woman seated at the table with the Widows Club called out to her.

"I don't know what Kitty's thinking, letting her stay on at the manor," another woman clucked.

Good to know her grandmother wasn't there yet, Theia thought as she placed a hand on the kitchen door.

"At least Marco found out what kind of woman she was before it was too late, Rosa. We—"

"You," a man bellowed, cutting off the older woman. Theia glanced to her right to see Daniel striding across the dining room toward her, red-faced and furious. There was no mistaking who he was talking about. His finger was pointed at her. This was not a discussion she wanted to have with the manor's guests and the Widows Club looking on.

She went to push open the door to the kitchen at the same time someone pushed from the other side. Clearly, she'd taken them by surprise. She heard the sounds of a tray, cutlery, and plates crashing to the floor. She wouldn't be welcome in there now. As she turned to head for the patio door, a heavy hand landed on her shoulder.

"Oh, no, you'll not be getting away from me that easily. Not after what you've done to me. It's your fault my family and my daughters have turned on me."

From under her lashes, Theia glanced around the room.

She couldn't believe he was doing this in the middle of the dining room. Everyone was staring at them. "I didn't do anything to you, Daniel. It's not my fault Ryan Wilson went to the—"

"Aye, it is. You forced me to make a devil's bargain with Caine Elliot and Wicklow Developments. Threatened me and my reputation unless I cooperated. If it weren't for you, I never would have sold out my family."

Theia stared at him, her shock at his lies rendering her speechless. But they didn't stun their audience into silence. Horrified gasps were accompanied by voices demanding she be held accountable for her sins.

Voices that quieted when a woman said, "That's enough." It was Daphne. She crossed the dining room to Theia's side. "You have no idea how she tried to protect you. How she painted you as a man who loved his family but got in over his head. All she's tried to do since we got here is bring us together, and this is how you repay her? In case you've forgotten, she's your daughter too. And my sister." She took Theia's hand. "Come on. Let's get Pen and go for a drink."

* * *

Marco sat on the porch at the manor's spa, pretending he didn't feel the weight of his mother's stare. He should have agreed to take part in the group massage for the groomsmen even if it seemed a little girlie to him. But he'd been afraid his mother would be the masseuse. He should just get it over with and talk to her. That's what Theia would tell him to do. He'd promised her he would.

He bowed his head as images of his night at the cove with Theia came to life behind his eyes. It was, bar none, the most fun he'd ever had on a date. It had been perfect until it wasn't. And maybe that's why the memories of that night on the beach were causing his head to ache. Not his heart. Never his heart. He hadn't fallen in love with her. He just, well, he'd really, really liked her. Dammit. He rubbed his eyes.

"Do you have a headache?" his mother asked quietly from behind him.

He pinched the bridge of his nose. *Here goes nothing*, he thought, glancing over his shoulder. "Yeah. Do you have some aspirin?"

Tina looked shocked that he'd spoken to her. He was about to call her out on the over-the-top reaction. It wasn't like he hadn't spoken to her since she'd moved back to town. But when he tried to recall the last time he'd said more than *hi* or *bye*, he couldn't.

"Yes. Yes, of course I do." She beamed like he'd asked her for the moon and she was able to deliver. "I'll get you an ice pack too. It helps when you put it on the back of your neck." She gestured to the spot. "It shrinks the blood vessels." She gave a flustered wave of her hand. "I don't know why I'm telling you. You being a paramedic and all. You always were a smart boy. I used to read you a book every night before bed. It wasn't long before you were reading them to me."

He remembered. It was their special time. No annoying big brother or little sister demanding her attention. His father or Rosa either. There was no denying she'd been a good mother when they were young. It might have been the reason it hurt so bad when years later she became someone he didn't recognize.

As though the conflicting emotions showed on his face, she said, "I'm sorry for the way I left, Marco. I should have at least tried to explain, but I wasn't sure I could leave if

I had to say goodbye to you." She looked away, inhaling a noisy breath.

The muscles in his chest tightened, and he wanted to hold up his hand and make her stop, but he'd promised Theia he'd talk to her. He didn't think six words qualified as a conversation. Though he still wasn't quite sure why he felt he had to keep his promise.

"I had to leave. Things between your father and me had gotten so bad, all we ever did was fight. Rosa couldn't stay out of it. She'd take his side, and they wouldn't let up on me. I could never do anything right in their eyes. I was the mangia-cake, and they never let me forget it."

"That's not true. You and Dad were happy. We all were. Until you…" He trailed off. He didn't want to get into this now. The wedding was in a few hours.

"Until I ruined everything? I know that's what you believed, Marco. But it's not true. We probably shouldn't have worked so hard to make you think everything was good. But the one thing your father and I did agree on was giving you kids a happy home."

"So all the memories, all the good times we had, they were just a lie?"

"No. We had good times. Lots of them. The last five years weren't great though, and they got worse. I was going through things, and so was your father. But everyone's good now." She touched his shoulder. "I'll get you that aspirin and ice pack. Your friends will be another twenty minutes."

Theia had been right about one thing: Talking to his mother had been enlightening. It helped put her leaving into perspective. But it wasn't his past that was the problem. It was his future. A future without a woman he couldn't stop thinking about.

"Marco, I know you don't think it's my place anymore, but I am still your mother, and I know you almost as well as anyone. It's why, even at the risk of alienating you again, I have to tell you you're making a mistake."

He stiffened. "Is that right?"

"Yes." Her voice quavered, and then she stood a little taller. "Yes. Yes, you are. I saw you and Theia together. You were happy. You both were. She deserves a second chance, and so do you." He went to stand up. "Please hear me out."

"I can't take anything you say on the matter seriously. You're dating her father."

"I'm not dating him anymore."

"Since when?"

"Since I found out what he said to Theia. Any man who could be so cruel to his own flesh and blood…" She winced. "That's a little like the pot calling the kettle black, isn't it? Although if you heard what he said to her, knew what she'd tried to do for him, you'd understand there's no comparison between him and me."

"What did he say to her?"

"From what Jasper said…He's how I heard about it. He stormed into the cottage." She made a face. "Good thing we weren't…well, you know."

He knew he'd regret asking. He regretted it even more when she told him what had happened in the dining room.

"Anyway," she continued, "I knew he had issues, but to out-and-out lie like that about his daughter?" She shook her head. "I have my own issues, and I was willing to turn a blind eye to some of his. He's a charmer, you know. Handsome as the devil, and you wouldn't believe what he—"

"Stop." He held up his hand before she said something he couldn't scrub from his brain. "So, what you're telling me is Daniel threw Theia to the wolves to save himself?"

"Exactly. And if I hadn't been about to dump the man, what Caine had to say to Daniel not five minutes after Jasper left would have decided it for me."

"Caine Elliot. He's Theia's boss, isn't he? The CEO of Wicklow Developments?" The man behind the plan to bring down the Gallaghers. The guy who'd dragged Theia into this mess.

"Yes, but she quit because he didn't tell her she was a Gallagher. He said he'd done it to protect her. They were the best of friends. Just like family from what he said."

Marco finally understood whom she'd been talking about that day she learned she was a Gallagher. It was Caine who'd betrayed her. Not Daniel like he'd thought. Though it sounded like her father had spent the past couple of days making up for lost time.

"What did Caine Elliot say that made you decide to dump Daniel?"

"Oh no, I'd already planned to dump him. But after hearing what Caine had to say, I wanted to tar and feather him."

He wasn't sure he could bear to hear much more. "What did he tell you?"

"Caine thanked Daniel for proving to Theia that he'd been right to keep Daniel's identity from her. Said how he wished Theia's mother had found Daniel because once she saw him for the man he really was, she wouldn't have wasted her time and love on him and would have given it to her daughter. From the sound of it, Theia's life with her aunt and uncle wasn't much better."

That wasn't news to him. But learning her mother had basically checked out for the first twelve years of Theia's life made Marco realize how easy he'd had it. How much he had to be grateful for. Whatever had been going on in his parents' marriage, they hadn't let it ruin his childhood. Unlike Theia's mother, they'd put their kids first.

"Um, Caine had a message for you."

"For me?"

"Yes. He knew you were my son. People used to say they could see the resemblance between us." Her wistful smile faded. "Rosa always shot them down. She…" His mother made a face. "Sorry. I've been trying to tap out my resentment toward Rosa, but I think it must be wired pretty deep in my brain."

He was afraid to even ask what that meant. "So, Caine…?" he prompted.

"I'm sure he didn't mean it. He was just feeling protective of Theia at the time. You can't really blame him—"

"Mom, what did he say?"

She pressed a hand to her chest. "Oh, Marco. You haven't called me 'Mom' in years." She blinked back tears, and he didn't think she could make him feel worse.

"I'm sorry. I've been a jerk."

"That's what Caine said. He also said if you're too stupid not to see the woman Theia is, you don't deserve her. But if you ever hurt her again, you'll join Daniel as shark bait." She wrinkled her nose. "I'm sure he didn't mean it."

He was pretty sure he did.

*   *   *

Theia had learned an interesting fact about sisters these past few days. While they could say any number of horrible things about her, Lord help anyone else who did. And there had been a rather large number of people in town and at the manor who had unfavorable opinions of her since Ryan Wilson had outed her in the *Gazette* and her sperm donor had spewed his vitriol in the dining room the other day. She no longer thought of him as her father. She'd rather not think about him at all.

Today's wedding at the manor made that easy to do, and it wasn't only because the bridal party was demanding or that the wedding planner had been missing in action for the past two days. It was because Marco was a groomsman.

She hadn't seen or spoken to him in days. She'd done a lot of dreaming about him though. She'd even considered hanging out by the fire station or calling in a false alarm at the manor. But she didn't have to do any of those things now because there he was, in perfect view of the window where she stood.

He wore a navy tux like the three other groomsmen on the beach. He was laughing, his white teeth flashing in his tanned face. She lifted her phone, hoping the glare from the glass wouldn't ruin the picture. She adjusted the aperture for a close-up. She wouldn't need a photo to remember him by if she'd figured out a way to make him understand that her feelings for him had nothing to do with the job she'd been sent here to do. If she'd been able to find the perfect words to tell him how she felt about him, she would have been down there, sitting on one of the chairs she and Jasper had set up early this morning.

His face blurred, and she blinked the tears away. She couldn't blink away her regret.

Her sisters came into view as they showed the guests to their seats. They looked gorgeous and confident in their red dresses. Daphne had insisted they wear the same color to make it easier for the guests to identify them. Theia had suggested they wear the same uniform as the waitstaff, but she'd been outvoted. It happened to her a lot, the outvoted thing.

Jasper had assumed because of her military background

and their birth order, Theia would be running the show. He
hadn't factored in that she was clueless when it came to all
the things girlie and sparkly. Her sisters were taking great
pleasure in educating her.

Just that morning, she'd endured a two-hour makeover
session. Penelope and Daphne had turned the bathroom in
Colleen's suite into a torture chamber. Still, they had the
best intentions. With their love lives more or less taken care
of—she'd flown Penelope's husband in from California
yesterday, and Daphne was officially dating Sully—they
were determined to help her win over Marco.

But the makeover was just step one. She would endure a
lifetime of plucking, prodding, and pampering if she could
bypass step two—sharing her feelings for Marco in a song.
And singing that song to him. At the wedding. It was,
she'd learned, a long-standing Gallagher-family tradition,
and one her sisters were positive would ensure she had a
second chance at love.

Marco's handsome face filled up her screen. He was
no longer smiling or laughing. She followed his narrowed
gaze to a dark-haired man staring down at the beach. She
zoomed in on his profile and gasped. Ryan Wilson. What
was he doing here?

She followed the direction of his gaze. At first she
thought he was staring at Penelope. But it was Jasper who
came into view. She turned the camera back on Ryan, shift-
ing to get a better angle and a close-up. She took several
photos, noting the self-satisfied smile on his face as she
sent them to Jasper.

Ryan Wilson was up to something. She thought about
what had happened the last time the man had taken his revenge out on the Gallaghers, and her heart began to race.
She needed to stop him before he hurt someone else. She

hurried from the atrium to the stairs into the dining room, walking fast instead of running so as not to draw attention from the guests enjoying Saturday high tea.

Once she'd made it out the French doors and onto the patio, she had a clear visual of Ryan. He was no longer alone. Jasper was with him, his stance aggressive.

Afraid things were about to get out of hand, she fast-walked along the garden path. Smiling at an older man and woman taking a stroll, she hopped over a bed of daylilies and cut across the lawn. Her right heel sank deep in the grass. She bent to pull it out, perhaps a little too forcefully because the heel remained in the soil, the shoe in her hand.

Her sisters would be heartbroken, but she wasn't. She lifted her left foot to slip off the other shoe and then took off at a run. Only the recently watered lawn was slick, and she slid about two feet. She wobbled but didn't fall down. With an inner cheer, she continued on.

Her quarry now in sight, Theia picked up speed. Which would have been fine if she'd been paying attention to where she was going instead of focusing intently on the two men. Her right foot sank into a hole, sending her into the air and flat on her face. It took her a couple of seconds to catch her breath. She pushed herself to her hands and knees. The grass really was wet, she thought as moisture seeped through her dress.

She reached the two men just as Ryan was about to walk away. "Because I'm a nice guy, I'll give you a second chance. A hundred grand before midnight tonight, or I go public." His eyes skimmed over her and then back to Jasper. "If you think what happened to her was bad, it's nothing compared to what will to happen to you."

"Be careful who you threaten, Mr. Wilson. Not everyone plays by the same rules," Jasper said, looking completely unruffled by the man and his threats. Except Theia picked up on the telltale tic in his jaw. Ryan had rattled him, and that rattled her.

She thought it only fair that Ryan with his smug grin was rattled too. "How's that lawsuit against HHPD going for you? I wonder what a judge will think when they discover just what you've been up to on behalf of Wicklow Developments? And now blackmail? It goes to character, doesn't it?"

His lip curled. "My price just went up. Two hundred grand."

She held up her phone. "Could you say that a little louder? I want to make sure the police hear it."

He laughed like she had no idea what she'd gotten herself into. "He's not going to let you go to the cops about this, are you, Jasper? Remember what I said. Before midnight."

"What was all that about? We should call the police," she said as the other man sauntered across the lawn. She wanted to throw her shoe at his head.

As though reading her mind, Jasper covered her hand with his. "Let it go. He's bluffing."

"No. He's desperate." She turned to face Jasper. "Tell me what he has on you. Please, I want to help."

"Believe me, if I needed help, you would be one of the first people I turned to. But at the moment we have bigger worries than Ryan Wilson."

"Like what?"

"For one, the wedding planner quit."

She grimaced. She'd been worried that was why the woman wouldn't answer her cell phone. "Don't believe anything she told you. She's jealous of Daphne and was trying to make her look bad. But Daphne has everything under control, so no worries there. And you'll save a pile of dough."

His lips twitched. "I see, and would you happen to know what happened to the swans? The bride was promised they would be available for her photo session by the pond."

"Um, that might be a problem. But I'm sure I can find some ducks. Would ducks do?"

"No. I don't believe they would."

"How about big ducks and I'll spray-paint them white?"

He sighed. "What did you do with the swans, Theia?"

"The twins like to fish in the pond, and the swans were terrorizing them, so I…"

"Please don't tell me you murdered the birds."

"No, but if I did, it would qualify as justifiable homicide. I captured them and brought them to the hotel in Bridgeport and put them in *their* pond. Just yesterday, one of the swans chased a woman, and she fell and broke her wrist. She's suing." She smiled. "You're welcome. Now that we've dealt with the problems, you can tell me—"

"Oh no, you have far bigger problems than I do. Here come your sisters. And they don't look particularly pleased with the state of your attire."

Chapter Twenty-Two

♥

Theia endured another session of pampering and polishing at her sisters' hands, but it wasn't as long as the first, mainly because they had a wedding to orchestrate. Well, Daphne orchestrated, and Penelope and Theia carried out her instructions. Most of which involved Theia acting as a liaison between kitchen- and waitstaff and ensuring the wedding guests found what they needed in the manor. Which meant Marco sightings were depressingly few and far between. But that was about to end when, through their headsets, Daphne ordered Theia to the tent.

She glanced at the bridal party's table as she walked by. She tried to catch a glimpse of Marco, but it was difficult to see past the floral arrangements. Daphne had told the wedding planner they were too high, and she'd been right.

Theia was just about to tell Daphne the same thing when she appeared by her side, taking her by the arm and dragging her to the far side of the tent. So instead of complimenting her, Theia said, "What's going on?"

"You know perfectly well what's going on, and don't even think about chickening out. This is your…What did you call it?" Daphne poked Penelope, who was talking to someone inside the tent.

She pulled her head out. "Her grand gesture. It's that moment in every book and movie where…well, usually it's the hero, but that's because the woman is rarely the bad guy in the story and has nothing to make up for. But you do, Theia. Everyone in Harmony Harbor thinks you used Marco, and that can be hurtful to the male ego."

She wished they'd stop talking. She was getting more nervous by the minute. She'd never done anything remotely like this before. Putting herself out there for a man, leaving herself open to rejection and ridicule. What the heck had she been thinking? "Seriously? Then he should grow a pair or get over himself," Theia said.

Daphne laughed. "Keep it up, Pen, and she'll be throwing the microphone at him instead of singing her little Gallagher heart out as she expresses her love for him."

"I don't know why you keep insisting I'm in love with him. I just like him a lot. We had fun together. He's the only guy who ever challenged me. The only guy who isn't threatened by me." The only guy who ever made her heart race. She couldn't remember missing someone as much as she missed him. She had to stop lying to herself. She was in love with him.

"Let's get this over with." She sounded as cranky as she felt. She also thought she might throw up.

"Okay, let's do it." Penelope looped her arm through Theia's right arm while Daphne looped her arm through the left.

"What are you guys doing?"

"This is our grand gesture too," Daphne said.

"Oh, come on. You can't sing to Marco. You've got your own guys."

"No, silly. It's our grand gesture to *you*," Penelope said.

Theia was pretty sure her mouth was still hanging open when they half-walked, half-dragged her through the curtains and into the bright lights.

Daphne released her and walked to the microphone at the center of the small stage. "Hi, everyone. We're the Gallagher girls, and we'd like to welcome you to the manor." Daphne shielded her eyes from the lights. "We hope you've all been enjoying yourselves. Before the band plays our lovely bride and groom's first dance, our sister, Lieutenant Theia Gallagher, has a very special song she'd like to sing for a very special man. Marco DiRossi, where are you?"

People looked around and then began to whisper, some wondering aloud why he'd respond after what Theia had done. Others wondering if he'd left. Someone else suggested they'd seen him with a blonde down at the beach. Another man chuckled and said it was a blonde and a redhead.

"I can't do this. He's not going to—" She tried to tug her arm free from Penelope's death grip.

"There he is. You're looking handsome tonight, Marco. Isn't he, Theia? Theia, get over here," Daphne said through a tight smile. "Now." She pointed to the spot beside her.

Penelope waved at the band to start the music with one hand while she pushed Theia with the other toward the front of the stage. Theia froze like a soldier caught behind enemy lines.

"*Cara.*"

She glanced down to where Marco stood in front of the stage in his navy tux, his white shirt open at the neck, his hands in his pockets.

He smiled. "You look beautiful."

"So do"—her voice cracked with nerves—"you."

"I've missed you."

She swallowed, fighting back tears. She would not cry. It was bad enough she was going to sing in front of a bunch of people who thought the gorgeous man in front of her deserved so much better. "I've missed you too."

"Sing," Penelope and Daphne hissed from behind her. It was then she noticed their audience had gotten antsy.

Marco turned, shooting a look at whoever was *boo*ing and telling her to get off the stage. She glanced back at her sisters, who nodded, mouthing, *You've got this.*

Theia focused on Marco, reminding herself why she was doing this. She wanted him in her life, and she hoped the song's lyrics would let him know how much. She held up the mic and opened her mouth, putting all her feelings for him into Wynonna Judd's rendition of "I Want to Know What Love Is."

She sang from her heart and from her soul, and maybe because she did, it touched not only Marco but her audience. As she ended on a last husky note, the wedding guests rose to their feet. Several people called for an encore, but by then Marco had joined her onstage.

He took the microphone from her. "Sorry, folks, but the only one she's singing for is me." He kissed her softly, sweetly, then whispered in her ear, "Come home with me tonight."

* * *

Marco glanced to where Theia talked to Johnny and Callie. The couple had seemed genuinely pleased for him and Theia, and for once they looked happy together. As though she knew what he was thinking, Theia gave him a discreet thumbs-up. He smiled, returning his attention to his best friend, who sat beside him. "Sorry. What did you say?"

"I asked if you're sure about this, but since you haven't heard a word anyone has said to you since she told you she loved you in a song, I'm guessing nothing any of us says will matter."

"You're right. It won't." Because she didn't sing a song of love; she sang a song of pain and loneliness and wanting to be loved, and she sang it in a voice that grabbed hold of his heart and showed no signs of letting go.

Liam turned to his wife. "Soph, talk to him."

She glanced from Theia to her husband and patted Liam's arm. "Don't worry. He's a big boy and can take care of himself, honey. Besides, Jasper supports Theia a hundred and fifty percent, and I've seen a lot I like about her over the past few days. She really pitched in with the wedding. Between her, Penelope, and Daphne, I didn't have to worry about a thing." She moved her head from side to side. "Other than the wedding planner quitting and the swans disappearing. But it looks like another wedding success for the manor. Right, Theia?" she said to the woman who walked their way.

Liam frowned. "What do you mean the wedding planner quit and the swans disappeared?"

Theia turned on her heel and headed in the opposite direction.

"Did you see that? I guarantee she had something to do with the missing wedding planner and the swans."

Marco had a feeling Liam was right and laughed. "You sound like a cranky old lady." He raised his hand to get Theia's attention and wave her back to the table.

"What is wrong with you two? Do you not remember that this woman worked for the same people who are trying to buy the manor out from under us? The same people who were responsible for—"

"Knock it off. She's your cousin. She's doing her best to help out at the manor, and she's coming back to the table." It didn't escape Marco that his relationship with Liam had been his biggest concern about getting involved with a Gallagher. And now that he was, he was more concerned about Theia than his best friend. "Have a little faith in me, man. I know what I'm doing."

"I wish I believed that," Liam grumbled, crossing his arms.

"Trust him like he's always trusted you," Sophie said with a wealth of meaning in her voice. Marco winked at her, appreciating her support. Though he had a feeling she was indirectly sticking up for Theia as much as she was for him. She credited Theia for Marco's improved relationship with their mother.

"Don't think I didn't catch the wink. I know what's going on—"

Marco picked up a mint and lobbed it at Liam's head to shut him up before Theia overheard him. If he didn't know better, he'd say his best friend was jealous of Theia. Maybe he felt like he'd been demoted to second-string. Marco could sympathize. He'd felt the same when Liam and Sophie got together.

"What's wrong?" his sister asked, casting him a worried frown.

"What's wrong is he shot a mint at my head."

Sophie sighed. "Not with you, with my brother. Look how pale he is."

Damn straight Marco was pale. He'd just realized what his inner dialogue said about him and Theia. He was thinking/acting like they were a done deal, like she was his plus one. His soul mate, his one true love, and all the other crap Rosa had been spouting for the past decade.

"I knew something was wrong with you. I told you he wasn't acting like himself. When are you going to realize I know him better than you do?" Liam reached over to feel Marco's forehead. "You don't have a fever. Are you—?"

"I'm not sick, *amico*." Lovesick maybe, but he didn't want Liam to faint, especially now that Theia had returned to the table. "Are you ready to leave?"

"No. We haven't danced…" Liam scowled. "I thought you were talking to me and your sister."

"Are you pouting?" Marco asked, sincerely shocked at how Liam was acting. Marco wasn't a serial dater, but he dated quite a bit. He'd also had a couple of long-term relationships, and not once had Liam acted this way. Marco almost laughed. If he needed another sign that Theia might be the woman for him, he had a feeling his best friend had provided it.

"I'm not pouting. It was a moue face."

Sophie looked at her husband. "A moue face is a pouty face. And, honey, it's not a good look for you."

"It's not a pouty face. It's a…a judgy face. He's one of the groomsmen. It looks bad if he leaves this early."

Marco started to laugh, and every time he tried to stop, he thought of Liam saying *moue face* and *pouty face* and laughed harder. His sister joined in.

"Okay, you two can stop now." Liam looked around. "No, I'm serious. You're drowning out the best man. See, you missed the announcement. They're doing the garter toss and then throwing the bouquet. Never mind, you guys wouldn't be…"

Marco got up from the table, mostly to mess with his best friend's head. He pulled out a chair for Theia and said,

"Sit. I'll be right back." He gave her a kiss that had Liam groaning and Marco lifting his head to say, "Get over it. I had to put up with you two."

Once out on the dance floor, Marco considered letting the lacy blue garter sail by, but he was too competitive and caught it. After accepting some good-natured ribbing from the other single guys on the floor, he said a couple of words to the groom, kissed the bride, and then walked back to the table. "Get up there," he said to Theia when they announced the bouquet toss.

"No. I need to…" She groaned when she saw her sister Daphne weaving her way through the tables toward them.

"Come on, big sis. Let's show these ladies how it's done." Daphne pulled Theia to her feet.

Marco smiled, watching the sisters squabble as they walked toward the dance floor. "Pen." Daphne waved their other sister over, laughing when the good-looking guy Penelope was standing with put a possessive arm around her shoulders.

Sophie smiled. "It looks like we might have a vow renewal at the manor."

"Is that Penelope's husband?" Marco asked.

His sister nodded. "Theia flew him in from LA yesterday. She kept the twins with her last night so their parents could have a romantic evening."

He raised his eyebrows at Liam, making a point. Family was as important to her as it was to them.

"Fine. She's a saint." Liam glanced at the dance floor, fighting a grin. "A saint who just took out her sister and two bridesmaids to catch the bouquet. She either wants to get married really bad or she's as competitive as you are."

"She's ten times more competitive than me," Marco said, laughing when she shoved the bouquet at her sister.

He stood up. "I said my goodbyes to the bride and groom, so if you two don't have any objections, I'm going to take Theia home."

"Good idea," his sister said. "She must be wiped. The twins were awake half the night saying they wanted to play with the ghost, and then they got up at five this morning. She'll probably fall asleep before her head hits the pillow."

He looked at his best friend, who started to laugh.

"Must have been a good joke," Theia said when Marco linked his fingers with hers.

"Liam thinks so. Do you feel like heading out, or do you have to stick around?"

"I'm good to go. Penelope's husband offered to take over for me. They owe me big-time for last night."

So much for his hopes that his sister had been yanking his chain. "So I heard."

She glanced over her shoulder. "Let me guess. Liam finds it hysterical that you may not get lucky tonight because I'm too tired."

"Got it in one."

She nodded. "Just a sec." She walked back to the table and bent to whisper in Liam's ear. Liam covered his face with one hand, looked through his fingers at Marco, and shook his head with a grin.

"What did you say to him?" Marco asked when she returned to his side to take his hand.

"I reminded him what kind of training I had as a fighter pilot. I can go on very little sleep."

"You're bad," he said.

"Or very, very good. Depends how you look at it."

"Either works for me." He waited until they were out of sight of the tent and wedding guests to take her in his arms. "I told you you're beautiful, and I told you I missed you, and you obviously have a good idea I want to be with you, but what I didn't say is I'm sorry. I shouldn't have left that night. I should have given you a chance to tell your side. I should have trusted that in the end you would do the honorable thing."

"You're giving me too much credit. The honorable thing would have been to quit my job last year when Caine asked me to go undercover at the manor. I'm sorry I didn't tell you. I promised Daniel I wouldn't tell anyone, but you were—you are—more than just anyone to me."

He kissed her long and deep and would have kept kissing her if he didn't get the feeling the entire wedding was walking past them. He lifted his head and looked around. They were. He realized why when the sky over the water lit up. The bride's special request had been fireworks. Her firefighter groom had given the idea a thumbs-down because they were a fire hazard, acquiescing only when the manor agreed to set them off on a barge. "Let's go to my place and set off a few fireworks of our own."

Early the next morning, Marco woke up to what sounded like fireworks going off in his apartment. The reality was much worse: His grandmother was pounding on his door.

Theia lifted her head from his chest. "Can she get in?"

As if in answer to her question, he heard Rosa open the door with a key, only to be stopped by the chain lock he'd thought to engage last night. "No, but we'll be able to hear her."

They were. But never in his life did he expect to hear her wail, "Murder. He murdered *amore mio*."

Chapter Twenty-Three

♥

Theia grabbed a quick shower while Marco tried to calm his grandmother down long enough to be able to understand her. Theia put on his white robe and then pulled a towel off the rack, straining to hear what was going on outside the bedroom door as she towel dried her hair. She stuck her head out of the en suite bathroom before walking into Marco's bedroom.

She hadn't gotten a good look at the room or the apartment last night. Her mind, mouth, and hands had been a little preoccupied. All she really cared about at the time was his bed. It met all her criteria: big with a good mattress and fresh-smelling sheets. Now, in the early-morning light, she saw that his room did too.

It looked like a guy's room, but not a frat boy's room. Functional but not cold and austere like her apartment. His comfortable king-size mattress sat in a sleek steel-gray bedframe, a moody seascape over the bed, a Berber area rug on the wide-planked hardwood floor, and thick wooden shelves on either side of the bed that served as nightstands with sleek reading lamps screwed into the walls above them. From the stacks of books on his nightstands, the reading lamps weren't for show. She checked out some of the titles and smiled. He wasn't just a handsome face.

At the sound of a muffled cell phone ring, she looked at the mattress. As it continued to ring, she lifted the sheets to look under the bed. The ringing grew louder, but there was still no sign of her phone. Then it stopped ringing.

Somewhere in the apartment another phone began to ring. Theia continued her search to the sound of Rosa wailing, which was quickly followed by Marco trying to calm her down. He sounded frustrated at his inability to comfort his grandmother, and Theia decided it was her duty as his girlfriend to offer support. Now she had to find her clothes. And her phone, she thought when it began to ring again. In the other room, someone else's did too.

She spotted a pile of clothes on the other side of the bed. Warm, she thought as the ringing grew louder. She crouched beside the tangled heap of both their clothes and found her phone in his jacket pocket. He'd insisted she wear it on the walk to his place last night.

"Hey, what's up?" she asked, taking Daphne's call. She frowned as the voices outside the bedroom grew in number and volume. If she wasn't mistaken, there were several angry women now in the apartment. They were also speaking in Italian.

"Why didn't you answer your phone? We've been calling you nonstop for the last twenty minutes."

"Sorry. I was in the shower. What's going on?"

"You haven't heard? I had visions of the DiRossis chasing you down Main Street with pizza pans."

Theia bowed her head. *What now?* she wondered, and

then she remembered Ryan Wilson's threat. "Did something happen to Jasper? Is he okay?"

"How did you...? Never mind. No, he's not okay. He's in jail. The police arrested him this morning for the murder of Antonio DiRossi, Rosa's husband."

It was a good thing she was crouched on the floor because it wasn't far to land on her bottom. The day Jasper picked her up on the side of the road, he'd said the truth would come out before this was over. This couldn't be what he meant. She didn't believe it.

"He didn't do it," she said as she moved off the floor to sit at the end of the bed. "Kitty and Rosa are best friends. There's no way Jasper killed her husband."

"This didn't happen recently. It happened close to half a century ago."

"It doesn't matter. I don't believe he did it."

"Word of advice, until you get back to the manor, I wouldn't be sharing your opinion. Right now you're in enemy territory. The lines have been drawn in the sand. Gallaghers on one side, DiRossis on the other."

Daphne had to be wrong. Theia wouldn't—couldn't—let her mind go to where this would come between her and Marco. "Don't be crazy. Sophie and Ava—"

"Have had issues with Jasper in the past, from what I understand. Now he's accused of killing Sophie's grandfather and Ava's uncle. They both took off from here fifteen minutes ago. I'm surprised they haven't shown up at Rosa's."

Theia listened more closely to the voices. "They're here. At Marco's. I'm in his bedroom."

"I'd stay there until the coast is clear."

Theia hoped Daphne was just being dramatic. But instead of worrying about the implications for her relationship with Marco, she focused on what they could do for the man she'd grown fond of. A man who, for all intents and purposes, was their step-grandfather. They needed to launch a strong defense. They'd prove to everyone he didn't do it, and they'd all be okay. "I know you're a divorce attorney, but you're also brilliant and ballsy. You need to get to the police station and protect Jasper's rights."

"Aw, thanks, sis," she said, and then the sweetness in her voice turned sour. "But I already tried and was told my services weren't required."

"Who told you that?" she asked, ticked on her sister's behalf.

"Our cousins. Two of whom are attorneys, just like their father." Daphne sighed. "You know what? They're excellent lawyers and have more experience than I do. It's just that the way they reacted to my offer hurt. It felt like neither our opinions or concerns matter because we didn't grow up here and don't know Jasper as well as they do."

She could identify a little too well with how Daphne felt. "We'll see about that. I'm going to the station."

"You won't beat anyone up on my behalf, will you?" Theia heard the smile in her sister's voice.

"I might if I don't get a coffee before I leave." She figured the breakfast in bed Marco had promised her last night was canceled. She hoped their relationship wasn't. It looked like she was about to find out, she thought when Marco opened the door to his bedroom.

"I've gotta go. I'll call you back." He wore a white T-shirt with a pair of black sweatpants. Not more than forty minutes ago she'd had high hopes of tearing off his clothes and picking up where they had left off at three this morning.

He looked from her face to her phone. "You heard?"

She nodded and patted the mattress. "How's Rosa?"

He sat beside her, dragging a hand down his face. "Shocked, hysterical, furious. It's difficult to pinpoint an exact emotion at any given moment."

"How are you doing?" she asked, linking her fingers with his.

"It's tough. I don't know what to do or say to make her feel better. You read about things like this happening, hear about it, but you never think it can happen to you or your family. I've known Jasper for most of my life, and to think he murdered my grandfather…"

She didn't think she'd made a sound or reacted in any way, but she must have because he looked at her and said, "You don't believe he did, do you?"

"I…No, I don't." He went to pull his hand away, and she tightened her grip. "That's not fair. You asked me a question, and I answered. You can't pull away from me. Last night we promised each other we'd tell the truth whether we wanted to hear it or not."

"I didn't need to hear it right now."

"You're mad at me."

"No. I'm mad at the situation. We're going to be on opposite sides of this, and I'm afraid it's going to get ugly."

"It doesn't have to. We don't have to let it."

"Really? Maybe you can explain to me exactly how we're supposed to do that when…"

She was about to respond until she noticed the doorknob turning. "Marco, we should talk about this later."

But obviously he was on a roll because he talked over her. "…you believe the man who was arrested for my grandfather's murder is innocent, Theia?"

Rosa strode into the room. "You believe a murderer over my grandson? Over the police? You know nothing! You—"

"Ma, stop. Theia is entitled—"

"No. She's entitled to nothing. She's a Gallagher. I want her out. I want her out of my house." She grabbed Theia's clothes and shoved them at her. "Go."

Marco put out his hand to stop her from getting up. "Theia, you don't have to—"

"No. It's okay," she said, and stood. "I'm sorry, Mrs. DiRossi. I didn't mean to upset you." She took Rosa by the arm and guided her to the bed.

Looking frail and disheveled, Rosa sat beside her grandson. She leaned her head against Marco's shoulder and began to softly weep.

Chapter Twenty-Four

♥

Thank the good Lord and the Holy Ghost, Colleen thought as Theia strode into the manor. Her sisters, apparently as relieved as Colleen, shot off the couch in the lobby where they'd been awaiting her return.

"Where have you been? I called you more than two hours ago," Daphne said as she hurried up the steps to the entryway. She didn't give Theia a chance to answer. Grabbing her by the hand, she dragged her down the hall toward the library.

"At the station." Theia tugged her hand from her sister's. "Look, I don't have time to sit around talking about this. I have to…There's something I need to do."

"Stop with the *I's*. You have us—sisters, a family. And that means when there's a family crisis, we deal with it together."

"Daphne's right, Theia. The past few days, working together, hanging out together, not to mention all the times you guys have helped me out with the boys, it's meant a lot to me. We kind of lost out in the father department, but it doesn't matter because we have each other now. And I for one think we won out in the sisters department."

Daphne glanced at Theia. "I think she wants us to hug." She sighed when Penelope smiled and opened her arms. They pulled a reluctant Theia in for a group hug.

"You know, Simon," Colleen said, looking at the black cat at her feet, "seeing these three together like this, acting like sisters…It goes to show that something good can come out of something bad. The Elliots thought to use the girls against us and bring the family down from within, but it turns out they underestimated them."

Simon looked at her like she'd missed a particularly salient point.

"I don't know why you're giving me that…" She briefly closed her eyes. "You're right, I suppose. I've been doing my best to put the image of Jasper being led away in handcuffs from my mind. I'm trapped here, unable to defend the lad. But as much as I'd like to lay the blame at the Elliots' feet, I can't. Their firing Ryan might have made him more volatile and vindictive, but he's just like his grandfather. The Wilsons were determined to bring down the Gallaghers, and it seems their wish is about to come true. Already the family is being torn apart. Although I believe Ava and Griffin's marriage, and Sophie and Liam's too, will be able to weather the storm. It's Theia and Marco I'm not sure about. Their relationship is too new."

Theia was the first to break free of her sisters' embrace. "I feel the same about you guys, but we don't have time for this now. We—"

"You're right. Grams needs us," Daphne said.

"Wait," Theia said when Penelope and Daphne continued toward the library. "Unless Kitty is spilling the beans about this—which I'm betting she isn't—you two stay with her and try to get her to talk. I have something—"

Daphne looked disheartened. "You've been gone so long that I just assumed you had some news to share with us, preferably good news."

"I don't know anything more than you. I spent the last hour at the police station basically being ignored by six of our cousins, seven if you count the doctor on FaceTime." Theia blew out a frustrated breath. "You'd think between a detective, a Secret Service agent, two lawyers, a member of the Coast Guard, and a firefighter, plus the doctor on the line, they'd have figured out what to do by now. But no, for all the combined brain power of the serve-and-protect Gallaghers, not one of them has come up with a plan as to how we're—excuse me, how *they're*—going to get Jasper out. Because even though they don't have a clue what to do, *we*—or I should probably say *I*—haven't been Gallaghers long enough to be allowed into the inner sanctum."

"What's wrong with my great-grandsons? They know better than to treat a woman as less than equal. Look who they had as a role model," Colleen grumbled, unhappy to learn they'd apparently forgotten all the lessons she'd drummed into them.

"Typical boys club. I've been dealing with that at the firm since I started."

"Then you should go out on your own or find a new firm," Penelope said to Daphne before giving Theia's arm a comforting pat. "Don't let it bother you. You're as much a Gallagher as we are. I'm sure they have no idea that they hurt your feelings."

"Come on, I'm thirty-four. They didn't hurt my feelings," Theia scoffed.

"Childhood wounds don't heal easily, Theia. Given your

history, I know how much their rejection hurt. It hurt us too, and we haven't had to deal with half of what you have. But they weren't rejecting you or us. They've basically grown up together. They've spent years operating as a unit. I'm sure they weren't purposely keeping you—"

Theia raised her hand to stop Penelope midstream. "I appreciate you trying to make me feel better, but you weren't there. I tried to get in to see Jasper, and our cousin the detective said he wasn't allowed visitors even though I saw Liam and Griffin coming out of lockup when I arrived." She lifted a shoulder. "They don't trust me, and I can't say I blame them."

"We do, and that's all that matters."

"Penelope's right. Who cares what they think. Better yet, let's prove them wrong. You have a plan, don't you?"

Colleen cast Theia a desperate look, praying Daphne was right.

"I have an idea, and, Pen, I'm going to need the twins."

"Why…? Oh. This is about our great-grandmother's ghost, isn't it?"

Colleen could see Theia was reluctant to admit she believed in ghosts and hoped the girl's pride stopped her from following through with her idea, because Colleen was fairly certain she knew what Theia was up to and she wasn't about to help her find *The Secret Keeper of Harmony Harbor*. The truth was there in black-and-white for all to see. Jasper's fate would be sealed. She also didn't relish the idea that the family's secrets—and hers—would be laid bare for her great-granddaughter to see. Between that and how her father and cousins were treating her, she might turn tail and run.

Theia gave a reluctant nod. "I know it sounds crazy, but if you slept in that room and saw and heard the things that I have, you'd believe in ghosts too."

"I believe you and my sons. Now I'll just have to convince them to get out of the water, which probably won't be difficult when I tell them they're going on a ghost-hunting expedition. Their father will be a different story. He's not really a fan of the whole 'woo-woo thing,' as he calls it."

"If he gives you a hard time, just tell him he can have you to himself for an hour."

"Her smile was about as wide as I imagine her husband's will be when he hears they get an hour to themselves," Daphne said as Penelope hurried off. "All they needed to work things out was some one-on-one time." She snorted. "If my ex and I had more time together, we probably would have wound up in divorce court a lot sooner."

"You and Sully spend a lot of time together. It doesn't seem to be hurting your relationship."

"No, it doesn't, does it?" Daphne grinned. "You know, I thought coming here was a really bad idea, but I'm beginning to think it was the best decision I ever made. In fact," she said, eyeing Theia in the clothes from the night before, "I'd go so far as to say it was the best decision the Gallagher girls have made in a long time."

Colleen smiled smugly. "It looks like my codicil worked exactly as I'd planned, Simon."

Her sidekick gave her a cheeky meow that seemed to say, "Don't get a swelled head." Apparently, Simon was of the same mind as the Gallagher family attorney and wasn't a fan of Colleen's habit of manipulating people and situations to her will. She was about to respond that she couldn't help if she was right ninety-five...perhaps ninety percent of the time was more accurate, but she was more interested in the conversation at hand.

"A few hours before, I would have agreed with you.

Now I'm not sure Marco can get past this," Theia said, looking dejected.

Despite the girl's obvious worry, Colleen was pleased. This was the first time Theia hadn't tried to deny her feelings for Marco.

Daphne put an arm around her sister's shoulders. "Don't worry. Penelope seems to have gotten back her relationship mojo. We'll put our heads together and come up with a strategy to help you win him back."

"We already did that, remember?"

At Theia's reminder, Daphne looked concerned. Theia had already used up her grand gesture. To Colleen's mind, it was Marco's turn. She understood that at this very moment the DiRossis were reeling from the shock of learning Antonio had been murdered. But if Marco was the man she thought him to be, he'd eventually come to his senses. He wouldn't let loyalty to his family override his loyalty to the woman he loved.

The twins saved Daphne from having to respond to Theia's worries about her love life. With a towel around each of their necks, floaties on their arms, bathing suits wet and feet bare and sandy, the boys hurried across the almost-empty lobby.

"W1, W2, walk," Theia called to them while looking in the direction of the dining room. "Where are your parents?"

"Mommy said you were babysitting us."

"Yeah, for two hours," his brother added, holding up two fingers. He peeked around Theia and smiled. "Hi, GG."

The other child waved.

"Is she standing right there?" Theia pointed to where Colleen stood.

William bit his lip and glanced at his brother.

"It's all right, laddie. You can tell her." Colleen nodded

and smiled so they'd know she wasn't upset they'd broken their promise. She should have known better than to try to swear them to secrecy anyway. Not that it had done her much good. By the sounds of it, they'd told their mother they could see her.

They both looked relieved and nodded.

Daphne swore in French. "She's been here all along, listening to us. I thought she only haunted the tower room."

"So did I." Theia crouched in front of the boys. "Can you tell GG that we need to find her book to help Jasper? I need to find *The Secret Keeper of Harmony Harbor*."

"I'm not good at keeping secrets," Weston said.

His brother nodded. "Mommy says we shouldn't keep secrets."

There had to be another way. Colleen shook her head.

William pointed at her. "She said no."

Theia stood, turning to face where Colleen stood by the stairs. "Now listen to me, and listen to me good, GG."

Daphne grabbed her arm. "Are you crazy? Have you not seen *The Amityville Horror*? Do not tick off the ghost."

"What's Amy...that thing you said?" William asked his aunt.

"It's nothing. Auntie Daphne didn't get her coffee this morning." Theia glanced from where Colleen was standing back to the boys. "Can you tell GG it's very important that I find—" She looked down at Simon, who pawed her leg.

"Simon! What do you think you're—" He cut Colleen off with a testy meow and then took off, stopping only to ensure that Theia, the twins, and Penelope gave chase. He ignored Colleen's threats as she followed them to Kitty's tower room.

"Now what?" Theia said. "I don't want Kitty to know—"

"I've got the key." Daphne removed it from the pocket of her white skirt. She lowered her voice. "Jasper gave it to me. Kitty wasn't up when they took him away. I had to break the news to her. It was awful."

"Once I find the book, you and the boys go to her. I can take care of the rest from there."

The boys got stubborn expressions on their faces that Colleen imagined matched her own. But the promise of sundaes wouldn't appease her as it did them. In the end though, she was no match for Simon's insistent meowing. There was a message in the way he looked from her to Theia. It just took her some time to understand what he was getting at. The girl was like her. They had a hard time trusting, to their own detriment at times. Now Colleen had to place her trust in her great-granddaughter.

After thirty minutes of the twins acting out the combination Colleen relayed to them, they were rewarded with the *beep* of the safe opening. Despite her sister's protest, Theia ushered Daphne and the boys from the room before removing the book. "There's a reason they've kept it locked away, Daph. I'm only looking for something that will save Jasper. If I find it, I'll tell you."

In that moment, Colleen knew she could trust Theia to protect the book's secrets. She sagged in relief. But she didn't have time to rest. Once she'd retrieved the leather-bound book, Theia shut the safe and spun the lock. Then she looked around the room. Hurrying to the unmade bed, she grabbed a pillow and shoved the book inside, carrying it, clutched to her chest, to Colleen's tower room.

Once she got inside, Theia dumped the book on the bed and sat down to read.

Colleen sat beside her. Focusing all her energy into her finger, she began moving the pages. As much as she trusted

Theia, she wouldn't mind if there were some things she didn't read.

Theia pinched herself. "Yep. I'm awake, and a ghost is sitting beside me, turning the pages of her book." When Colleen found what she was looking for, Theia leaned forward. Moments later, she muttered, "Crap. Crap. Crap." She stood up. "I need Daphne to teach me to swear in French." She looked down at the page again. "Crap. Now what am I supposed to do with…?"

She hurried over to Colleen's desk. Rummaging through the open drawers, she patted underneath, searching for the key to the locked top drawer.

"Smart girl," Colleen said when she found it, opening it to pull out loose-leaf paper and a fountain pen. She checked the color to the one in the book. Colleen could have told her it was one and the same, but she'd used up too much energy turning the pages in her book to shout in her ear.

Theia pulled out the chair and sat. She rubbed the paper between her fingers. "Too new." She grimaced and then murmured, "Sorry," before ripping a blank page from the back of Colleen's memoir.

"What are you up to, lass?" Colleen wondered, looking over Theia's shoulder as she wrote on the other piece of paper. She appeared to be trying to perfect Colleen's handwriting. It wasn't until she started to write in earnest that Colleen was clued in to what she was about.

She was writing Colleen's confession to the murder of Antonio DiRossi. Colleen shook her head. "You have no idea what you've done, Theia."

As though she sensed her standing over her, Theia said, "I'm sorry, but it's the only way I can think to save him."

"I'm not mad. Far from it. I'm grateful. You've allowed

me to do in death what I couldn't do in life. You've found a way for me to make amends for all that Jasper lost. I don't care that I'll go down in history as a murderess if it means he goes free."

Theia looked weary and troubled once she'd finished the letter. She got up and went to the dresser, pulling out a change of clothes. She wasn't one to fuss and left the bathroom a few moments later wearing a pair of jeans and a white T-shirt, her hair tousled, her face makeup free.

She took a picture from her wallet and placed it on the desk. "I don't know how all this heaven stuff works, but if you see this man, can you tell him I'm sorry? Sorrier than he'll ever know. Tell him I'm keeping my promise. I'm looking after his wife and son. His boy's going to college just like he wanted."

The lock on the door *beep*ed. Theia grabbed Colleen's memoir, papers, and fountain pen and shoved everything in the top draw. She locked it just as the door to Colleen's suite opened.

"Any luck?" Daphne asked, peeking her head into the room.

Theia nodded. "We have to get to the police station right away. Jasper didn't do it. Colleen did." She held up an envelope. "I found her confession. There was a false bottom in the locked drawer in her desk." Her fingers lightly grazed the photo of her friend, and then she walked to the door. Just as she was about to close it, she whispered, "I'll bring him home for you."

"Thank you," Colleen murmured as she touched the photo of the handsome young man in uniform. "I'll try to find a way to ease your guilt as you have eased mine."

Chapter Twenty-Five

♥

Marco glanced at his grandmother, who was curled in on herself on the passenger seat of his truck. She'd refused to change out of her threadbare blue housedress or take off the white sweater she wore despite it being eighty degrees in the shade.

He hoped to God he didn't see Jasper at the station. He wasn't sure what he'd do if he did. Wasn't sure what Rosa would do. Or what his sister and cousin would do for that matter, he thought as he glanced at them following behind in his rearview mirror.

At least he didn't have to worry about his brother and father descending upon them to seek their revenge. When they'd finally gotten through to them a few hours before, they'd made it clear they wouldn't be coming to Harmony Harbor for the trial. There'd been something in his father's voice that had given Marco pause. He'd almost sounded… satisfied.

With his grandmother, sister, and cousin huddled close

to him as he spoke on the phone, Marco hadn't wanted to dig deeper. He would though. Later. Once they'd gotten Rosa through the interview. He'd wanted to hire a lawyer for her, but the only ones he knew that were any good and in the area were Gallaghers, so he decided to see how it went. He could always put a stop to the interview if Rosa got upset or he didn't like the questions.

He found a parking spot around the block from the station. It was busy for a Sunday. He didn't realize how busy until he'd rounded the hood of his truck to help Rosa out and got a look at the front of the building. Press. Just what they didn't need. Of course, with the Gallaghers involved, it made the news.

"Ma, don't get out," he said when she opened her door. "We'll park around the other side."

"No. We go in the front. They should be ashamed, not us."

He didn't need to ask who *they* were. She'd been railing against the Gallaghers for most of the morning. It made for an uncomfortable few hours for not only his sister and cousin but for him too. Especially when his grandmother basically threw Theia out of the house. She'd handled it better than he'd expected. She didn't seem hurt or offended, though it had been obvious she was worried what it meant for their relationship. He didn't tell her then that so was he. But as the morning progressed, he realized just how bad it could get.

Word had spread in town. They'd been fielding calls for the past several hours. The lines had been drawn— DiRossi supporters on one side, Gallagher supporters on the other. From what he could tell, the majority of folks in town sided with the DiRossis. Not really a surprise given Rosa was the victim.

And Jasper wasn't exactly a man who'd gone out of

his way to make friends in town. He was standoffish and mostly stuck close to the manor. He wasn't known by a lot of people, and those who did know him didn't seem surprised by the charges brought against him.

Some of the reactions of those who called to check on Rosa struck Marco as odd, just like his father's had. They weren't outraged or mourning the death of his grandfather. It's possible the length of time he'd been dead played a part in their lack of remorse. Still, it felt like something else was going on. He just needed a moment to look into it, but his grandmother wouldn't let him out of her sight or hearing, which was why he'd been letting Theia's calls go to voice mail. Or was it? he wondered.

Sophie and Ava joined them by the truck, cutting off any more thoughts about the woman he was pretty sure he was in love with. If only he'd known a couple of weeks ago what he knew now…

"How did this get leaked to the press so—"

Marco turned to see what had caused Sophie to stop midquestion and for her eyes to go wide. Theia and her sisters were walking Jasper from the police station. An angry shout came from a man in the crowd gathered near the doors. It was followed by another. Things were about to get ugly.

"Get Ma in the car and take her home. I'll talk to the chief. Get him to reschedule her interview," Marco whispered to his sister, and then took off at a run toward the station.

He hoped to God his sister and Ava blocked Rosa's view of Jasper leaving the building a free man. He glanced over his shoulder. He wasn't the only who knew Rosa. They were hustling her from the truck to the car. He held his breath until he heard the car doors shut.

"Marco! Hold up!" Liam ran down the road. "What's going on? I thought Rosa was supposed to be—" He looked at the station when the shouting intensified. "Who let Jasper out?"

"If you ask me, it looks like Theia and her sisters did." He glanced at Liam as they ran to the station. "So you're telling me you had no idea?"

"Yeah, that's what I'm telling you. I told your sister the same thing, but it looks like if Jasper's guilty, we all are in the DiRossis' eyes."

"Walk in our shoes, *amico*, and tell me how'd you'd feel." At a loud bellow, their gazes shot to the parking lot. Someone had made a move on Jasper, and Theia had inserted herself between them. The shout came from Daniel, who'd just jumped from a car. Marco's mother's car, to be precise. He didn't have time to think about that because Daniel was now threatening the man who'd threatened his daughter.

The police officers, who'd been trying to hold back the crowd, must have radioed for help, as several officers, including Liam's cousin, piled out of the station. Just in time to see Daniel knock out the man who'd threatened Theia.

Liam shrugged. "He used to be a boxer."

"He can tell that to the cop who's about to cuff him," Marco observed as they approached the scene.

"Liam, get them out of here." Aidan Gallagher gestured at Theia, Jasper, and her sisters.

As much as he wanted to check on Theia, Marco didn't trust himself around Jasper. He turned toward the station. He had to speak to the chief and find out how the hell Jasper was out of jail.

"Marco, wait."

He bowed his head at the sound of Theia's voice and then stopped walking and turned.

"So that's it. You're just going to shut me out. Not take my calls." She stood a few feet away from him, her hands in the pockets of her jeans, her dark hair falling in her eyes. He took a step toward her. All he wanted to do was brush the hair from face and take her in his arms. But then the press started shouting questions, reminding him why they were there.

"I was going to call you back after my grandmother talked to the chief." His jaw clenched as he looked over her head. He lifted his chin. "How did you do it? How did you get him off?"

She glanced over her shoulder. "He didn't do it. Colleen did."

Marco reached out to lift her chin with his knuckle, forcing her to look at him. "No more lies, remember? Look at me and tell me how you got him off."

Theia covered his hand with hers. "It's not what you think. There's more to the story, Marco. You have to talk to Rosa."

He freed his hand from hers. "So what, you're trying to tell me my grandmother had something to do with it? That she's somehow to blame for my grandfather's—"

"No, not at all. She's the real victim in this. Jasp—I mean Colleen was trying to protect Rosa. It was an accident. It had been raining. They were down on the rocks. Antonio, your grandfather, had come looking for Ronan. As I understand it, Antonio had been jealous of Ronan for a very long time." She rubbed the back of her neck. "It's not my story to tell. You have to talk to your grandmother about this."

"I'm not going to talk to her about a bunch of lies that were made up for the sole purpose of getting Jasper off."

"I understand you're angry on Rosa's behalf, that your

family is in shock. But I wouldn't be here if I didn't believe what happened that night wasn't a horrible accident. People have been carrying a lot of guilt and a lot of pain over that night for decades. Your grandmother included. It's important that you to talk to her about this, Marco. For her sake." She turned to walk away.

"Did Kitty know?"

Shoulders bowed, she nodded. "Yes. I don't think she's known for long though. She wasn't just protecting… Colleen. She was protecting Rosa too."

"*Cara*, look at me." She slowly turned to face him. "Tell me the truth. Did Jasper kill my grandfather, or did Colleen?"

She lifted her chin. "Ninety percent of the confession is the absolute truth. Call me once you've talked to your grandmother and I'll tell you, and only you, the ten percent that isn't."

"How do you know I won't go to the chief right now and tell him what you just said?"

"Because I trust you. Now you have to trust me to know that while I will do what I can to protect my family, I wouldn't do it at the expense of yours. You have my number," she said, and then walked away.

His mother, who'd gotten out of her car, said something to Theia before continuing toward him.

"I thought you said you were no longer dating Daniel," he said to his mother while watching Theia walk to the black limo at the far end of the parking lot. The crowds had dissipated, but the press was still crowded around the door to the station, waiting for a statement. It was a statement Marco would like to hear. But he'd get his directly from the chief, not the communications officer.

"We're not dating, but it doesn't mean I can't try to help

him. He's deeply ashamed and afraid. Emotions all of us have faced at one time or another." She glanced around before saying, "I overheard a little of your conversation with Theia. She's right. You need to talk to Rosa. And if she won't talk to you, ask your father. He remembers some of it, but he doesn't like to talk about it. I think your uncle Gino does too. And Dr. Bishop. But you'd need Rosa's consent for him to speak to you."

"You obviously know, so why don't you tell me?"

"Because your father made me promise I would never tell you kids. You should hear it from Rosa. Maybe it will help her exorcise the demons once and for all."

"He beat her? Is that what you're not saying? My grandfather beat my grandmother?"

"Keep your voice down," she said, once again glancing the reporters' way. "Yes, he did. The night that Antonio disappeared—died, as we now know—he put your grandmother in the hospital. She said she fell down the stairs."

If his grandfather weren't already dead, Marco would have been sorely tempted to kill him himself.

* * *

For the past two days, Theia had been waiting for the other shoe to drop. She'd basically told Marco she'd lied about Colleen's confession. She didn't feel like she had any other choice. Still, she didn't have a clue what she'd say or do should the police arrive at the manor.

Now that forty-eight hours had passed, she felt herself relaxing. At least about the likelihood of her being arrested for falsifying evidence.

But the police weren't the only ones who hadn't shown up on her doorstep. Neither had Marco. Which was why she was loitering outside Sophie's office, hoping to have a word with his sister.

"Can I help you with something, Theia?"

She yelped and placed a hand on her chest, turning to glare at Jasper. "You can't sneak up on people like that. You nearly gave me a heart attack."

"You're too young and fit to have a heart attack. And I wasn't sneaking about." She heard the accusing *unlike you* in his voice.

She groaned. "How many times do I have to tell you I did exactly what Colleen would have wanted me to? The last thing she'd want is you rotting in a cell because you accidently killed a man who routinely beat his wife. She loved you, and they owed you."

He cupped her elbow with his hand and shepherded her into the library.

"It's true," she said when he closed the door. "Maybe not Colleen, but your father certainly owed you. You're a Gallagher. The manor and everything in it should have been yours." She sat heavily in the chair by the window.

Jasper took the seat beside her. "I don't care about that. But I do care about Madam's reputation. I won't have everyone believing she's a murderer."

"She didn't confess to being a murderer. She confessed to exactly what happened that night. You had no choice. You confronted him about putting Rosa in the hospital, and he attacked you. It wasn't your fault he slipped on the rocks in the rain. I'm sure everyone in Harmony Harbor will be glad you stood up to him once the truth gets out about Antonio."

"From what I've observed the past two days, the majority of Harmony Harborites are feeling less than supportive of the Gallaghers and the manor. The dining room is nearly empty. The Widows Club just canceled Wednesday Wing

Night, and I wouldn't hold your breath waiting for Rosa to confirm the rumors of Antonio's abuse. She kept it a secret while it was going on, and she's worked hard to put the past behind her. The last thing she wants is to have it all out in the open."

"I'd say that ship has sailed."

"I suppose you're right."

"I am, and I'm right about something else. This is what Colleen wanted. I felt it, Jasper. There's no other way I can describe it. You also care about more than Colleen's reputation. You care about Kitty. She needs you now more than ever. The Widows Club and Rosa have turned against her."

He flexed the fingers of his right hand. "If Ryan Wilson knows what's good for him, he'll stay far from Harmony Harbor."

"You haven't seen him since the day you were released?" He'd been screaming at them from the front of the police station, livid to be denied his revenge. Theia had been nervous he might try something else. As the days passed her worry had subsided, but it was instantly renewed by the mere mention of his name.

"No. But as you know, I've been sticking close to the manor."

Given the feelings in town, the chief of police had advised Jasper to keep a low profile for a while. All the Gallaghers, really.

At Jasper's solemn expression, Theia thought a change of subject was in order. "Tomorrow's the big day. Penelope's and Daphne's month of servitude is up, and I only have a couple of weeks to go."

That earned her a small smile. "Your grandmother couldn't be happier that you girls are voting to keep the manor in the family."

"Well, Daphne and I have some news that we hope will make her even happier. We've both decided to stay in Harmony Harbor." She'd made her decision the night she'd spent at Marco's. With everything that had happened, she hadn't had a chance to tell him. Now she wasn't sure he'd care. She forced her lips to curve. Although it wasn't that hard when she thought about her sister and the twins. "Pen's booked one of the cottages for the entire summer next year."

"That's wonderful news. We'll celebrate tomorrow."

"Do you think Sophie and Ava will come? I haven't seen them around."

"No. I think it will just be your sisters, the twins, Kitty, and myself."

"Really? I thought by now things would have begun to get back to normal. At least with Ava, Sophie, and the family. I guess I was being overly optimistic."

"It will take some time for things to return to normal, if they ever do. But Sophie and Ava are back home with their husbands." He reached over and patted her hand. "Give him time, Theia. Rosa has been Marco's sole responsibility for more than a decade now. This will be difficult for him to come back from. But like Liam and Griffin, he's been busy at work. Both the fire department and the Coast Guard are preparing for the possibility the storm may change course. It's why I believe a small celebration would be best."

Damaging winds and heavy rains were scheduled to make landfall fifty miles up the coast early the next morning.

"You're right, of course." She was talking about keeping the celebration small, but she hoped he was right about Marco too.

"You know, there's still time to join your father and

sisters on the whale-watching tour. The twins wanted Ronan Jr. and Mia to join them, so Sophie will be there. It will give you a chance to get better acquainted. Maybe find out how Marco is?"

"You're not very subtle, you know. But I think I'll pass." Her sisters had begged her to go, stooping so low as to have the twins fake cry. Daniel had been disappointed too. She felt bad that her fears were keeping her from an afternoon with the boys and her sisters, and she felt even worse now knowing that Sophie would be onboard. But the thought of being that far out to sea, with the dark water and the sharks, made her stomach turn and her knees weak.

"It leaves the dock in ten minutes. Say the word, and I'll call the captain and have him hold the boat for you."

"Maybe next time. I have a call in to my landlord in New York that I can't afford to miss."

Four hours later, Theia discovered there was something much scarier than sharks and black water on the ocean that day.

Chapter Twenty-Six

♥

Marco strode to the end of the wharf, barely able to hold himself together. Sophie, Mia, and Ronan were in the hands of a madman. A man who hated the Gallaghers so much he'd hijacked the tour boat they were on this afternoon, holding them for ransom.

Ryan Wilson had let anyone unrelated to the Gallaghers off at Bridgeport. Detectives from HHPD had been interviewing them for the past several hours, hoping for clues as to where Wilson had taken them. So far they hadn't had a break in the case.

It wasn't for a lack of volunteers. Anyone who had a boat was on the water searching for the tour boat. But moments ago, the Coast Guard had ordered everyone but the professionals off the water because of the turn in the weather.

The storm that been slated to reach landfall fifty miles down the coast had intensified over the last several hours, turning at the last minute so that it was now barreling toward them. Dusk had fallen, and the winds had picked up. The night would only get worse.

And somewhere out on the vast ocean were his family…and Liam's, he thought as he spotted his best friend getting ready to board the Coast Guard cutter. Liam turned at his approach. The fear thrumming through Marco's body was reflected on his best friend's face.

Liam walked to him, pulling him into a fierce hug. Marco hugged him back just as hard, unable to get the words out. They'd been here before. Terrified they were going to lose Sophie and Mia in the carriage house fire. The reminder helped. They'd survived.

Marco stepped back and put his hands on his best friend's shoulders. "They've gotten out of worse. They're smart and strong."

Liam looked away, wiped his eyes, and nodded. "I know. How's Rosa?"

He glanced at his grandmother, wrapped in a blanket and surrounded by her friends. She looked old and beaten down. "It's been a lot. I'm worried about her. How's Kitty?"

"Same. It's taken a toll."

He didn't want to voice his fear that this was one crisis too many for the two older women. He had to stay positive not only for Rosa and Liam but for himself. "How's Theia holding up?"

"You haven't talked to her?"

"Between Rosa and the storm and now this, I haven't had a minute to myself."

"Give me a break. You can't take what's going on with our families out on her." Liam's eyes narrowed. "Unless she was just a summer fling to you."

"You know better." Marco didn't want to tell him that Rosa was being difficult about his relationship with Theia.

She'd made him promise not to have anything to do with her. At any other time, he would have told her to butt out of his love life. But this wasn't one of those times. "I thought she'd be down here."

"She was." Liam frowned, turning as a seaplane cruised to the dock one over from them.

Marco walked to the edge of the wharf. "I think I just found her." He tried to get a better look at the man getting out of the plane. He had a duffel bag in his hand. "I recognize him. That's the guy she used to work for at Wicklow Developments. What's he doing here?"

Liam swore. "Sully, Griff, I think we have a problem." He lifted his chin at the other dock.

"What's going on?" Marco asked, keeping an eye on Theia and Caine, stiffening when the other man hugged her. He'd been dying to have her in his arms again, and now because he'd been trying to keep the peace at home, afraid to deny his grandmother anything in the state she was in, he worried he might have lost his chance. No, he realized at the familiar suffocating tightness in his chest. He was beyond worried.

Liam's voice penetrated his near panic. "We were instructed by HHPD not to pay the ransom. Which we probably couldn't have come up with anyway, since Wilson is asking for half a million—"

Marco took off down the wharf before Liam got the last words out. He slowed as he reached his grandmother. "They'll be okay. We all will." He kissed the top of her head, tucking the blanket around her shoulders. "Take care of her," he told her friends.

He heard Rosa and Liam calling to him, but he couldn't stop. He had to get to Theia. She was going to play hero. Fly off on her own into the rainy night over the dark ocean and deliver the ransom to Ryan Wilson. There were people and press everywhere, slowing him down.

He bobbed and weaved. "Theia!" he shouted from the end of the dock as she went to get in the plane. She had the duffel bag in her hand.

Caine, Jasper, and Kitty turned. Jasper put a protective arm around Kitty's shoulders, his expression daring Marco to say one hurtful word. Caine moved to stand beside Theia, placing a hand on her shoulder. Marco wanted to rip it off.

Then he looked at Theia, and everyone else faded away. He walked toward her, holding her gaze. "I know what you're doing, and you're not doing it alone. I'm coming with you."

Whoa. He didn't just say that, did he? If he went by Theia's shocked expression, he did. He had just volunteered to climb into that extraordinarily small space and fly. In the sky. Over the ocean.

He wasn't sure, but he thought her eyes filled with amusement for a second. It didn't last long though. The risks involved, the lives of those she hoped to save superseded all else, even his terror. Which was why he repeated himself. "I'm serious. I'm going with you. You can't go alone."

"She's not. I'm going with her," Caine said.

"Yeah. So, what's the plan? You're going to just drop the money wherever he tells you? No backup because the police won't agree to the ransom being paid and no doubt Wilson has already warned against involving them. You two are in this alone. So the way I see it, while one of you drops off the money, one of you will have to swim to the tour boat and, using the element of surprise, take out Wilson."

"That's exactly what we're going to do. So, if you don't mind, you're wasting—"

He interrupted Caine. "Who's doing the drop-off, and who's doing the swimming?"

"Marco, don't," Theia said.

"Theia will fly us close to the drop-off point, and then she'll swim to the boat. She's better trained than I am." He looked from Marco to Theia. "Is there something I'm not aware of?"

"Yeah, a hell of a lot." Pushing past his nearly paralyzing fear, he walked to the plane. "Neither of you knows this area or the water like I do, and neither of you swim as well as me. And if that's not enough to get you to back off, Elliot, I'm in love with her. And if—"

Caine clapped him on the back, a lot harder than Marco was prepared for, and he may have stumbled a bit. He blamed it on his weak knees. He was feeling a little dizzy too. "About bloody time," the other man said, and stepped aside.

"Marco, you can't do this." Theia glanced around and then went up on her toes, placing a hand on his shoulder. Then she said so only he could hear, "Look, I appreciate what you're trying to do, but—"

He slid his arm around her waist, holding her close. "Did you not hear me two seconds ago? I said I love you. I'm not letting you do this alone, and there's no way I'm letting you swim at night."

"I love that you want to do this for me, but, Marco, you look like you're going to faint. I know you're terrified of flying."

"It doesn't matter. My family is out there with a madman. Just like yours. There's no one better than me for the job, and you know it. I trust you to get me there in one piece."

"I trust you too." She briefly touched her mouth to his but then drew away to hold open the door. "It's a little cramped."

He cursed in Italian as he climbed inside. Once he got strapped in, he drew his arm across his sweaty brow. "It's starting to rain," he told Theia as she settled in beside him.

Her lips pressed together, she nodded and put on a headset. She pointed to his, glancing at him when he didn't move. She dug around by her seat and pulled out a plastic bag, placing it on his lap. "Just in case."

At that moment, he thought a paper bag might be more appropriate. He felt like he was hyperventilating. He cupped his hands over his mouth.

"Marco, you'll be fine. Just try to relax and breathe."

"Keep talking. Listening to you helps."

As Theia maneuvered the plane into the harbor, Rosa and the Widows Club reached the dock. He closed his eyes, not just because he was terrified but because he didn't want to see his grandmother and Kitty fighting. They'd had their ups and downs over the past couple of years, but in the end they'd always been there for each other when times got tough.

Warm fingers wrapped around his. "Look."

He cracked an eye open to see his grandmother and Kitty standing side by side, the Widows Club huddled around them. He nodded and gave Theia's fingers a relieved squeeze in return.

"It's okay to be scared, you know. Even pilots get scared. If anyone tells you they don't, they're lying."

"If you're trying to make me feel better, it's not working." He had to raise his voice to be heard over the noise. His stomach felt like it was riding a wave, rolling over as the plane lifted off. "Are you afraid?" he asked.

"I..." She glanced at him. "There was a time not so long that I was terrified. I didn't think I'd fly again."

"What happened?"

"An accident. My plane was shot down during a joint operation in the Pacific. Friendly fire. I lost my NFO. My naval flight officer. For years I was terrified I'd make a mistake and someone else would die on my watch. Healthy fear is one thing, but terror is a completely different beast. So, to answer your question, no, other than for our families, I'm not afraid. If the weather holds for another couple of hours, we'll be good."

"What was your friend's name?" he asked, keeping his eyes on her.

"Holden. I called him Maverick. Corny, but he loved *Top Gun*. He swore his wife married him because of the movie."

"It was a great movie. What did he call you?"

She smiled. "Ice. We'd flown together for three years. His ejection seat didn't deploy right away. The explosion took out our emergency equipment. We crashed late at night in the western Pacific. It took a while for them to find us."

"So Holden was still alive?"

She nodded. "He'd go in and out of consciousness. He died about an hour before they rescued us."

"How long were you out there?"

"Eight hours."

His heart ached for her. "Theia."

She lifted a shoulder. "So now you know why I have a problem swimming in the middle of the ocean. And because I know how difficult it is to deal with that kind of fear, I hate to ask you this, Marco, but I need you to take those night-vision goggles and start looking for the tour boat. I've mapped out the coordinates Wilson gave Jasper, but we're pretty sure there will be some distance between the drop-off point and where he's stashed the boat and passengers."

He put on the goggles, working hard to convince himself he was in a boat, not a plane. "Give me the coordinates." He'd plug them into his phone.

"Jasper said it's around Twilight Bay."

He nodded. "Makes sense. He probably ran the tour boat aground on one of the small islands. He might have a speed boat stashed on another one to make his getaway. What time did he schedule the drop-off?"

"Two hours from now."

"It's only going to take…Got it. You don't want him to take hostages when he makes his getaway." He shifted in the seat. "Don't get me wrong. I think your plan was well thought out, but you didn't factor in the weather. We have to get them off the island before the storm hits, and from what I can see, it's moving in faster than we expected. So as much as you don't want to involve the police or the Coast Guard, we don't have a choice."

She smiled. "It's already taken care of. The Coast Guard cutter left shortly after us."

"Sully. Should have known. Liam and Griff with him?"

"I think so."

"Okay, we've got this." And for the first time since he'd learned the whale-watching boat was missing, the vise-like grip on his chest relaxed. He leaned in and kissed the corner of her mouth before he began stripping out of his clothes. He pulled the wet suit from behind the seat. "This should be interesting," he said wryly.

"Wait until I land. You can sit on the float and change."

"At least one of us is thinking."

"Fear has a way of short-circuiting our brains. You're doing great. We'll be landing here." She pointed to the smallest of the three islands. "As far as Caine's IT can tell, there's no heat source and nothing that looks like a speed-boat or the tour boat."

"Okay. So I'll swim to the second island, disable the speedboat if it's there, and then find the best way to get to the third island and the tour boat undetected."

She nodded as the plane began its descent. "How long do you figure it will take you to do that?"

"Forty-five minutes tops."

"Okay, so once you're in the water, I'll set my alarm for forty-five minutes. When it goes off, I'll contact Wilson using the megaphone so you'll hear me. If you get in trouble, you have flares in the waterproof knapsack. There's also a gun, a knife, and a first aid kit."

"Good to know," he said, praying he didn't have to use the weapons or the first aid kit.

As though she read his mind, Theia said, "He's desperate, which makes him dangerous. Go in armed."

The plane bounced along the ocean, water spraying the windows. Theia shot past the small island and then brought the plane back around. Something came over him as he opened the door to the plane. He'd never felt as close to anyone as he did to Theia in that moment.

He shifted in the seat to look at her. "There have been two women in my life I thought I was in love with. But when I went to propose to them, I couldn't get the words out. I used to think it was because I was a commitment-phobe. Now I know it's because I've been waiting for you. Will you marry me, *amore mio*?" At her wide-eyed expression, he quickly amended, "Not now, but one day."

"This is crazy. We're going to rescue our family, and

you're asking me to marry you?" She tilted her head to the side. "Are you asking because you think we're going to die? We won't, Marco. We're all getting out of this alive." She leaned across the seat and kissed him. "Be safe."

"You too," he said, unwilling to tell her that fear of dying had nothing to do with his proposal.

The swim to the second island didn't take Marco as long as he'd expected, but the hunt for the speedboat did. It wasn't there. The unsuccessful search had eaten up more time than he'd thought. Just as he rose from the water to walk onto the shore of the third island, Theia's voice came over the megaphone. He scrambled up the rocky shore, listening closely as he did.

"You're early." Wilson's voice cut through the sound of the wind and waves.

"I don't know the area well. I didn't want to be late. I have your money," Theia called back.

Wilson directed her to the other side of the third island and the tour boat. Marco didn't like it. He set the knapsack beside a tree and pulled out a pair of sneakers and the gun. He heard the seaplane coming around the island and rushed to get the sneakers on.

"Slow down, Theia. Slow down." His heart raced as he began to run through the undergrowth, grimacing at the snap of branches, the rustle of leaves. He needn't have worried, he thought as he got closer and heard the kids' anxious voices, the women trying to comfort them.

"What are you about, Ryan?" he heard Daniel ask.

"Shut up, old man, and stay in your seat." The sound of the plane grew louder, and then seconds later the engine shut off. Theia was there, and he was at least a few minutes out. "Step onto the float with the money and hold up your hands."

Marco cleared the trees, crouching behind a rock. As they'd expected, Wilson had grounded the boat on the shore. Theia left on the seaplane's lights, and he could see the outlines of adults and children inside the boat.

Wilson stood at the helm. His hand came up. He held the gun straight-armed in front of him, pointed at the plane. At Theia. Marco opened his mouth to call a warning just as the door to the seaplane opened. There was a loud bellow, and Daniel threw himself in front of Wilson. The gun went off. Daniel cried out, stumbled, and then crashed onto the deck.

There was a splash near the plane. Theia must have dove into the water. Marco stayed low and ran alongside the boat, shutting out his fear for Theia, the sound of the women and children crying, and Daniel moaning.

"You've got two minutes to give me my money or more people start dying," Wilson yelled, scanning the water.

Marco stood and raised his gun. "Drop it, Wilson."

The other man spun around. Marco didn't hesitate. He fired. Wilson got a stunned look on his face. Then he pressed a hand to his chest, fumbling with his gun.

* * *

Deep beneath the cold, dark water, Theia's jacket snagged on the boat's hull. With her clothes weighing her down, she struggled to breathe. She didn't know how much longer she had left. She'd already used up a lot of oxygen swimming under the water to the boat.

Panic tightened her limbs, and she forced her thoughts to Marco. He'd come with her despite his fear of flying. She thought about the fears she'd battled over the years. She could do this. Her family was depending on her. Maybe Marco was too.

Afraid they might need the ransom money, she couldn't drop the duffel bag, so she placed the handles between her teeth. Then she struggled to get her arms out of her jacket. She didn't have much time left. She was losing feeling in her limbs. But just when she was about to give up hope, she managed to free herself from her jacket. On a sudden burst of energy, she kicked her way to the surface, gasping for air when her head cleared the water.

"Everyone, stay in your seats," she heard Marco call out, the sound of his voice filling her with dizzying relief.

"Theia! Theia, where…?" He leaned over the side of the boat. "Thank God," he said, reaching for her. "Here, give me that." He took the duffel bag, dropping it on the deck beside him, and then he hauled her from the water.

"Sorry," she said at her inability to help; her arms and legs felt like waterlogged noodles.

"That's okay. I've got you." He lifted her over the side, and she wrapped her arms around him, holding on as tightly as she could.

He drew back and framed her face with his hands. "Are you okay?"

She nodded and went to look past him, but he held her in place. "Daniel's been shot. I've done what I could to stop the bleeding and keep him from going into shock. Sully is less than a mile out, and there's another cutter on the way. Everyone else is okay. I don't want them out here until Daniel and Wilson have been taken off."

"Right. Of course. Wilson?"

"Dead."

She nodded. "You didn't have a choice."

He gave her a quick kiss. "I'll stay here with Daniel. You go back with your sisters and the kids and get warm."

"I'll check on them, but I'd rather stay with you." And as she looked into the eyes of the man she'd fallen head-over-heels in love with, a man who made her see stars when he kissed her, she said, "I'll marry you someday, Marco DiRossi. If you still want me."

Chapter Twenty-Seven

♥

Colleen had been waiting impatiently for Theia to return to the tower. It had been two days since the rescue. Daniel remained in the hospital recovering from his gunshot wound. He'd been a hero from what she'd heard, risking his life to protect Theia. Colleen imagined that went a ways to making amends for how he'd behaved when Theia's relationship with Wicklow Developments had been made public.

And wasn't that a pickle. How was Colleen supposed to hold on to her anger against Caine when he'd played a prominent role in the rescue of her family, providing them with the ransom money? She didn't know what to make of the lad. She'd give it more thought later. At the moment, she had more important things to occupy her mind. Like the manor.

They'd weathered many a storm, and they'd weathered this one, but they'd paid a high price. The winds had uprooted centuries-old trees and the surf had risen to frightening levels, flooding the tunnels for the first time in distant memory.

Still, she smiled from where she stood by the window in her suite, looking down over the hive of activity. The kidnapping had brought the DiRossis and the Gallaghers together, and now the damage to Greystone had brought out the town.

"You have to endure the storm to appreciate the rainbow." She murmured her mother's favorite saying and then turned at the *beep* of the door's lock, smiling at the sight of a sleepy-eyed Theia coming into the room. From what Daphne and Penelope had said, Theia had spent the past two nights with Marco, grabbing what little time the two had together in the aftermath of the kidnapping and the storm.

Theia glanced around the room. "Hey, I'm back. You probably already know this, but in case you've been…I don't know, hanging around someplace else, everyone's fine. Well, Daniel isn't exactly fine, but don't worry; the doctors say he'll be okay. He seems different though. Brushes with death have a way of changing people, I know, but Pen, Daph, and I are in wait-and-see mode."

Her phone rang, and she answered. "No. That's blackmail. Okay, fine. But only one song." She shook her head as she disconnected and then pointed her phone at the room. "You better appreciate this, GG. I've agreed to a sing-off with my cousins tonight after the clambake." She half-laughed. "You probably have no idea what I'm talking about. The clambake is to thank everyone in town who's come out to help at the manor. The sing-off is to raise funds to pay for the manor's repairs." She rubbed her hair. "I guess I'd better grab a shower and get changed…You stay out here, okay? I won't be long."

Colleen chuckled when Theia grabbed her clothes and walked into the bathroom, saying, "I was right all along. Love really does make you crazy."

She wondered what Theia would think when Colleen delivered the message she'd received early this morning. It was from a man named Holden. Colleen believed he was Theia's friend in the photo. She'd begun to think she wouldn't hear from him. Which wouldn't have been surprising since she'd never communed with the dead before. Though, truth be told, she'd never thought to try. In all this time, she'd only ever seen one other ghost, so she wasn't sure how to go about it.

After spending time meditating on the photo, Colleen had decided to pray. She'd asked every saint and angel she could think of to intercede on Theia's behalf. This morning, she'd received what she believed was an answer to her prayers.

Maybe because she'd been waiting impatiently for Theia's return to relay the news, Colleen leaned in as soon as her great-granddaughter opened the door to the steam-filled bathroom and yelled the words imprinted on her brain, "Nothing to be sorry about, Ice. You did everything you could. Let it go. Fly high."

Theia grabbed the doorframe. "Holden. Is that you?"

Colleen smiled, relieved that she'd reached the right man after all.

Theia rested her head against the doorframe, a tear trickling down her cheek. "Thank you, GG," she whispered as she absently wiped it away.

"I hope you're able to do as your friend says, Theia. Life is too short to be weighed down by things you can't change." Colleen turned at the loud *ping* of something hitting the French doors that led on to the balcony. "What in the…?" she began when it was followed by another *ping* and a muffled male voice calling Theia's name.

Theia wiped at her eyes, unable to contain her smile as she tightened the ties of her robe. She tugged the gaping neckline closed and walked across the room. Opening the door, she stepped onto the balcony, a warm summer breeze rushing into the room. Colleen inhaled the heady scent of the climbing roses and the salty tang of sea air. She loved this time of year.

And if she wasn't mistaken, Theia loved the man standing somewhere beneath the balcony.

"What are you doing? I thought you were digging the fire pit for the clambake," Theia said.

"We're done," Marco said. "We were just putting the seaweed over the lobster and clams when your crazy sisters dragged me over here."

Holding her breath, Colleen put a toe onto the balcony, stunned when she wasn't immediately sent flying backward into the room. She'd never been able to venture outside the manor before. Oh, what a gift, she thought as she tentatively crossed the balcony to Theia's side. Though a small part of her worried about why she was able to do this now, she wouldn't let it steal her joy at the moment. Which only grew when she caught sight of Marco looking up at her great-granddaughter with an expression on his face that Colleen had seen many times before. The lad was head-over-heels in love with the woman at her side.

He jerked his thumb to where Theia's sisters stood a few feet away. "We're not crazy," Penelope said.

"Right. You just keep talking about some grand gesture I'm supposed to make." He looked at Theia. "Do you know what they're talking about, *amore mio*?"

"Daph, Pen, would you leave the poor man—" Theia began.

"Sorry, there's a rumor out there that he freezes at the big moment—"

Theia cut Daphne off with a horrified gasp. "Uh, no, he doesn't. Everything is perfectly fine in that department." Marco let out a mortified groan. "Better than fine," she corrected.

Marco placed a palm over his face and shook his head while her sisters laughed.

Liam appeared. "Hey, bro, what are you doing over here? You're supposed to be making the fish chowder."

"You have got to be kidding me," Marco muttered when one by one the entire DiRossi and Gallagher families joined him under the balcony.

"What a picture," Colleen murmured at the sight of them standing there together, all looking up at Theia.

"Would someone remind me why I wanted sisters?" Theia grumbled beside her.

"Okay, just so we're clear, Theia, it wasn't the big O we were concerned about," Daphne said.

"What big O is she talking about?" Rosa asked Kitty.

"No, not a big O, a big moment," Penelope corrected, to everyone's relief. "Marco freezes at the big moment, Theia. As your sisters, we just want to be sure that when the time comes he can propose to you. He's zero for two."

Rosa turned to Marco. "What's she talking about?"

Marco looked up at Theia. "Are you going to tell them, or am I?"

Theia sighed. "Marco asked me to marry him two nights ago."

"And?" several people called out.

"I said yes. Wait. No." She anxiously waved her hands

when half the crowd congratulated them while the other half began planning the wedding. "It's not what you think."

Marco whistled, quieting the crowd. "We're not getting married." There were a couple of *boo*s and several disappointed sighs. "This week or the next one or the one after that." He smiled up at Theia. "But I love you, Theia Gallagher, and one day I plan to make you my wife."

"And the mother of his children," Rosa called up with a smile.

"Yeah, that too," he said, putting his arm around his grandmother. He leaned around her to glance at Theia's sisters. "Are we good?"

Penelope and Daphne looked at each other and then up at Theia.

"I'm good. I love him," she said to her sisters before her gaze moved to Marco. "I love you. I want to marry you and have your babies."

He stared up at her as he stepped away from the crowd. "Now? I thought you wanted to wait."

Colleen noted her great-grandsons' faces. They thought Marco was going to choke. Colleen thought the woman who stood frozen by her side might also, but she surprised her. "I don't want to wait anymore. Months maybe, but not years."

A slow smile spread across Marco's face. "Okay, then. Let the wedding planning begin."

"*Madonna mia*, it's a miracle," Rosa said, raising the cross she wore to her lips.

"*Nonna*, our wishes really did come true!" Mia said.

Colleen stood on the balcony long after the orange ball had sunk into the turquoise sea. Down on the beach, standing in the warm glow from the bonfire, Theia, Penelope, and Daphne sang "I'll Stand by You" to celebrate winning the sing-off.

Colleen smiled as halfway through the first verse, one by one, her great-grandsons joined her great-granddaughters. Colleen pressed a hand to her chest as they all stood together, voices like angels raised in song. She couldn't have wished for a more perfect ending to the night, a more perfect beginning to Theia and Marco's life together in Harmony Harbor.

Have you tried Debbie Mason's Christmas, Colorado series?

As her thirtieth birthday approaches, deputy Jill Flaherty decides it's time to live a little. When she walks into Sawyer Anderson's bar in her sexiest dress, she's not thinking that he's her brother's best friend or about the many women he dated during his years as a pro hockey player. All she's thinking is that it's finally time to confess to her longtime crush how she truly feels.

Please turn the page for an excerpt from *Happy Ever After in Christmas*.

Chapter One

♥

Deputy Jill Flaherty sat at her desk wrapping her brother's birthday present for his surprise party that night. The yellow helium balloons she'd ordered were currently bouncing in front of her face. She lifted her hand to bat them away, ripping the paper off the present in the process. A present that she'd been painstakingly wrapping for the last ten minutes. Frustrated, she swore under her breath while shaking her fingers to free them of the tape and brightly colored tissue paper.

"You're stuck," Suze announced in an authoritative voice from behind her computer.

"Thank you for your insightful observation," Jill grumbled at the forty-something woman sitting at the dispatcher's desk across the room as she bent her head to pull the tape off her fingers with her teeth.

Suze leaned around her computer and grinned. "I didn't mean literally. I mean you're stuck, stuck. That's why you've been so bitchy lately. You have the pre-thirtieth-birthday blues."

"It's my fingers that are stuck, not me. And I'm not…" Jill sighed. "Okay, so maybe I have been a little bitchy. But it's because of all the overtime I've been putting in the past couple of weeks. I'm tired."

She ignored the reference to her thirtieth birthday. She wouldn't admit to Suze that she was partially right. Like an ominous black cloud, the big three-o loomed large in Jill's mind. It always had. Her mother had died two days before her thirtieth. Preparations for Jack's thirty-seventh birthday had served to remind Jill that *her* thirtieth was only five months away.

"Because you don't have a life."

Jill lifted a hand still covered in tape and paper in an are-you-kidding-me gesture. "I do so. I have—"

"Yeah, yeah, I know. You have friends and family and a job you love. Still doesn't mean you have a life. You put yours on hold when Jack was MIA. I had a front-row seat so I know what I'm talking about." Suze held up her hand when Jill opened her mouth to defend herself. "I get it. We all knew how hard it was for you dealing with Jack being missing while working two jobs and taking care of Grace and little Jack. It's why I cut you some slack. But here we are two years later, and you still haven't pressed the restart button."

"I have a life," Jill reiterated without elaborating. Suze had stolen her ammunition. If having friends, family, and a job she loved didn't count, Jill didn't know what else to say.

As another balloon danced in front of her face, she thought back to Jack's birthday two years earlier. The Penalty Box, the local sports bar, had been decorated with a hundred yellow balloons that warm night in May. Half the residents of the small town of Christmas, Colorado, had shown up to share their memories of Jack and pray for his safe return. By then it had been seventeen months since his Black Hawk had been shot down over the mountains of Afghanistan.

In all that time they hadn't received a single word as to whether he was alive or dead, not even a ransom demand. They'd had nothing to hold on to but hope and faith. At least Jill had been holding on. Right after they'd sung "Happy Birthday" in honor of her brother, she'd found out she was the only one who was.

Still tough to think about, Jill thought as she rubbed the phantom pain in her chest. The memory of the raw, ugly emotions that had cut through her that night. Anger and hurt that his wife Grace planned to move on with her life. The searing burn of jealousy and betrayal that she'd planned to move on with Sawyer Anderson, Jack's best friend and the man Jill'd had a crush on since she was ten, and had fallen in love with when he'd kissed her at her brother's wedding. Not that Grace and Sawyer had ever come out and admitted their intentions or feelings, but Jill had recognized the signs.

And then, within seconds of discovering Grace's betrayal, one of the worst moments in Jill's life had turned into the best. Breaking news had flashed across the television screen behind the bar that Jack and his crew had been found alive.

A chair scraped noisily on the tile floor and drew Jill back from that night. Suze moved the bouquet of balloons and took a seat across from her. "Okay, so tell me, when was the last time you hid the salami?" she asked.

Jill frowned. "What…"

Suze rolled her brown eyes as she peeled the last of the tape and tissue paper from Jill's fingers. "Bumped uglies…Did the horizontal mumbo?"

"I have no idea what you're—"

"Oh for godsakes, when was the last time you got laid?"

Since the answer didn't immediately pop into her head, Jill hedged, "What does that have to do with anything?"

"And there's your problem. You can't remember, can you?" Suze said as she rolled the paper and tape into a ball.

"Yes, I can. Seven months ago," she said, taking a guess. Then realizing the number of months might unwittingly validate Suze's no-life pronouncement, Jill added, "Before you say anything, I've been busy."

Suze pursed her lips and tossed the ball into the garbage can. "Don't buy two-sided tape again. And it was eight months ago with that accountant from Logan County."

"Really? Huh. I could have sworn…" She took in the I-told-you-so look on Suze's lightly freckled face. "Oh, come on, that doesn't mean anything."

"Yeah, it does. It says it all. You have unmemorable sex with unmemorable men. And do you know why you do?"

"No, but I'm sure you're going to enlighten me," Jill said, carefully working the rest of the paper off Jack's present with a pair of scissors.

"Fear," Suze said, taking the scissors from Jill's hand and looking her in the eyes. "You're afraid to get your heart broken. That's why you spend your time fantasizing about the man and life you want and not doing anything about it."

"I do not fantasize about Sawyer," Jill blurted without thinking. She caught the triumphant look in Suze's eyes and quickly added, "Or any other man in town."

"Umhm," Suze said as she opened the gift box, carefully removing the framed photos from inside. It was a collage of Jill's favorite pictures of Grace and Jack with Jill's nephew. "You want this, don't you? The house, the baby, the man of your dreams, the whole enchilada. I want that for you, too, girlfriend."

Jill looked away from the photos and shrugged, turning to pull another roll of gift wrap from the bag at her feet. "I guess. Someday," she said in an offhand manner, unwilling to admit how much she did. But Suze knew her too well to be fooled. She needed a distraction. "What about you? You won't be able to use the boys as an excuse for much longer. They'll be heading to college in a couple years."

Suze arched an eyebrow while sliding the framed photos back into the box. "You wanna play it that way, fine. Here's what we'll do." She taped the box shut, then leaned across the desk to grab two pieces of paper out of the printer. She handed one to Jill.

"What's this for?"

"We're making our life-goal lists. Or in your case, get-a-life list." She took the gift wrap from Jill. "I'll take care of this while you write down yours. I have to think about mine for a bit seeing as how I already have the kids and house."

"Don't be smug," Jill said, looking at the paper like it was a bomb about to detonate and she didn't have the code. Maybe because there was a part of her that knew Suze was right. If Jill wrote down what she really wanted, she'd actually have to do something about it. Sometimes living in a fantasy world was easier. You didn't have to deal with rejection, the hurt and disappointment.

By the time Suze had wrapped the present, Jill had one item on her list. It was the only one she felt comfortable enough to write down.

"I knew you wanted to be sheriff," Suze said with a self-satisfied smile, then grimaced. "Make sure you don't show anyone your list. No one's supposed to know Gage isn't running for another term. He'll figure out I accidently over-heard his conversation." Suze put her hand over Jill's to stop her from ripping up the sheet of paper. "Don't. You have to write them down. There's a higher percentage that they'll happen if you do."

"Yeah? Where did you read that, Facebook?" Jill asked her friend and coworker who spent more time on social media than anyone she knew.

"Oprah. Now come on. No more stalling. Stop editing yourself and just write them down."

Jill bent over the paper, shielding it with her arm, and wrote down the rest.

"You have to let me see," Suze complained, but before she could take the list from Jill, the phone rang. "Sheriff's department, how can I …Oh, hi, Boss. What's up? Jill? Yeah, of course she's here. Where else would she be?"

Jill scowled at her and took the phone, rolling her eyes when Suze pressed the speaker button. "Hey, Gage, what's up?"

"I need a favor. The seniors' hockey league are playing the last game of the season today, and I need you to take my place."

"Ha! Good one. Now, what are you really calling about?"

"I'm serious. We've got two guys down, including me. You know how competitive Ethan is. If we lose the game, he's gonna blame me, and I'll never hear the end of it. Brad already agreed to fill in for one of the other guys."

Brad was a recent hire. Young, smart, and ambitious, Jill had no doubt when word got out Gage wasn't seeking reelection, he'd throw his hat in the ring. Since the guy was also handsome and charming, he could pose a serious threat. Which was probably why Suze was widening her eyes at Jill and nodding like a bobble-head doll. But there was no way Jill was volunteering to play. "I'd like to help you out, but I promised to decorate the Penalty Box for Jack's—"

"Don't worry about it, girlfriend. I'll go over after my shift and decorate," Suze said, stabbing the first line on Jill's list.

"Wow, thanks, Suze," Jill said through clenched teeth. "But I'm sure you have more important things to do. Besides, you'd be better off getting someone who actually knew how to play the game, Gage."

"Come on, you practically lived at the arena and spent more than half your life around Sawyer. You know hockey."

She'd lived at the arena because she had a crush on Sawyer, not because she loved hockey. Though she kinda did now. "Yes, I know how the game is played, but I don't play the game. You need to find someone who does." And they better be good, because former NHL superstar Sawyer Anderson was on the opposing team. So was Jill's brother.

"He's found someone. You. Don't worry, Gage. She'll be there."

Jill stared at Suze.

"Great. Thanks, Jill. I owe you," Gage said.

"Dammit, Suze, why did you do that?" Jill demanded as soon as her boss hung up.

"Did you not just hear Gage say he owed you? You've had five complaints filed against you this month alone. You need—"

"Four. Mrs. Burnett was exaggerating. The tree branch was a hazard, and I didn't cut her phone line. I tripped over the wire and it came out of the wall." Which was one of the reasons Jill was feeling a little stressed and over-worked these days. Since most of her complaints had come from the seniors in town, Gage had volunteered Jill to work twenty hours a week at the nursing home in hopes she'd learn a kinder and gentler approach.

"Regardless, it's in your file until she withdraws the complaint. But you're missing the point. Brad's a suck-up, and he hasn't been written up. You need to do some sucking up of your own. The only way you'll be elected sheriff is if you have Gage's full support."

"Well, he's not going to feel very supportive if I lose the game for them. Suze, the only hockey I've ever played is street hockey with Sawyer and Jack when I was nine."

"You'll be fine. You're as athletic and as competitive as Brad. You'll get the hang of it in no time." She wiggled Jill's list out from under her arm. "And this is a great opportunity for you to prove to Sawyer that you're perfect for him."

Jill grabbed the paper from Suze and folded it in half. "I didn't write, *prove to Sawyer I'm perfect for him* on my list. I wrote, *ask him out*." Saying it out loud caused Jill's stomach to heave. But the more time she'd spent on the list, the more obvious it became that she really had put her life on hold. And clearly, with the approach of the big three-o, she wasn't getting any younger.

"Maybe you should have, because you are. He just doesn't know it yet. And you know why he doesn't, Jill?"

"No, but I'm sure you're going to tell me," she said under her breath.

"He doesn't because you're so busy working, the only time he sees you is in uniform or at Grace and Jack's. You need to show him another side of you. Not the cop or his best friend's baby sister."

About the Author

Debbie Mason is the *USA Today* bestselling author of the Christmas, Colorado, and the Harmony Harbor series. Her books have been praised for their "likable characters, clever dialogue, and juicy plots" (RTBookReviews.com). When she isn't writing or reading, Debbie enjoys spending time with her very own real-life hero, their three wonderful children and their son-in-law, and two adorable grandbabies in Ottawa, Canada.

You can learn more at:
    AuthorDebbieMason.com
    Twitter @AuthorDebMason
    Facebook.com/DebbieMasonBooks/

Fall in love with these charming small-town romances!

USA TODAY BESTSELLING AUTHOR
DEBBIE MASON
Barefoot Beach

"Heartfelt and delightful!"
—RAEANNE THAYNE

BAREFOOT BEACH
By Debbie Mason

Theia Lawson and Marco DiRossi are determined to beat the matchmakers of Harmony Harbor at their own game. Both lone wolves, the two conspire to pretend that they've already fallen in love. But just when they want to make their relationship real, a secret is revealed that puts everything Marco and Theia have fought for in jeopardy.

Discover exclusive content and more on
read-forever.com.

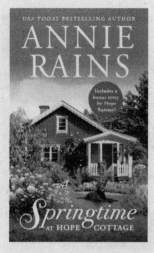

SPRINGTIME AT HOPE COTTAGE
By Annie Rains

In Sweetwater Springs, love has a way of mending even the most damaged heart. When Josie Kellum is sidelined in a small town, she focuses on her rehab to get back to the big city ASAP. But that becomes awfully difficult when she falls for her hunky physical therapist. Includes a bonus story by Hope Ramsay!

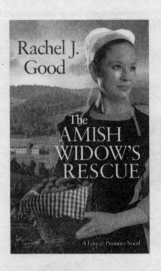

THE AMISH WIDOW'S RESCUE
By Rachel J. Good

Pregnant and recently widowed, Grace Fisher is determined to provide for her family on her own. Elijah Beiler has always admired his neighbor Grace, so standing by while she struggles to support her family isn't an option. Determined to help, Elijah finds it difficult to remain detached. Can he overcome past hurts and open his heart to this ready-made family?

WELCOME TO LAST CHANCE (REISSUE)
By Hope Ramsay

When Wanda Jane Coblentz arrives in Last Chance with five dollars in her pocket, all she wants is a hot meal and a fresh start. But when she falls for sexy musician Clay Rhodes, she never expects a bad boy like Clay to rescue a damsel in distress. Thank goodness Jane plans on rescuing herself. Includes a bonus story!

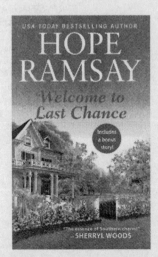

Follow @ReadForeverPub on Twitter and join the conversation using #ReadForever.

THE WAY YOU LOVE ME
By Miranda Liasson

Gabby Langdon secretly dreams of being a writer, so for once she does something for herself—she signs up for a writing class taught by bestselling novelist Caden Marshall. There's only one problem: Her brooding, sexy professor is a distraction she can't afford if she's finally going to get the life she truly wants. Includes a bonus story by Alison Bliss!

THREE LITTLE WORDS
By Jenny Holiday

Stranded in New York with her best friend's wedding dress, Gia Gallo has six days to make it to Florida in time for the ceremony. And oh-so-charming best man Bennett Buchanan has taken the last available rental car. Looks like she's in for one long road trip with the sexiest—and most irritating—Southern gentleman she's ever met.

Connect with us at Facebook.com/ReadForeverPub.

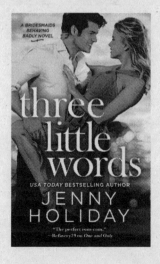